For Rachel

Let food be thy medicine and medicine be thy food.
— Hippocrates

Chapter 1

Dante Palermo walked along the Las Vegas strip desperately trying to hold in the biggest secret of his life. None of his friends or family knew. But among the brilliant lights, the faux architectural wonders of New York, Paris, Venice, Egypt, the eyes of every passer-by seemed to try to coax Dante's secret out of him.

He took the hand of the woman by his side—Abby, the most incredible woman he'd ever known. His grin grew wider, and he couldn't help singing and snapping his fingers like Bobby Darin back in 1962.

"I'm dancin' all over the world. And singing along. And singing along. Ah, go get 'em Eddy."

Abby looked at him with an arched eyebrow. "And who's Eddy?"

"I made him up. He's the leader of the band in my head. We play every weekend at the Joker Lounge."

The older couple walking a few yards ahead, who wore matching Iowa State Fair T-shirts, turned and regarded Dante as though he'd forgotten to take his Ritalin.

"Hey," Dante said to them, "I'm originally from Des Moines."

The couple nodded and smiled.

"And you know what else?" Again, Dante's singing rang out in the Las Vegas night. "I'm dancin' all over the world."

Abby rolled her eyes, but Dante grinned. And why not? In a week, back home in San Francisco, he would sign the lease on his first restaurant, Pane e Vino. He'd be chef and co-owner of a restaurant in one of the great food cities of the world, in one of its historic neighborhoods, North Beach.

His Nonna Isabella, who died when he was eighteen, would be so proud. Much of what he knew about food, and even about life, he'd learned from her. She taught him to cook with her favorite ingredient: love. Without her, he might not be a chef, and certainly would not be as successful.

But the restaurant was only half the reason for Dante's euphoria. The other was about to happen in just a few minutes. He fingered the small velvet bag in his pocket that held a one-carat diamond engagement ring.

He had known he'd be in this place, at this time, maybe from the first moment he saw Abby standing in the lobby of the Monte Carlo Hotel two years before. He hadn't been looking for his true love that night. In fact, he'd given up on finding anyone to share his heart with. But when he saw Abby's green eyes, the way she looked at him, the way she smiled, Nonna's words rang in his ears: *Fidati dell'imprevisto*—trust the unexpected. Now, here they were.

He squeezed Abby's hand.

She smiled weakly.

"You worried about Zoe?" Dante said. An hour earlier, when they had been sweaty and naked in bed, she hadn't seemed worried.

"A little I guess." Abby had spent the last week in New York on a business trip, and she had brought her four-year-old daughter, Zoe, with her to spend time with her dad, Abby's ex, who had moved back there earlier in the year. "She loves getting to stay with her dad, and she had a great visit with my parents. But I still worry that since her dad moved, it's been a little hard on her."

"Well, I'm glad you were able to make it here."

They approached a giant bright red neon Coke bottle where a street musician, whom Dante had earlier paid fifty bucks to be there, honked and wailed on his saxophone with his eyes closed in be-bop bliss. Dante directed Abby to sit on a nearby bench, then went over to the sax player.

Dante glared at him. "You're supposed to be playing romantic music."

"Sorry, didn't see you coming." The sax player's breath smelled of Swisher Sweets and Hennessy.

"That's okay. Now just wait for my signal."

Dante went back and sat next to Abby, then nodded to the musician, who started playing "That's Amore."

Dante's eyes crossed six different ways. "Hold on," he said to Abby. He jumped up and ran over to the musician. "What are you doing?"

"Playing the song you requested."

"I requested 'That's All.'"

The performer smiled sheepishly. "Oh yeah." Then he played a mellifluous rendition of "That's All" that the great Lester Young would have been proud of.

Dante went back to his place next to Abby, and took both her hands.

"What's going on, Dante?"

"It was right here," he said, "exactly two years ago tonight that we had our first kiss. It was the most extraordinary kiss I've ever experienced." Dante's voice broke. "It changed my life."

Abby turned and looked at the ground. Dante tucked her dark hair behind her ear. Then a tiny drop of water fell onto the back of his hand. He looked up to see if it had started raining, but the sky above was clear darkness. Another drop hit his wrist. This time he saw that it came from Abby's cheek.

A tear of joy, maybe?

A closer look at her face revealed the truth.

Dante squeezed her hand. "What's wrong?"

Now Abby's tears flowed freely. She put the back of her hand to her mouth. "I didn't mean to do this tonight."

"Do what?" A chill ran down his spine like a streaking Jack Frost, naked, arms in the air. The shiver went all the way down to the heels of his feet.

Abby stared at the sidewalk for what seemed like an hour, then finally said, "I have a job offer with Cook Network in New York."

The rest of the strip went dark and Dante just stared at Abby. He couldn't feel his hands or his feet. His arms or legs. And it felt like his heart had stopped beating.

She wiped the tears from her cheek. "It's a huge promotion for me, VP of Marketing."

Dante forced his heart out of his throat. "So what does that mean for us?"

Abby took a deep breath. "I wasn't sure I was going to take the job. But the other morning I was sitting in my parents' kitchen, watching the two of them. They seemed older than I thought they should be. Do you know what I mean?"

Dante could hardly breathe, let alone speak. He finally said, "I guess."

"And I want Zoe to have time with them. My grandparents were such an important part of my life growing up, and I know what your nonna meant to you. So I've decided to take the job."

Dante closed his eyes. He felt like his entire body was shaking.

Abby put her hand on his shoulder. "You're going to be so busy with the new restaurant. I do love you. But I have to move back home to New York and I can't ask you to leave your dream behind. That doesn't give us much of a future together."

Dante could only nod. He sat in silence as Abby kept talking. She didn't want to try to maintain their relationship long-distance. She thought a clean break was best.

Finally, Abby said she would find another room that night, then fly home in the morning. She didn't say they'd talk more about it later. When she said goodbye, it sounded like forever.

Dante sat with his head in his hands until the street musician sat next to him and handed him the bottle of Hennessy. Dante swigged the cognac and handed it back.

"Thanks."

"I didn't mess that up, did I?"

Dante shook his head, then returned his head to his hands.

"I was married once," the sax man said. "Long time ago. I wasn't ready. Or I wasn't ready to marry my wife, and she was a fine woman. Getting married just made me miserable. Made her even more miserable. I always think how much luckier we'd've been if she'd said 'no' when I proposed."

Dante didn't say a word. The saxophonist held out the bottle of Hennessy again.

"No, thanks."

The musician stood. "Good luck to you, my brother." He patted Dante on the back, then left.

Dante sat on that bench, imagining that his heart was a black tumor in his chest. After an hour, he wondered if perhaps he was dreaming. He shook himself, but did not awaken in his bed, relieved to find the situation had only been a nightmare. He had been rejected. Dumped.

Chapter 2

When Dante saw Abby that first time in the Monte Carlo, he probably should have kept walking right on by. Instead, he stopped about five feet from her. She glanced at her watch, surely waiting for some lucky guy to meet her. Dante looked at her, but she was facing the other direction. Probably on purpose, he thought. A wave of embarrassment ran through him as he imagined that she cringed to herself and thought, "Oh, God, please don't let this dork talk to me." He started to walk away. But Abby turned and smiled.

"Hello," she said. Her voice was smooth and resonant, like a radio announcer.

"Hi." Dante's ears burned and his mouth filled with cotton.

She ran her hand over her opposite shoulder. Dante's fingers tingled with envy. "The air conditioning is always too cold in these places," she said.

Sweat formed on Dante's upper lip. "I guess because we're in the desert."

A woman with curly hair that spread like a nun's habit from each side of her head came over. "Abby, we're over there." She pointed toward the entrance to the casino and gave Dante a definite *back off, buddy* glare.

"Okay, be there in a sec."

The flying nun peered over her glasses at Dante before walking away.

Abby looked directly into his eyes. "I have to go. Work dinner." She extended her hand. "Abby Drivakis."

"Nice to meet you, Abby." He took her hand. The moment he touched her skin, an emptiness opened in his chest and his stomach turned into a block of cement. "D-Dante," he said. "Dante Palermo."

"Nice to meet you, too, Dante Palermo." In one fluid motion, she turned and walked away. Dante stared as she rounded a pillar. Abby didn't look back.

That night, after his own dinner, after he'd left his fellow food conventioneers to their karaoke, their casinos, their shows, Dante hung around the bar near where he'd met Abby. Why hadn't he asked her to meet him? Why hadn't he told her where he'd be? He nursed beers until well past 1:00 A.M., then went up to his room and crawled into bed. The scent of her perfume lingered in his memory. His hand still tingled from her touch.

He stared at the dark ceiling. He hadn't been on a date in three years and he wasn't sure if he ever would go on another one. But something in Abby's eyes got him, made him want to take one more chance.

The next day, Dante went about his business, attending seminars on the latest food preparation technologies, restaurant business practices and the like. He got next to nothing out of any of them. Each presenter may as well have been saying, "Abby Abby Abby. Abby Abby Abby Abby Abby."

That following evening, he meandered about the lobby of the Monte Carlo trying to run into Abby accidentally. He went to the same place he'd seen her the night before, at around the same time. He browsed the shops. He stepped into the casino, and took a quick look around. He walked back and forth past the front desk. After the third round, the staff started giving him suspicious looks.

One of the clerks, a tiny Filipina woman with graying hair and half specs resting on the end of her nose said, "Sir, are you in need of help?"

"No." He forced a smile. "I'm waiting for a friend."

The clerk regarded Dante with an air of pity. She'd probably seen more than her share of people "waiting for friends."

You've been at this for an hour. You're not going to see her.

He headed to the Monte Carlo Pub and Brewery and sat at the bar. The Yankees were on television. Between food, beer, and baseball, he was distracted enough to keep thoughts about Abby to one every seven seconds.

As Dante was finishing the last of his beer, he saw, from the corner of his eye, someone with dark hair take the seat next to him. Before he could lower the glass, the dark-haired person nudged him with a shoulder. It was Abby. Her hair danced on her shoulders.

Yeeeeeeeee Hawww!

She looked at him as she had the night before and said, "There you are." Those eyes.

"Here I am." Dante dropped his hands under the bar to hide their shaking.

She looked at the TV. "What's the score?"

"Yankees are up five to two."

"Yes!"

"You're a Yankee fan?"

"New Yorker born and raised. Been a Yankee fan all my life."

A Yankee fan? That was enough to marry her right there.

A leathery bartender stepped over and looked at Dante. With a Texas drawl she said, "Seeing as how you have such a big crush on this pretty lady, are you gonna buy her a drink?"

Abby smiled and leaned over the bar. "Does he have a big crush on me?"

"I never seen a boy so smitten."

"What do you think I should do about it?"

They both looked at Dante, who was turning a brighter shade of red. "He is kind of cute," the bartender said. "Tall. And look at those hazel eyes. That nice thick dark hair." She stroked her chin. "He has a certain Mediterranean look about him, like you. I think I'd go for it."

"I don't know. He could be a serial killer."

Dante threw his hands up. "I'm right here."

The bartender put her finger to her lips. "*Shhhhh*, I'm working it for you, honey." Then she turned back to Abby. "He seems harmless to me. Plus you'll have beautiful children."

Abby laughed. Not a small, demure giggle. Nor a cackle. Like her voice, her laugh was smooth, silky, but with body. "Hmmm. Maybe I should let him buy me a drink." She put her hand on his shoulder. "How about a cosmo?"

After Abby got her drink, they toasted with a "cheers."

"So you're out here for work?" Dante said.

"Yeah, big PBS meeting. I work for KQED in San Francisco."

"You live in San Francisco?"

"Yeah."

"I'm the chef at Santino's in Union Square."

"I've been there. A few months ago. I even remember what I had. It was cod sautéed with anchovies, tomatoes, olives, and capers. It was really good."

Dante blushed. "Wow. I'm flattered you still remember it."

"I went to culinary school," she said, "so I tend to remember good food."

She had graduated from the French Culinary Institute in New York and worked as a chef for a couple of years. "But you know restaurant hours are brutal. Especially in New York. So when I met my future ex-husband, I decided to go back to school and get a marketing and broadcasting degree."

After Abby finished her drink, the bartender came over. She said to Dante, "Hey, Bright Eyes, another round for you and Beauty?"

"Those bright eyes could be masking some sinister personality disorder," Abby said. "But what do you think, Bright Eyes? Another drink?"

Dante looked at his watch. "As long as we're not out late. I have a strangulation at eleven."

The bartender narrowed her eyes. "You know what? I think y'all should get out of here. I have a sixth sense about these things, and when I look at the two of you, I see two pieces of a jigsaw puzzle fitting together. And that ain't something I see a lot of in this town. Go get to know each other without alcohol involved. It'll be worth it."

Dante and Abby looked at each other. The bartender's corroboration of what he had felt since he first saw Abby made Dante almost pop with exhilaration.

"Well, what do you think, Bright Eyes?" Abby said.

"I think we should hit the strip."

Over the next four hours, Abby and Dante took in Las Vegas. They rode the Manhattan Express roller coaster at New York-New York, saw the Lion Habitat at the MGM Grand, did oxygen shots and took a gondola ride at the Venetian. Everywhere they went, Abby struck up a conversation with someone. Their gondolier had tried out for *American Idol*, the young woman working the roller coaster line had just moved to Vegas the month before, the guy behind them for the lions was seventy and had never been to Las Vegas before.

As they left the Venetian, the smile left Abby's eyes. She said, "I have a serious question."

Dante's stomach tightened. "Okay."

"What's your all-time favorite *Far Side* cartoon?" She smiled.

Dante let his breath out. "Hmmm." He narrowed his eyes, and after a few seconds said, "There are so many. But right now I'm going with *Beware of Doug*."

"Nice! I'd say mine is the one with the aliens having just landed on Earth, and one of them has fallen down the stairs. Another one says, 'So much for instilling them with a sense of awe.'"

"Ooh, that was almost my choice. I actually say that every time there's a screw-up in the kitchen."

"Okay, what's your favorite cheese?"

"Velveeta!" Dante grinned.

Abby smacked his arm. "Come on. Mine is a cave-aged gruyere."

"Well, I love Humboldt Fog. And my latest cheese crush is Casatica di Bufala."

"I haven't had that one."

"It's a water buffalo milk cheese. Creamy and sweet, really subtle herb. So good."

Abby asked lots of other questions. She asked what the last song he'd listened to on his iPod had been. She asked him to describe his worst date. She also talked a lot about Zoe. She showed Dante pictures and glowed when recounting how Zoe danced to 80's music and loved being read to. "I'm sorry. I'm probably totally boring you with kid stories."

Dante smiled. "Not at all."

After a couple of hours of walking, they stopped and sat on a bench near the giant neon Coke bottle. Abby's forearm touched Dante's. Her skin was like a ripe peach. They sat quietly for a few seconds, then Abby said, "So." She pressed her shoulder against his. "Do you have a crush on me?"

Dante tucked her hair behind her ear and let his fingers graze her cheek. Then he leaned over and kissed her. When their lips met, time stopped. When her mouth opened slightly and their tongues touched, a tiny moan escaped her throat.

She pulled back. "You are a great kisser."

"I couldn't do it alone."

Then she put her hand on his face and stared into his eyes. Stared. Dante felt like he could conquer the universe. He'd never felt so confident and calm. The moment was perfect and nothing else seemed to matter.

For the next few days, they were together every spare moment, and the more time Dante spent with her, the further he fell. On their fourth and final evening together, they had dinner at Delmonico's. Abby said, "You've paid for the last three dinners. It's my turn." Dante opened his mouth to protest but she said, "Don't worry, I'll take it out in trade." Then she winked. To that point, they had only kissed and it seemed that Abby wasn't into public displays of affection. They had held hands while walking on the strip and even kissed in a dark corner here or there, so Dante assumed she was just a little reserved. But he learned otherwise that night.

As soon as they were back at the hotel, Abby took him straight to her room. The door was barely closed before she had him pinned against it, pressing her body against his. Her tongue was in his mouth. Her hands ran over his chest. She looked into his eyes. The look was one he hadn't seen. It was mischievous, playful, uninhibited.

She ran her hand down his stomach. "That was an expensive dinner, you know."

"Then I'll have to do my best to give you your money's worth." Within minutes, they were both undressed. They spent the next two hours exploring each other's body until they were both spent and floated into sleep.

The next morning, Dante awoke with Abby in his arms.

"Hi there," she said. She rubbed her cheek against his chest and kissed him. He stroked her hair. "Mmm, that feels nice."

"You feel so good in my arms." Dante took a deep breath.

"I can feel your heartbeat against my face."

This woman is your fate. Tell her you love her.

He kissed her head forehead.

Come on. You're in love. You can do this. One word at a time.

"Abby—"

It's simple. I Love You. Pretend you're singing a Wings tune.

"Yes?" Abby said.

He ran his hand along her arm. "We better get up if you're going to make your flight."

Gutless punk.

Abby lifted her head and looked at him. "Did you just hit yourself in the head?"

"I was swatting at a gnat."

Later that morning they took different flights home. Before she left, Abby said she would have to spend time with Zoe. "I have to make up for being gone for the last week. So no babysitters this week." It seemed reasonable, but Dante could see that things were going to turn out just as he suspected, and he'd probably never see Abby again.

But she called the next night. Dante was winding down the dinner shift when his cell phone rang. When he saw Abby's name come up, he nearly jumped in the air. She said, "I just put Zoe to bed and thought I'd call to say hello."

"I'm glad you did. I know it's only been a day, but I already miss you."

She hesitated and Dante thought he might have revealed too much. "Really?" she said.

Dante cringed and squeaked out, "Yeah."

"That's nice to hear."

Only a couple of weeks after meeting her, he told Abby he loved her, that he had probably loved her since the first time he saw her. Abby said she had to be a little more careful because of Zoe.

A couple of weeks later, Dante and Abby stood on the front door step after a date that had included champagne and oysters, and a musicless slow dance on a Fort Mason pier under a full moon in the clear sky. At Abby's front door, they kissed. She placed her hand on his cheek. Then she pressed her forehead to his and sighed.

"I don't want to go in. But the sitter is waiting." She kissed him again. "I wish you could come in."

Dante smiled. "I'm free tonight."

"Ha. You know what I mean. I don't want Zoe to meet you for the first time coming out of my bedroom."

"I see your point."

"But I think it's time for Zoe to meet you. Because I think—" She bit her lip. "I think I'm falling in love with you."

The rush of emotion that went through Dante nearly buckled his knees. It was unlike anything he'd ever felt before and nothing like he ever could have imagined. It was like euphoria on ecstasy.

The next day, Dante met Zoe, and in the days and weeks to come, he became more and more a part of Abby's life. Though they both had very busy schedules, they spent as much time together as they could. They went to the opera, they saw live jazz. They went to a private screening of a new feature film about the 1906 San Francisco earthquake. They saw plays and went to comedy shows. They went to rare book shops and even took a ballroom dancing class. And between the two of them, they knew about or discovered every great place to eat within a three hundred mile radius.

To the rest of the world, Abby was a sophisticated professional, maybe a little conservative, aloof. But in private, she was anything but conservative. One night, Dante and Abby were at the Bubble Lounge. They sat in a dark corner, Abby in a skirt. She'd gone to the bathroom, then returned and handed Dante her panties.

Dante looked at the underwear, then sighed and half shrugged.

"Are you okay?" Abby asked. Her eyes seemed worried.

"Oh, don't get me wrong, they're nice. But I usually wear a thong."

Abby laughed, then kissed Dante and said, "I'm so glad I can be myself with you."

"I'm glad you're comfortable being yourself with me."

A few weeks later, Abby asked Dante to meet her at a bar, the Irish Bank at 5:30. When Dante got there, she had a shot of Jameson's waiting for him. "You're going to need this," she said.

"And why am I going to need this?"

She smiled salaciously.

"I see."

After he finished, she ordered one more. "You'll probably need this one, too."

They went straight from the Irish Bank to a skin care spa called BellaPelle. They sat in the waiting room and Abby leaned over to Dante. "You don't have to do anything you don't want, but if you do,

I'll make it so worth your while. Victor's got Zoe for the week, so . . ."

"What exactly is it you want me to do?"

"Have you ever heard of a Boyzilian?"

Dante cringed. "No. But I can guess what it is."

She raised her eyebrows. "What do you think?"

"I think it'll hurt like hell."

"So you're willing to do it?"

Dante bit his lip. "What do I get in return again?"

"Anything you want." She looked into his eyes. "Anything."

Dante took a deep breath. "That sounds like an offer I can't refuse."

A few minutes later, Dante and Abby entered one of the rooms with a woman named Liz. "She does my Brazilian," Abby said. "And she's the best there is."

Liz smiled. "I promise this'll be quick and as painless as I can make it."

After some discussion, the consensus was that, given the rest of Dante's body hair, a full Boyzilian wouldn't look quite right. Instead, Liz would only remove the hair on the main equipment.

With no time for modesty, Dante was unceremoniously on his back, legs apart. Abby smiled and Liz walked him through the procedure. Her soothing voice and professional attitude put Dante at as much ease as was possible in the situation. He'd suffered through needles to his face as part of acne treatments and the cutting of skin tags from his eyelids at the dermatologist, so how much worse could this pain be?

Abby sat next to him and said. "You are truly an amazing man to do this for me." She kissed his cheek. "Which is why I love you so much."

Then with surprising acumen and alacrity, Liz applied warm wax and ripped it away. The resulting pain, a combination of burning and tearing, caused every muscle in his body to tense. Dante had hoped not to make a sound, but a stifled grunt escaped his throat.

When it was all over, he wasn't sure his pecker would feel anything again. He and Abby went home and though he had to give it a day to recover, Abby spent the rest of the week fulfilling every fantasy Dante could come up with.

When his Sous Chef and best friend, Larry "Bird" Johnson, heard about it, he said, "Oh my god, D. I've been looking for someone like that all my life. You better ask that woman to marry you."

Chapter 3

Dante returned home the day after the breakup in Las Vegas. His jaw was clenched so tightly it ached, and he felt like his brain was trying to push his eyeballs out of their sockets.

For the rest of the day, which took forever to end, Abby's words echoed in his brain. *Doesn't give us much of a future . . .* He walked around like a corpse pulled from the ground and set in motion by some witch's spell.

Around eight that night, he decided to self-medicate. After half a bottle of Bowmore Scotch whiskey, followed by retching the entire contents of his body through his throat, he finally passed out.

The next morning, Dante felt like a squished prune left to harden in the sun. He drank a big glass of water, then a pot of espresso.

The rest of the day was not much better than the previous one, except that between glasses of whiskey he had equal moments of optimism that he would be able to win Abby back. He was sure the breakup was temporary and that she would come to her senses. But then he would tell himself that she was leaving him for her family, and that nothing he could do would get Abby back.

That night he passed out without the vomiting.

On Monday, Dante went back to work, his final week at Santino's. When he arrived, Bird was at the grill, flipping chicken breasts. His cocoa skin glistened from the heat. A drop of sweat ran down his dimpled cheeks, and into his perennial two day growth of beard. He caught the droplet on his shoulder before it could dive into the food.

"Yo, D," he said. "How was Vegas? You and Abby have a good time?"

Dante removed the seventy-two knives stabbing his gut and said, "Yeah. We did."

Bird narrowed his eyes and a devious little smile crossed his lips. "Did you get a little freaky deaky? Come on. I know you did. Did you do it against the hotel room window? She hire a prostitute for a little *ménage à trois*?"

"No." Dante shook his head then turned and grabbed the invoices from the morning's deliveries.

"No, none of that happened or no, you won't give me the details?"

Dante just continued looking at the paperwork.

"Come on, D. Details."

"Did you say something?"

"I see." Bird shook his head. "I need me a girlfriend like Abby so I don't have to rely on you for all the good stories."

"How'd everything go here?"

"I met this Ukrainian woman at DragonBar—"

"I meant here at the restaurant."

"Nothing out of the ordinary. Oh but Gordon was in here looking for you Saturday night. Seemed to be tweaking." Gordon Mayo, hotshot investment advisor, was Dante's business partner in the new restaurant.

"Yeah, he left me a couple of voicemails. Not sure what's up."

For the next three days, Dante held himself together. At least in public. Sixteen-hour work days did their part in keeping him on his nut. But at home, in the quiet of the night, he carried on the same unending conversation in his head.

Should I call her? I think it could be a good idea. She needs to know how much I love her.

I should just propose to her. That'd prove she means more to me than anything else, including my restaurant.

Yeah, I'll call her. Not now. It's too late. But tomorrow.

The one thing Dante couldn't reconcile was why Abby had even applied for a job in New York. She said she hadn't been sure she'd take it, but a person doesn't apply for a job and go through the interview process without having a serious willingness to make the move. And why had she never even mentioned anything about it before she broke up with him?

Or had she? Had he been so busy trying to get his new restaurant that he wasn't really listening or paying attention to what was happening with their relationship?

No, she hadn't said anything explicitly, he knew that much. Abby said she was going to New York for work, and to see her family. Nothing about interviews or job possibilities or Cook Network.

But the signs of strain were there. After Victor moved back to New York, Dante barely saw Abby more than once a week. She'd say she didn't want to leave Zoe with a babysitter all the time. Or with Dante's hours, she didn't want him coming over late and waking up Zoe. All of that had also been true when Victor still lived in San Francisco, but at least then, because Victor had Zoe every other week, Dante and Abby could spend much more time together on her "off" weeks.

And then, about a month before the breakup, Dante went to Abby's for their usual Sunday dinner. When he arrived, Zoe ran into the living room. "Hi, Dante!" Her dark hair was pulled back from her forehead with a hair band and her green eyes sparkled just like her mom's. Dante swooped her up over his head and made airplane noises as Zoe giggled. He put her down and she said, "I picked my own outfit tonight." She wore a pink Yankees sweatshirt with blue jeans and pink sneakers.

Dante patted her head. "It's perfect."

"My dad gave me this shirt and I get to wear it when we go to Yankee Stadium."

"Can I borrow it when I go to a baseball game? I think pink is a good color for me."

Zoe laughed. "You won't fit."

"Oh. I guess I'll have to get a bigger one of my own." Dante mock frowned.

When Abby and he had started dating, Dante quickly became attached to Zoe. She was smart and sweet and he loved spending time with her. He and Abby would often cook dinner with Zoe as their tiny helper. She made her own miniature pizzas and lasagnas. She also had a good appetite and was a connoisseur of the finest hot dogs and french fries. She would even eat things other four-year-olds might not touch, like rapini (as long as it was sautéed with garlic in olive oil) and eggplant parmesan.

But when they sat down for dinner that night, Zoe absolutely refused to eat her four-cheese pasta. She said she wasn't hungry and wanted to watch cartoons.

Abby rolled her eyes. "You haven't eaten anything since lunch."

Zoe held her nose. "I hate this pasta."

"No you don't. This is your favorite." Abby rubbed her temples with both hands.

"I want a hot dog."

"Well, when I asked what you wanted for dinner you should have said a hot dog, not four-cheese pasta."

"Dad lets me have hot dogs."

Abby's face turned near crimson. "Your dad's not here!" She slammed her hand on the table so hard it made Dante jump.

Zoe put her head down and started to sob quietly. Giant tears fell from her eyes. Then she picked up her fork, pierced one piece of pasta and put it in her mouth.

Abby closed her eyes and took a deep breath. She went over and stroked her daughter's hair. "I'm sorry, sweetheart. Do you want me to make you a hot dog?"

Zoe swallowed and wiped her eyes. "No mommy. I like the pasta."

After Zoe went to bed, Abby and Dante sat on the couch.

"I can't believe I lost it like that," Abby said.

Dante put his arm around her.

Abby shook her head. "I thought I could handle this on my own, but I'm beginning to wonder. It just feels like I never get a break. Like I'm isolated from my family, from everything but work and Zoe. I know I'm not the only person who's ever gone through this, but I wonder how people keep their sanity."

"You know I'd love to help in any way I can."

She just smiled and put her head on his shoulder.

At that point, Dante's plan to propose was already in motion, and he knew that once they were married, he could help raise Zoe. They would be a family. They could share responsibilities. And be together all the time.

Thursday night, Dante was at work at Santino's at the height of the dinner rush. He stepped into the kitchen after making the rounds to greet guests in the dining room.

Fire flashed off the grill. With a flip of the pasta guy's wrist, shrimp, scallops and fettuccine danced in a skillet. Line cooks in white coats, smudged with red, yellow, black and green, prepared pasta, poultry, and pizzas, steaks, and seafood.

One of the wait staff was nearly in tears over the fact that Gloria Sierra, wife of the beloved regular and San Francisco real estate heavyweight, John Sierra, had just sent her grilled salmon in caper butter back a second time. Ramon, five-foot-six, two-hundred thirty pounds, suggested that before sending the next one out, they place the fish squarely on his sweaty ass.

"If I ever catch anyone's ass on any food," Dante said, "you're all fired."

Ramon laughed. "Not after this weekend!"

Amid the kitchen cacophony, Dante's cell phone buzzed. He

yanked it from his pocket, hoping it might be Abby. It was his lawyer, Susan.

What he heard when he answered was that Gordon slept with Muntry and sled on the hefty mine.

Dante shook his head. Why would he care who his business partner slept with? He pressed the phone harder to his ear. "Gordon did what?"

This time his lawyer's voice was completely drowned out by a waiter screaming for his Sicilian chicken salad.

"Hold on a second, Susan, let me get out of here."

When he got into the office, he said, "I'm sorry, what was that again?"

"Gordon has left the country. And just ahead of the FBI."

"What? Left the country? For good?"

"I assume he'll be away for a while."

Dante placed his hand on his forehead. "What the hell did he do?"

"Apparently a lot. And with other people's money."

"Any of mine?" Dante sat behind the desk and felt as though his head was in a vice.

"Did you give him any?"

"No."

"Smart move. So the only thing you have to worry about is how you're going to replace his investment and raise the working capital you need to secure the lease for the restaurant."

Dante's stomach tightened. He choked back the rising acid and said, "Then he might as well have taken my money."

He had always thought Gordon was a little too clean. Slick, but not obviously so. He looked more like a shortstop for the Yankees than a finance guy. The kind of charmer who could talk a nun out of her panties. One night at a bar when Dante mentioned he was looking for an investor to help him open a new restaurant, Gordon rode up on his white horse. He promised money, support. He said, "Whatever you need—no, whatever you *want*—you'll have." And Dante would run the whole thing without any interference from Gordon. They'd have the best restaurant in North Beach. In San Francisco. Dante had known there was something off about Gordon, but he'd let himself get carried away by his dream.

After hanging up with Susan, Dante took a moment to pick up the pieces of his exploded head. Then he called the property management company.

"One of my investors unexpectedly backed out so I was hoping I could get another week before I sign the lease."

"I'm sorry Mr. Palermo, but we have strong interest in that property from at least two other parties. And the building owner is eager to get this done."

"Okay then, what can you do for me?"

"We can give you a twenty-four hour extension. Ten o'clock Saturday morning."

Dante wasn't sure whether another twenty-four hours would do him any damn good, but it was worth a shot. His replacement at Santino's had already been hired, a young lion coming up from the three-star Azzurro in Beverly Hills. So no Gordon, no Pane e Vino, no job.

Santino's owner, Arthur Ho, burst through the office door.

"Is everything set for tomorrow night?"

"It is."

"I want it perfect. The Speaker of the House of the United States is coming to my restaurant and I want it to be perfect," Arthur said.

"Perfect," Dante said. "Got it."

Arthur removed his glasses, and ran his hand down his face. "Do you?"

"Jesus, Arthur. First of all, she wouldn't be coming here if it wasn't for Charly." Dante's friend, Charly, was the District Chief of Staff for Gina Farello who represented California's Eighth District, San Francisco, in the House of Representatives and was Speaker of the House. "And second, if she has any complaints, you can fire me, okay?"

Arthur glared a second and huffed off.

Maybe he should call Charly. She'd be all over his investment problem.

On second thought, though, she'd be so all over this problem he wouldn't have a chance to breathe.

Bird peeked into the office. "John Sierra wants to say hello. You available?"

Dante's eyes lit up. John had money. Lots of it. He was a great guy and he loved Dante's food. He'd be the perfect business partner. "Absolutely," Dante said.

On the way to the dining room, Dante explained the Gordon situation to Bird. "Damn, D. I guess it's good he didn't rip *you* off. But, to be completely selfish about it, I don't want to be stuck here if you don't get to open your new place."

"Then let's just hope John wants to invest in a restaurant."

In the dining room, the woman on the piano played the ballad, "Here's That Rainy Day." Dante walked by white-clothed tables, smiling and nodding at the votive candle-lit faces. The dining room was too dimly lit for Dante's taste—people shouldn't have to ask for a flashlight to see what they're having for dinner. And the maroon carpet and dark wood didn't help.

At a back table, the best one in the house, the top of John's balding head and his wife's gray hair were just visible above a border of ferns.

"John, Gloria, how are you?"

John pushed his six-foot-four, two-hundred-fifty-pound frame back from the table in an attempt to stand, but Dante walked over to shake his hand. "Just grand," John said. He mopped sweat beads from his forehead. "I just wanted to tell you that red chili Alfredo sauce was something. I hope you'll have it at your new place."

"Glad you liked it." Dante went to the wife. "How are you tonight, Gloria?" He placed his hand lightly on her bony shoulder but could feel her recoil from his touch. Dante had never made physical contact with Gloria before and now he knew he wouldn't try it ever again. He removed his hand and smiled. His fingers felt blackened by frostbite.

Gloria looked up and faked a smile. Her weather-worn face nearly cracked from the effort. "I'm doing well, thank you." Her accent was all southern gentility. "Though the salmon tonight was not up to your usual standards."

"I'm sorry, Gloria. I've spoken to the staff about it. And your dinners tonight are on me."

She faked another smile. "Thank you."

"You're welcome." Dante turned back to John and paused a moment. The thought of asking a favor stuck in his throat. And now they were just looking at him as he stood, silent, no doubt with a stupid expression on his face. "Uhm, John?" John raised his eyebrows and smiled. "Would it be possible to meet with you tomorrow? I have—"

"I'm sorry. I'm flying to Seattle in the morning. But I'd be happy to meet with you next week."

"Unfortunately, what I'd like to talk to you about won't make any difference after tomorrow."

"Then what about tonight? We're finished here." He turned to his wife. "Gloria, you don't mind, do you?"

She clearly did mind. But she looked at her watch and said, "It's only 8:45. I'm sure I can pass the time across the street at Bloomingdale's jewelry counter." She slowly took a last sip of coffee, then meticulously dabbed the corners of her mouth with her napkin. She fussed with her blouse, fidgeted with her purse, and finally stood. She smoothed herself over one last time then, stepped over to kiss John's head, then sauntered out of the restaurant. Dante swore he saw a few people shiver as she passed.

John gestured for Dante to sit.

"Please give Gloria my sincere apologies for interrupting your evening," Dante said.

John smiled. "She'll make up for the inconvenience with something expensive, I'm sure."

"In that case, my sincerest apologies to you."

John chuckled. His eyes danced with utter happiness, as though he always expected things to turn out the way he wanted. "So what can I do for you?"

Dante swallowed hard. "You know I'm leaving Santino's to open a new place in North Beach."

"Yes, and I look forward to trying it out. You'll be so close to my office." The Transamerica Building, where John's office was on the 45th floor, was only about four blocks from the proposed location for Pane e Vino. "I'm sure you'll see a lot of me."

Dante's face burned. He cleared his throat. "The problem is, my partner backed out tonight. Well, not so much backed out as ran out. Of the entire country."

"That wouldn't be Gordon Mayo, would it?"

"How'd you know?"

"I've seen him here a few times and I heard the news earlier this evening that he had skipped the country. What a shyster. I'm sorry you got mixed up with him."

"I haven't lost any money, but it leaves me without a partner. And I only have until Saturday morning to resolve the situation."

Dante looked down at the tablecloth, brushed some imaginary crumbs away, almost grabbed Gloria's coffee cup to take a sip. "So I thought I'd ask if you were interested in investing."

"Hmm." John stroked his chin. "You know I love your food, and—"

"I've worked in restaurants since I was fourteen. After culinary school, I worked for a year in Rome. Here in San Francisco, I've been at Napoleon's and Il Pagliaccio. And I've been executive chef here for five years. Opening my own place is my biggest dream and I would never let that dream or your investment in it fail."

"I have no doubt, Dante, I have no doubt." John placed his hand over his mouth and squeezed. "How much of an investment are you looking for?"

Dante took a deep breath. "$250,000."

"Not a small amount of money. I'd need to see a business plan, a budget."

"I have the business plan on my laptop in the office. Do you mind if I go print it off?"

A minute later, Dante returned with his business plan. He handed it to John, who flipped through the pages.

"Very impressive," John said. "You've done your research and you know your market." He turned pages back and forth a few more times, then said, "But I just don't think it can be done by Saturday morning. I'm sorry."

Dante tried to smile. "I understand." He thanked John for his time and apologized again for interrupting his evening. He walked back to his office on numb legs.

Chapter 4

Dante and Bird sat at Santino's bar after the kitchen closed. The restaurant was nearly empty and thankfully Arthur had gone home. Dante had requested the pianist play "Everything Happens to Me" and the gentle music drifted through the dining room. He held up his glass of Bowmore, his second, and swirled the amber liquid.

"I'm sorry, D," Bird said. "But maybe you'll be able to find someone else."

"I doubt it. And maybe it's just not the right time." Dante took a sip, letting the smokiness of the whiskey fill his mouth then run down his throat. "There is special providence in the fall of a sparrow. If it be now, 'tis not to come; if it be not to come, it will be now; if it be not now, yet it will come: the readiness is all."

"What's that from?" Bird asked.

"Hamlet."

Charly came up from behind Dante and put her arms around him. Her blue eyes danced. She placed her flawless cheek again his. "I love it when you talk dirty." She looked at Bird. "Must be bad if he's quoting Shakespeare." She removed her hairclip and let her blonde hair fall over her ears. "Sorry I'm late. Did you get my text?"

Dante pulled out his phone. It was dead.

Charly shook her head. "Dante, do you know what a charger is? You know, that thing that keeps your phone powered?"

"I guess I should get one for here."

"Anyway, I had a meeting run late, so sorry. You know how it is when the boss is in town."

Bird half-snorted. "Yeah, we know how it is when she isn't in town. You're still a workaholic."

"What's your point?"

The bartender handed her a Grey Goose martini and the three of them toasted.

"Cheers."

Bird glanced over her shoulder. "What'd you do with your hunky mayor boyfriend tonight?"

"He was still working when I left the office. I'm going to his place after I leave here."

"For some hot mayor monkey love."

Charly rolled her eyes. "Nice, Bird." She turned to Dante. "Okay, let's see who we can find to invest in your restaurant."

Dante took another sip, closed his eyes, and swallowed. "Not tonight, Charly."

"What? Are you just going to mope?" She sipped her drink. "If I hadn't just bought my house, I might have been able to help."

"And if this place paid me more," Bird said, "I might be able to help." He grinned.

"Okay," Charly said as she pulled a small pad of paper and pen from her purse. "We can take John Sierra and Gordon Mayo off the list of potential investors. Who else did you pitch? What about banks?"

"Charly, I'm not going to do this now."

"Oh, get off the pity pot."

"Charly."

She took the olive from her martini. "You know, Dante, if you shrink from every tough challenge—"

"Jesus Christ, Charly! Give me a fucking break. I've never shrunk from any challenge. I'm just not doing this tonight. I need a chance to think."

Charly looked at Bird and put the olive back in her drink. "He's such a hothead." She turned to Dante. "I was just trying to help."

"I know. But you only have one speed: full steam ahead. I need to get my head around the situation and figure out what I really want. Maybe this is a sign from the universe that I'm supposed to wait for a better opportunity."

"First of all, that New Age stuff is a dangerous way to go. Signs, fate, all that crap—next you'll be consulting a psychic."

"Charly, shut the hell up."

Charly focused all the intensity of her blue eyes on Dante's face. "Okay, what's up? Something else is going on."

Dante stared into his drink.

"Abby? The Ice Queen still giving you the icebox treatment?"

"This has nothing to do with Abby. And she's not an ice queen."

"She's always cold to me."

Bird rolled his eyes. "Well of course she is. No woman likes her man to have a beautiful woman as a friend. Especially when he's always staring at her butt."

Charly's face reddened. "Shut up, Bird!"

"If it makes you feel any better, Charly" Bird said, "Abby's kind of cold to me, too. And D ain't never given my ass a second glance."

Dante rolled his eyes.

They finished their drinks and Charly offered Dante a ride home. She was silent as they walked through the parking garage and Dante knew it was too good to last once they drove out to the street. "So what's up with you and Abby, anyway?"

Dante looked out the window, watching the lights of downtown San Francisco pass. "There's nothing up."

"It seems like you two never see each other."

"It's been hard for her to take care of Zoe on her own."

"I don't know. Seems like a good reason to let you more into her life, not shut you out."

Dante shrugged.

"But I guess you have more immediate issues to deal with." She put her hand on his arm. "I can probably make a few calls."

"No, that's okay. I do appreciate the offer, though."

Charly smiled. Again, Dante turned and looked out the window as they drove up Columbus Avenue, right through the heart of North Beach. They crossed Broadway and he shifted in his seat. Pane e Vino would have been just a block down.

"So," Charly said, "how's everything for tomorrow night? Everybody in the office is looking forward to the dinner."

"We're all set. I think you'll enjoy it."

"You sure you're okay?"

Dante nodded. "Just a lot going on in my head."

Charly stopped in front of Dante's house. "You know, if you need anything, just give me a call."

"I will. Now go and get you some of that hot mayor monkey love."

Charly just looked at him for a second, then said, "I'm glad to see you embracing your inner sixteen-year-old."

"You're only as young as the adolescent comments you make."

They sat silently for another couple of seconds. Then Charly said, "Dante?"

"Yes?"

Again she hesitated. Finally she said, "Well, just call if you need anything."

"Thanks, Charly."

He got out of the car and watched as she drove away.

Dante first met Charly at a fundraiser for the North Beach Homeless Coalition. She was a volunteer and he helped with the catering. The event coordinator was a high-strung pain in the ass, so Charly kept hiding out in the kitchen.

He and Charly talked most of the evening and exchanged cards afterward. She called first and they met for drinks at Vesuvio. One story Dante remembered in particular from that night was an incident at Charly's first job out of college, a management consulting company in Dallas.

"They killed me at that place," she said, "and I totally hated it. My boss was such a jerk. Former college quarterback, arrogant as hell, this buttoned-down, wife-and-two-kids, go-to-church-every-Sunday guy. Anyway, I was working late one night on a presentation *he* was giving the next day. It was like eleven o'clock when I finished printing and binding them all and I went to leave them in his office. I opened his door and there he was on his knees, performing fellatio on his admin."

"Oh my God!" Dante laughed. "What'd you do?"

"I said, 'Hey, I thought we weren't getting bonuses this quarter!'"

"You did not."

"It's my proudest snap comment ever. I don't even know where it came from."

"Did you get fired?"

"No, but I left after a month. That's when I moved to California."

Dante held up his glass. "Cheers to that."

For the next year-and-a-half, Thursday at Vesuvio became a regular Charly and Dante night. Others often joined them—Bird, other restaurant people, Charly's friends—but if it was Thursday and you went to Vesuvio, you'd always see Charly and Dante there.

Dante got into the house, tossed his keys onto the dining room table, then plopped down in his favorite chair. In the silence of his living room that annoying voice in his head finally got a chance to really start talking.

This has been a pretty damn good week. You lost your restaurant, you lost the woman you love. Maybe tomorrow you'll wake up with cancer of the ass.

He leaned back and closed his eyes.

A second later, he jolted upright. How could he have been so stupid? *Fidati dell'imprevisto*—trust the unexpected. Maybe Gordon leaving was *supposed* to happen. Without a restaurant or job in San Francisco, he was free to go with Abby to New York.

He looked at his watch. 10:30. It was late but he knew he had to talk to Abby.

As her phone rang, he whispered, "Please pick up, please pick up, please pick up."

"Hello," she said, a lot less irritably than Dante thought she might.

"Hi. I'm sorry to call so late, but I really need to talk to you. Can I come over?"

"I don't think it's a good idea."

"But something major has changed, and—"

"Zoe's asleep. Can't you tell me over the phone?"

"Please. Just let me see you for a few minutes. I don't even have to come in. I'll call when I get there and we can talk on your front steps."

Abby sighed. "Alright."

Dante grabbed the engagement ring and drove over to Abby's place in the Marina district. When he walked up to her house, she was outside waiting for him, her arms hugged closely to her body. She smiled slightly when he got to the top of the stairs.

"Hi," he said

"Hi."

"Thanks for letting me come over."

She nodded.

"So tonight I found out Gordon has skipped the country."

"Oh?"

"Leaving me without the money to open the restaurant."

"I'm sorry. That's terrible." She furrowed her forehead. "But what—"

"I don't have any reason to stay here in San Francisco."

Abby didn't seem to follow.

He reached in his pocket. "I don't have any dreams to leave behind here. My dream is you. I can come to New York."

Abby closed her eyes and bit her lip.

Dante's heart dropped. "Unless . . . you don't want me to."

Abby opened her eyes but said nothing.

Dante looked into her perfect green eyes and felt the weight of this mammoth mistake pressing down on his heart.

"I see," he said. "Can I ask just one question? Did you ever love me?"

"That's so not fair. You know I did."

"Did?"

"Maybe still do. But this is about more than me. I've got Zoe to think about."

"Don't hide behind Zoe."

Abby looked up to the sky. "I knew this was a bad idea. I knew letting you come over would just make things worse."

"You're right. I should have left it alone. You made a nice clean cut and I had to go and dig around in the wound. That's my fault."

He turned and walked down the stairs.

Chapter 5

When Dante got home, he didn't turn on the lights. He just collapsed in a chair as every bit of energy, every ounce of power, every fragment of his shattered soul were sucked from his body into a pit of thick black tar that burned and froze him at the same time. He couldn't even cry. He just felt like he was melting away from existence.

He wasn't sure how long he sat like that, and when or if he had fallen asleep, but a noise in the kitchen brought him back to the dark room. He didn't move as consciousness settled on him. When he heard the noise again, he sat up. A peppery aroma wafted from the kitchen. And now someone was humming. He vaguely recognized the tune. Something from when he was young. Something his Nonna Isabella would sing when she was cooking.

The humming started to form into words. Sicilian. He walked toward the kitchen. A woman's voice sang, "*Ciuri, ciuri, ciuri di tuttu l'annu, l'amuri ca, mi dasti ti lu tornu . . . Lah lah la-la la, la la, la la, la lah . . .*"

Dante rounded the corner to the kitchen. "What the fuck?"

Nonna Isabella stood at the stove, stirring a pot.

Dante jumped, and stumbled back. He ran into a side table and knocked several pans to the floor. He stepped on the handle of a dented old saucepan, which slipped out from under him and he landed flat on his ass with a jaw-jacking thud.

Nonna looked over and raised an eyebrow. "Watch your mouth, Dantelino."

Hearing her voice and the nickname she always called him sent a wave of calm through him as he stood up. "Nonna, is that really you?"

Nonna smiled. "*Siediti*," she said, pointing at the kitchen chair.

On the other burner opposite the pot she stirred, a tomato mixture simmered in a large skillet. Something pungent and sharp. Spicy. Nonna's Puttanesca sauce.

She pulled a strand of spaghetti from the pot and tasted it. "*Perfetto*." She took the pot to the sink and dumped the spaghetti into the colander. Then she dropped the pasta into the skillet and mixed the spaghetti into the sauce with a spoon and a fork. She put some in a pasta bowl, and placed the food in front of Dante. The smell alone—anchovies, garlic, olives, and red pepper—was like a salve for his wounded heart.

Nonna put her hand on Dante's shoulder and said, "I always knew I'd have to come here for you."

"Come here for me? *Do* I have cancer? Am I dying?"

She shook her head and pointed at the pasta. "*Mangia*."

"I'm not hungry, Nonna."

Her glare let him know a slap on the back of the head would soon follow. He took a bite. The tangy heat filled his mouth. And like so many times when he was young, eating this simple, common dish, he tasted Nonna's true expression of love and care.

"You remember," Nonna said, "I made this when you were thirteen and that girl broke your heart. *Qual'era il suo nome*? Amy Leonardo, *sì*?"

Amy's brown hair and her big brown eyes seemed to shine unlike anything Dante had seen before. Her dimples melted him every time she smiled. Of course he had never spoken to her. But one day his science teacher asked him to be a last-minute addition to the Science Bowl team for the city tournament. At first, Dante declined the invitation, but when his teacher explained he'd be paired with Amy as the freshman members of the team, Dante's disinclination disappeared.

Throughout the afternoon, as the two of them studied everything from pi out to ten digits to E=mc2, from cloud formations to human cell structures, Amy smiled and laughed with him. She nudged him and put her hand on his arm.

That night, he happily did not sleep. His heart pounded and he felt like a bright golden light was shining out from his chest.

The next morning, Dante couldn't wait to get to school. He arrived a full half hour early, and waited in the hall not far from Amy's locker. When he saw her, his heart swelled to three times its normal size. He took a deep breath and went to say hi.

He got there just as her friends, Sue and Carmen, did. They looked at him like he was in the wrong place. Then Carmen said, "Eww, look at the zits on his face." Dante looked to Amy's eyes, but when she laughed, he turned and walked away.

Now back in Dante's kitchen, Nonna said, "When you came home from school that day, you were only a shadow. I knew then that when you truly fell in love, you would give your entire heart and soul. And if your heart was broken, it would shatter into a million pieces. So I come tonight."

"I don't understand."

"I'm going to tell you the story of your great-great-great-great-great-grandmother, Marietta. *Ascoltare*," she said, and Dante knew she had set aside her normal macaronic English. It was time to listen to her tale.

"C'era una volta in Sicilia, appena fuori dalla città di Trapani, un cuoco che aveva una figlia dai capelli dorati . . ."

Once upon a time, just outside the town of Trapani, Sicily, there lived a cook who had a golden-haired daughter with a face of honey cream and eyes like crystal molasses. Her name was Marietta and all her life, her father told her that, because of her beautiful heart, someday a handsome prince would come and marry her. And all her life, she waited for that day.

Over the years, Marietta grew into a beautiful young woman. One day she was out for a stroll in the countryside when a young man came thundering through the meadow on his black stallion. His silver boar-hound raced alongside. Marietta knew at once it was her prince.

And indeed, he was Prince Giuliano of Trapani. He, his horse, Ventonero, and his dog, Argento, were in pursuit of their favorite prey, the wind. They flew towards the entrance to the woods where the trunk of a long-since-fallen oak lay in their path. Argento sailed over the tree first and a second later, Ventonero was airborne. At the height of the horse's jump, Giuliano caught sight of Marietta near a patch of pink and yellow and red flowers. The prince turned and so absorbed was he in the sight of Marietta that when the horse hit the ground on the other side of the tree trunk, Giuliano lost his balance and catapulted from the saddle. He hit the ground, face down, on a large patch of moss. He did not move.

Marietta, rushed over. "Are you hurt?"

"Only my pride."

One look into Giuliano's eyes and Marietta knew he was as beautiful inside as he was out. She asked him to walk with her awhile, knowing that once he saw in her eyes what she had seen in his, he would ask her to marry him. They talked and laughed and at the end of the day, Marietta was truly in love. The young prince was also very much in love, but was already arranged to marry another in two days time.

But Giuliano couldn't tell Marietta. Instead, he asked her to meet him again tomorrow, determined he would find a way to marry Marietta instead of his betrothed. At home, he told his father, the King of Trapani, of meeting his true love. But the king scolded him. "Foolish boy, what do you know of love? Love comes out of duty and your duty is to marry the one to whom you are engaged."

The next day, Prince Giuliano met Marietta again in the country-side, and the moment he saw her, he broke down. "You are my one true love, but I am to wed another. One of royal blood."

Marietta cried, "Alas, all I can offer is my eternal love and devotion."

"Then I will marry you no matter what my father says!" The prince rushed home, but the king would hear nothing of Giuliano's true love. "Foolish boy, kingdom comes before love. You were born a prince and must marry royal blood. Your fate is your fate and cannot be changed."

"You are the one trying to change my fate!" said the prince. "I will marry my true love and duty be damned!" At that, the king had his son locked away. The next day, the prince's brother took his place and married their father's choice.

Marietta waited for days, but when Giuliano did not return all hope died inside her. Soon she fell ill with a broken heart, and became so sick that it was feared she would soon pass from this world—

Dante said, "And you're sure I'm not dying?"

Nonna gave him that same glare that told him to be quiet or be hit in the head. She continued, *"Ma una fata venne da lei di notte . . ."*

But a fairy came to her in the night and said, "You have a truly loving heart, but you have now lost hope for love. And when that happens, there is nothing sadder in all of creation." To fix this, the fairy said she would grant Marietta the power to heal the broken hearted with her cooking.

But Marietta would not be able to heal herself with her food. "You must learn to overcome your grief. Make peace with your heartache, allow it to heal, and bring hope back into your heart. If you can, your reward will be a true love of your own. For only a heart with hope can truly love again."

At first, the cook's daughter did not believe the fairy was real. Just the next week, however, Marietta saw the power of her food. A woman in the village whose husband had died six months before became very sick. Everyone knew she was dying of heartbreak over the loss of her husband. Hearing this, Marietta made a simple soup of chicken and vegetables and brought it to the woman. After only one spoonful, the color returned to the woman's face and by that evening her strength returned.

Word spread that it was Marietta's soup that had cured the woman's broken heart and soon all of the village's heartsick were coming to her. In a matter of months, people from neighboring villages started coming to her and after just a year, she was world-renowned for her ability to cure heartache.

Now in all this time, Giuliano was still in Marietta's heart, though she had made peace with her heartache. She knew that one day she would be with her true love. When asked why she would not marry, she always had the same answer: "The heart of my true love awaits. We will be together in this world or the next."

After ten years passed, the newly crowned King of Trapani summoned Marietta. He said, "My brother has not spoken since my father denied him his true love. Now that my father is dead and I am King, I wish for you to cure my brother's heart."

She was led to a room where a broken man sat gazing out of the window. What little light came into the room was obscured by the sadness that hung over him. When Giuliano turned and saw Marietta, all the color retuned to his face. He looked to the sky. "You see, father! Foolish old man, you could not deny me my love. My fate is my fate and cannot be changed." He embraced Marietta and pledged he would never again leave her side. The King cried out in joy and gave them the town of San Vito lo Capo as a wedding gift. The next day Giuliano and Marietta were married and lived out the rest of their days happy and content by the sea.

"San Vito lo Capo?" Dante said. "Isn't that where you were born?"

"It is."

She began washing the pots and pans she had cooked with. "When I was a young girl, just eighteen, I thought I had found the one I was to marry. He was a soldier and a beautiful man. But a month before we were to wed, I found out he had another woman in Marsala. I spit in his pig face and told him never to come near me again. Then I cried for three months, and I too lost all hope for love. My Uncle Agostino, dead ten years, came to me in the night. He told me because I had a truly loving heart, but had lost hope for love, he would grant me the power to heal the broken hearted with my cooking. But I would not be able to heal myself. I would have to learn to overcome my grief. Make peace with my heartache, allow it to heal, and bring hope back into my heart. And if I did, my reward would be a true love of my own.

"After that night, it took my heart three months to heal. I knew that man had been wrong for me and I would find someone better someday. And for five years, my food cured the heartsick. I told no one about this and my mother worried I would never marry because I had suffered such a terrible broken heart so young. But hope had indeed returned to my heart, and I knew my love was on his way."

Nonna Isabella smiled and a tear ran down her cheek. "Then I met your Nonno Giorgio. He worked on a fishing boat that came into town one afternoon in May. The moment I saw him, I knew he was my true love. I said, 'Hello' and his heart belonged to me for the rest of his life."

She cleared her throat and continued, "So tonight I come to give you the gift that has been in our family for generations." She took his hand as she had so many times when he was a boy and looked at him with those great brown eyes of wisdom. "From now on, your food will have the power to cure broken hearts. But you must learn to overcome your grief. Make peace with your heartache, allow it to heal, and bring hope back into your heart. If you can, your reward for being a heart healer will be your own true love. For only a heart with hope can truly love again."

Dante shook his head trying to awaken from the dream.

"You're not dreaming, Dante. You will see." Nonna touched his cheek one more time and faded away before his eyes.

Dante stood in the kitchen. He smiled and placed his hand where she had touched his face. A tear ran down his cheek. "Thank you, Nonna."

Chapter 6

Dante woke up the next morning and tried to shake the blur out of his eyes, but his neck was too stiff. He took several deep breaths and blinked hard. Eventually his eyes focused.

He straightened up in the chair and felt like a cast iron skillet sat on top of his head. He unclenched his jaw and felt a vague nausea envelop him.

He stumbled to the kitchen to make espresso. The scent of garlic, anchovies, and peppers hung in the air. The skillet and pot his Nonna used sat in the dish rack. And when he opened the refrigerator, leftover Puttanesca was in a clear plastic container on the top shelf.

That confirmed Nonna's visit.

For a moment he considered another possibility: he was out of his fucking mind. Maybe he had developed multiple personality disorder and Nonna was just a new character in his head. Good lord, how many others would come out now? Or would it just be the two of them carrying on with cooking and Italian folktales in the night? Then they could slowly start a movement: Cooking Club. *The first rule of Cooking Club is you do not talk about Cooking Club.*

"I need a cold shower."

The cold shower seemed to help bring him back to a semi-normal mental state. And though it was only 6:30 A.M., he decided to walk to work. Maybe the fresh air would further the return of his sanity. He stepped outside under the ceiling of gray that covered the sky above San Francisco. About halfway through the trip, Dante's cell phone rang. As he dug in his jacket pocket, he wondered who the hell would be calling him this early.

Maybe Abby? Yes, of course. After seeing you last night, she decided she can't let you go. She's going to stay in San Francisco, not take the huge job, you knob.

The call was from a number he didn't recognize. Normally, he'd let it go to voicemail. This time, however, something made him answer.

"Sorry to call so early." It was John Sierra. "But I wanted to make sure I got a hold of you this morning before I left."

"No worries. I'm glad you called. What can I do for you?"

"I got to thinking last night that maybe I'd missed a great opportunity with you. So I looked at your business plan again, and I think we can actually put this together quickly. I have to leave for the airport at ten, but if you can come over to my office right now, we can talk about what you need and how I can help."

Dante, head spinning, hailed a cab and took a short ride downtown.

John's office was the size of Dante's living room and dining room put together, and had a view of the Bay Bridge. John, who was on the phone, was parked behind a mammoth mahogany desk.

John said into the phone, "Just grand, just grand." He waived Dante in and motioned for him to have a seat. "I'll be there this afternoon. Thank you so much, Bill. This has come together nicely."

He hung up the phone and said, "So, Dante, here we are."

"I have to admit, I'm in shock."

"I'm sorry for the drama. But sometimes, even in business, you have to go with your heart." He smiled. "And just so you know, I like to keep it simple and I operate on handshakes and contracts that aren't longer than a page."

"That sounds great."

“So,” John said, “Gordon’s investment was to be $250,000?”

“Yes. Working capital. I’m sure we can get by with less—”

“Let’s not think about ‘getting by.’ If we’re going to do this, let’s do it right.”

Dante breathed an inaudible sigh of relief. “We’ll need to gut the place and the kitchen needs a lot of work, so $250,000 should do it.”

John nodded. “I assume you’ll be the managing partner in this arrangement.”

“As long as you’re comfortable with it. I’ll handle all the day-to-day operations, the staffing, menus, catering.”

“There is one thing,” John said. “My wife likes to dabble in design.”

Dante suppressed a cream-curdling scream.

“And when I told her my plan to become your business partner, she got very excited. I have to tell you, not a lot excites her these days. She would like to be involved in the restaurant’s design.”

Damn it! How do I get out of this?

“Hmm.”

“I know you’ve budgeted for a professional restaurant designer, so I’m not suggesting Gloria actually design the place. But she would like to hire the designer and to give her input about décor and the like.”

What could he say? Was he going to let the chance to open his restaurant slip away because he didn’t want a bored rich woman to give her input about how the place looked?

“That should be fine.”

“And the name is Pane a Vino?” John said.

“That was the name I’d planned. But something about it doesn’t feel right now.”

“I agree.”

They both thought for a moment, then John said, “What’s the Italian word for ‘stolen’?”

“*Rubato.*” Then Dante’s eyes lit up. “What about Pane Rubato? Stolen Bread.”

John’s face lit up. He clapped his hands and said, “I love it!”

At the end of the brief meeting, Dante left with a check and later that day, he signed the lease, making the location on Broadway at Kearny officially the new home of Pane Rubato.

Chapter 7

After signing the lease on his new restaurant, Dante called his mom, brother, and sister in Des Moines to tell them the big news. He e-mailed his cousin Marcello, whose restaurant, Quattro Uccelli, he'd worked at in Rome.

He also texted his friend, Savio, whom he worked with on the line at Quattro Uccelli. Dante and Savio were like brothers and spent most of their time at work trying to one-up each other. For the past couple of years, they had had a running bet which one would open a place of his own first. Dante's text was two words: "I win!"

At work that night, Bird slapped him on the back. "Yo, D, smile! All your dreams are coming true."

Dante turned up the corners of his lips and hoped it looked genuine enough. "I guess the last couple of days have taken a lot out of me."

Bird grabbed his shoulders and looked him in the eye. "Well remember all you got right now and let that put something back into you, man! This is a *great* day."

"Okay, okay. You're right."

That night at work, even though images of Abby pierced Dante's heart, gut, and mind unremittingly, he managed to stay focused on Speaker Farello's staff dinner. For the main course, he prepared a filet mignon wrapped around a mixture of gorgonzola, pignoli nuts, basil, parsley, black pepper, and parmigiano cheese. He wrapped the steak in speck, a smoked prosciutto, and rolled the whole thing in flour, browned it in butter, then finished it off in the oven. Dessert, inspired by something he'd had his first time in Palermo when he was twelve, was a simple spongy brioche roll cut in half and filled with two scoops of pistachio gelato, a dollop of whipped cream, and topped with chocolate sauce.

The staff knocked that out, along with the regular dinner orders, without a hitch. After the Speaker's dessert went out, Dante clapped his hands to get the staff's attention. "Hey everyone, great job on Speaker Farello's dinner tonight. That might have been your best performance yet. Thank you."

A few minutes later, he headed to the back party room at Speaker Farello's request. He entered the room to a group of smiling faces (and a few not-so-smiley security agents). Speaker Farello wore a red turtleneck that clung to her liberal bosom. She stood and made her way around the table with politicianly authority, her shoulders barely visible above the heads of her seated staff. Her smile seemed genuine to Dante, but how could you tell with someone who held such a high office? Sincerity must be something politicians learn to simulate very early in their careers. Her dark eyes burned with confidence and intensity, but warmth, too. Dante couldn't help but feel as though the Speaker was greeting him as she would a friend.

"That was a truly wonderful dinner and I wanted to thank you personally." She shook Dante's hand in a tiny vice-like grip. "Charly was right. That was some of the best Italian food I've ever had."

"Thank you, that's so nice of you to say. It was an honor to cook for you."

"I only hope I'll have the pleasure of your cooking again soon."

After the Speaker's party broke up, Dante met Charly at the bar. "You told your boss I make some of the best Italian food?" he said.

Charly's face turned a very light shade of pink. "Of course."

"I'm a little surprised."

"Why? I love your food."

Dante laughed. “Then why do you only ever order the grilled chicken breast with whole wheat fettuccine and steamed veggies when you come in here?”

“I like to eat healthy. And I know this is shocking to you, but not everyone lives to eat. For some of us food is just the way we get the energy we need to function. If I could get it in a pill, I would.”

Dante acted like he'd been stabbed in the chest. “I'm glad not everyone thinks like you.”

“The world would be such a wonderful place if everyone thought like me.”

“I don't even want to imagine the world according to Charly.” He smiled.

“So you and Abby celebrating tonight?”

Dante looked at his watch, then the floor. “Um, yeah.”

“Then I'd better get out of here. I don't want to mess up your good day by having Abby find me here with you. Congratulations on everything. I'm so excited for you.”

Chapter 8

By the following week, when Dante took possession of his new restaurant, his pants were getting loose, and he realized he probably hadn't eaten a regular meal since his return from Las Vegas.

That morning, he arrived at the new place to start the major cleanup. The kitchen smelled of moldy, rotting food, and the dining room had the mustiness of disuse. It all still seemed haunted by the previous tenant, Vinny's Fine Italian Cuisine. Shadows of doughy pizzas topped with rubbery mozzarella and mushy pasta covered in tasteless, runny alfredo sauce or marinara from a can crept out of the kitchen. The echoes of trite mandolins and accordions rang in the dining room. But he saw past all of it and imagined how his restaurant would be on the day they opened. The space at the back was perfect for a small jazz combo. He'd expand the tiny bar just before the entrance to the kitchen.

Bird stepped inside and said, "We got a lot of work to do, D."

"Yeah."

"And what's up with that menu you sent me yesterday?" Dante had e-mailed Bird his ideas for entrees like spaghetti alla Calabrese (spaghetti tossed with sardines, olives, capers, and breadcrumbs) and morseddu (a spicy dish of pork with offal—heart, lungs, spleen, liver—in tomato sauce).

"They're southern Italian specialties."

"The spaghetti is fine. But you think offal is going to fly?"

"I learned it in Rome. My cousin Marcello was a master with Calabrese food."

"Maybe. But not a lot of people are going to eat lungs and spleen. Least of all, her." He motioned toward the front door where Gloria approached with a look on her face as though she smelled rotten eggs.

Bird held the door open for her and said, "Mrs. Sierra, how are you?"

"I didn't realize we were *right next door* to the strip clubs." Her eyes seemed to indict Dante.

He smiled. "This part of North Beach has a different charm than up the block."

John came through the door, grinning. "This is perfect. I can already see the patio packed every night."

"I suppose we'll make do," Gloria said. "But once we're established, we'll probably want to move to a more dignified location."

"I think I'll go check out the back," Bird said.

He was barely ten feet away when Gloria whispered, "Are you sure he should be running the kitchen? Shouldn't we have someone with a better culinary pedigree?"

"Bird's been working in restaurants since he was sixteen and knows as much about food as anyone who graduated from culinary school. I can't think of anyone I trust more to handle this job."

"Bird's a good man, dear," John said. When John came into Santino's alone, he'd often have a drink at the bar after dinner, usually staying until near closing time. At the bar, he and Bird would talk Giants baseball, 49ers football, Warriors basketball, and Sharks hockey. "If Dante trusts him, so do I."

Gloria didn't look impressed and she was just about to say something when Dante's choice to run the front of the house, Sal Verzino, walked in. Silver hair, wire-rimmed glasses, and a slight frame that belied his nickname, the Brooklyn Bull.

Sal and Dante had worked together at Napoleon's, Dante's first restaurant job in San Francisco. Dante got the gig on the day after he moved into a studio apartment on Filbert, his second full day in the city. Dante was twenty-three and had spent the previous year in Rome. He walked into Napoleon's, across the street from Washington Square Park, and there was Sal. Dante inquired about the line cook job ad in the paper, and Sal said they didn't hire homeless kids off the street then turned and walked away. Dante called after him, "You own this place?"

The owner, Aldo Napoleon, sitting at the bar, said, "No, I do." He appeared to be in his early sixties, barrel-chested, with a Cuban cigar stub stuffed between his yellow teeth.

Dante handed Aldo his resume.

Without looking at it, Aldo placed the resume on the bar. He looked Dante up and down and said, "Come back when you grow some pubes."

Dante said, "I'll cook in your kitchen tonight for free. If I don't impress you, I'll go away."

Sal, who had picked up Dante's resume, said, "You went to culinary school in Des Moines? And you want to cook in the best Italian restaurant in San Francisco? Do they even know what Italians look like in Des Moines?"

Dante glared. "*Mia madre proviene da Cariati, mio padre proveniva da Palermo. Ho appena passato l'anno scorso a lavorare a Roma. Sono Italiano. Tu cosa se?*"

Sal and Aldo looked dumbfounded. Dante said, "Let me translate for you. I said that my mother is from Cariati, and that my father was from Palermo. I just spent the last year working in Rome. I *am* Italian. What are you?"

"You got balls," Aldo said. "I'll give you that much. So let's see what you can do."

"He's a cocky bastard," Sal said. "Put him on the pasta station. He'll be crying for his Italian mama by eight o'clock."

Aldo nodded.

Dante went back to the kitchen, got a quick rundown of the pasta menu and how things were prepared, then waited for the onslaught. At the time, Napoleon's was widely regarded as one of the best restaurants in North Beach, and they were packed every night of the week. Pasta was the specialty of the house, and they would normally knock out nearly a hundred plates during dinner service. That night, Dante stood in among the taunts and jeers of the other kitchen staff, the screaming and whining of the wait staff, and the deluge of orders. He handled it all with the finesse he'd learned doing the same thing night after night in Rome. And not only did his food taste great but his plates were beautiful.

When the kitchen closed, Aldo hired him on the spot, and told him he'd never been so impressed by anyone's moves in the kitchen as he had been by Dante's. Even the surly Sal shook his hand and said, "Nice job in there."

Over the next three years, Sal and Dante became good friends. Dante would soak up every word of what Sal had to say about running the front of the restaurant, how the service should be so good it was almost invisible. No customer should ever have to look around to catch someone's eye to ask for something. The staff should be paying attention and anticipating anything a table might need. When Dante left to become the Chef de Cuisine at Il Pagliaccio, he said to Sal, "When I open my own place, I want you out front." And now here they were.

Sal took Dante aside. "Jesus, this place is a real dump." He smiled.

Dante chuckled. "I know. But we're going to make it brilliant."

Long after everyone left, Dante remained, sitting at the old Vinny's bar. The sun had gone down and the house lights were up. He chewed a pen and stared at a blank pad of paper on which he'd meant to write up some promotion ideas.

She loves me. I know she loves me. She just let her head get in the way of her heart.

A large figure outside the front door caught Dante's eye. He looked up to see John peering in.

When Dante opened the door, John said, "I thought you'd still be here." In his hand, he held a bottle. "You're a Bowmore man, right?"

"Indeed I am."

They sat at the bar and Dante grabbed a couple of the plastic glasses he'd brought in earlier. John held up his Scotch and said, "To Pane Rubato."

"Cheers." Dante sipped his whiskey, then said, "So what brought you out here?"

"Gloria's off at one of her functions, and since we haven't had a chance to officially celebrate our new business relationship, I thought I'd stop by."

"I want to thank you again, John. It means a lot to me that you invested in this place."

The two of them sat and talked for the next couple of hours, John saying things like, "It's much easier getting what you want when everybody in the room is smiling," and "I didn't get where I am by stepping on people, and fighting all the way. I got here because I always knew I would and never let anyone tell me differently. There are lots of people who will tell you what you *can't* do. And not a lot of them are truly successful."

He also told the story of how he met Gloria. "I was twenty five, on a business trip to Charleston. She was a secretary—it was the sixties, so we still called them secretaries—and when she walked into that room to take notes, I couldn't stop looking at her. She kept smiling back at me and all I could think was I needed to talk to this girl. So I asked her to dinner." He smiled. "Her boss never forgave me for stealing his best secretary."

Over the next two months Dante and John spent many evenings together. While the restaurant was being renovated, John would often stop by after he left his office and he and Dante would share stories late into the night.

One night, they got on the subject of family.

"When I was a kid in Des Moines," Dante said, "before my Nonna died, all of my aunts and uncles and cousins would go over to our house on Sundays. We'd have these great big meals and everyone would sit around talking for hours. My younger cousins and I would play tag and when it got dark, hide-and-go-seek. A lot of the families around us were Italian, too, and on summer nights they'd join us. Someone would break out a guitar and they'd sing folk songs. I was so lucky to have such a close family. Most of my friends in high school never knew much about their heritage, and they certainly didn't get to experience it as directly as I did mine."

"I'm glad we went into business together," John said. "I've enjoyed getting to know you, hearing your family stories. Reminds me of my family when I was growing up. Crazy Irish—"

"Wait. Sierra is an Irish name?"

"Our family name was originally O'Sullivan. My great grandfather came to California from Listowel, Ireland right at the beginning of the gold rush. He was in Nevada City picking up supplies and heard a group of men bashing the Irish, saying they should be run out of the hills and mines. They apparently gave great-granddad the stinkeye and asked him his name. He faked his best American accent and said, 'Sierra. John Sierra.' And the name stuck. So we may have gotten rid of the name but all the Irish remained." He sipped his bourbon. "My son and daughter are much more like Gloria. Brilliant kids but they don't often let their guard down."

A rapping came from the front door where a couple of young women—one blonde, one brunette—smiled and waved. Dante opened the door and they said they had often seen him inside when they were on their way to work and wanted to stop by to say hello.

The blonde's name was Lisa, but at Showgirls, the club down the street, she went by Luna. The brunette's stage name was Star, but her real name was Val.

They didn't stay long, but after that night they stopped by every so often, and Dante learned a lot about the neighborhood from them. Even though he had been in North Beach since he moved to San Francisco, and had been to the clubs a time or two, this little strip had character and politics all its own. So they gave Dante the lowdown on Broadway people, who was okay, who to watch out for, and who had done what to whom.

Over the two months of renovation, Dante got first-hand experience of Gloria's idea of input on design and décor. "Why do we need to have jazz?" she said. "Who even understands that music?" Sal had suggested putting the wait staff in black shirts and blue jeans, but Gloria said, "Oh, we really mustn't have blue jeans. I think the classic white shirt and black pants are much more suitable."

Dante's menu included *arancini ai gamberetti* (fried rice balls, stuffed with shrimp), and fried eggplant cakes with tomato and basil as appetizers, spaghetti with artichokes and *battarga di tonno* (cured tuna roe sacs), and *triglie di scoglio* (red mullet in onion sauce). When Gloria and John saw the menu, Gloria said, "Can't we have something a little more elegant for an appetizer? Some nice canapés?"

Dante forced a smile. "Oh, what did you have in mind?"

Gloria brightened up. "You know I just love those cucumber rounds with salmon mousse."

"That sounds awful," John said.

"Well," Dante said, "I'm not sure it works in our menu, but I'll see what I can come up with, okay?"

One afternoon, Gloria had Tina, the designer whom *she* had hired, in tears when she rejected the third round of design comps. Gloria made notes all over the sketches, changing the color of the walls, the lighting, the chairs and the floors. All the modifications would have given the place a sterility and stuffiness that only she would have enjoyed eating in.

Dante begged the designer not to quit and said to Gloria, "We're going for a more laid back style. Something reminiscent of North Beach in its heyday and new San Francisco. Warmer colors, not so much of the brass and marble or the ornate chandeliers." He pointed to the marred sketch of the dining room and said, "This is perfect. There's a certain elegance without being pretentious. And to be fair, it incorporates a lot of your requests and previous changes."

"I suppose it does."

"Exactly. Now we're already three weeks behind schedule, so I say we go with this as it was before you made your notes."

"Oh, alright," Gloria said. "But I'm starting to wonder if I get to have any say at all in this restaurant." She left without waiting for Dante's response and didn't come back to the restaurant for another two weeks.

She reappeared on the day the kitchen was finished. The dining room was still probably two weeks away, but the kitchen was ready to go. Gleaming new appliances and stainless steel counters and tables. It made Dante nervous to see it all unused. And he still felt like the presence of Vinny's haunted the place. So he decided to cook a meal in the new kitchen that night to exorcise any evil spirits.

At that moment, however, Gloria was fast approaching and appeared to have something Dante didn't want to hear about on her mind. She had in tow a young man with a crooked nose, oversized ears, and the scars of severe acne.

"This is my nephew, Darryl," she said. "He wants to move here from Atlanta. He works in a restaurant there and I think he'd be a wonderful member of our kitchen team."

Darryl glanced around the half-finished dining room with a sneer-like smile. Dante was shocked that Gloria would even admit to him being a relative.

"So Darryl," Dante said. "Where do you work in Atlanta?"

"I manage the kitchen at a Chicken-n-Dumplins."

"I don't think I've heard of it," Dante said.

"They got stores in Georgia, Florida, and South Carolina. My dad owns it."

"Wow," Dante said. "The whole chain?"

Gloria's face turned a little pink.

"No," Darryl said. "Just our store. But it's the busiest out of all thirty-seven."

"I see. And did you actually do any of the cooking there?"

"Of course I did." His eyes added, *You goddamn idiot.*

"Hmm." Dante did the best he could to stifle all the petty thoughts. He'd never been to a Chicken-n-Dumplins so he couldn't really judge a cook's talent without having ever had the food. He suspected, however, that most of the preparation involved opening boxes, bags, and cans. Still, he wasn't in need of a kitchen manager.

Gloria took Dante's arm. "Excuse us Darryl, I would like to talk to Dante in private a moment." They walked to the other side of the room and Gloria said, "He needs to get out of Atlanta and away from those so-called friends of his. I'm asking you as a favor." She paused a moment. "His father says he's really good on the grill at family barbeques."

Asking Dante for a favor must have been hard for Gloria. Her eyes practically pleaded.

"Let me talk to Bird. Have Darryl come back tomorrow so we can give him a few things to make and see how he does."

"Thank you."

After they left, Bird came over to Dante. "What was that all about?"

"Her nephew. She wants us to hire him."

Bird smirked. "Dishwasher?"

"Chef du cuisine."

"I knew she didn't like me. And she wants to put that—"

"Relax. I'm kidding."

"You're an asshole."

§ § §

Around seven that night, Charly arrived at Pane Rubato. Dante had invited her and the mayor but the mayor had an event to appear at. Charly said she'd love to come as long as Abby was okay with her being there. Dante told her Abby would be out of town, so not to worry about it.

"Hey strangers," Charly said to Bird and Dante, then hugged each of them. "Thanks for inviting me."

She looked at Dante. "Hey, have you lost weight?"

Dante shrugged. "I don't know."

"You have. It's got to be at least ten pounds." It was fifteen, but who was counting?

"I keep telling him he's working too damn hard," Bird said, "but he doesn't listen."

"So what do you think of the place?" Dante said.

"Seems to be getting there. When are you planning to open?"

"I'm hoping for the 18th. But it still feels like we have a long way to go. And the liquor license is taking forever."

"Don't worry, it'll all come together." She looked over Bird's shoulder. "Is it just us?"

"I invited John and Gloria, but she'd rather wait for our proper grand opening."

"And Abby's out of town again?"

Dante looked away. "Yeah. I guess KQED's got some big new initiative going."

Charly narrowed her eyes. "Dante, what's up?"

"Nothing's up."

"Abby seems to spend a lot of time out of town. And you look like shit. What's going on with you two?"

Dante tried to steady his voice. "We broke up."

"I *knew* it. When?"

"Oh, I guess it was almost three months ago."

"Damn it, D," Bird said. "Why didn't you say something?"

"Because." He took a deep breath. "Because I couldn't."

"Why?" Charly said. "Did you not think we'd understand? Did you think we wouldn't know how to help? That we wouldn't know how to be your friends?"

"No."

"Then why?"

"Because I knew that as soon as I told someone. If I said it out loud." He closed his eyes and bit his lip. "I'd completely . . . fall . . . apart."

Charly put her arms around him. "I'm so sorry." She put her hand on the back of his head and held him close. Bird patted his shoulder.

Then Charly kissed his cheek. "Let's sit down," she said.

His eyes were blurred and his cheeks were wet. "Sorry." He couldn't look Bird or Charly in the face as they guided him to the dining room table.

"There's nothing to be sorry for," Bird said.

"I'll be fine." He forced a smile.

The three of them went back to the kitchen where Dante had set up a prep table with a table cloth, candles, and place settings for the three of them. Bird poured three glasses of red wine. They all sat, and Dante gave them the basics of the Abby breakup story. To her credit, Charly mostly listened and when it was clear Dante had had enough of talking about Abby, she said, "So, what's on the menu for tonight?"

Dante picked up a glass, "First, let's toast to our first dinner." They all clinked glasses. "Now just a sec while I get the *polipo*."

A minute later, Dante produced a plate of octopus salad with potatoes and black olives. "We did this one at Quattro Uccelli, my cousin's restaurant in Rome."

Charly looked at the plate and arched an eyebrow.

"Don't worry," Dante said, "you'll like it."

Charly put a little of the octopus on her plate. She gave it a long look. "Here goes nothin'." She put a forkful of the salad in her mouth, then nodded her head and raised her eyebrows. "Wow, who knew octopus was so tasty?"

Dante stood and said, "Eat up and I'll get the rest ready."

He went to the stovetop where a pot of water was on the verge of boiling. He dropped butter in a large skillet, and a sautéed a clove of minced garlic. When the garlic was soft, he poured a cup of cream in. The pot on the other burner was now boiling and he dropped three side-servings of fresh fettuccine into the rolling water. He turned his attention back to the skillet. He stirred the cream, butter, and garlic until the mixture started to boil. Then he added a couple of tablespoons of freshly grated parmesan cheese into the mixture and waited for it to thicken. Finally, he added salt and freshly ground black pepper, then took the fettuccine with his tongs directly from the pot to the cream sauce. A few tosses of the pasta and sauce and everything was nicely coated.

He pulled roasted brussels sprouts from the oven and tossed them in a bowl with olive oil, sautéed garlic and red pepper flakes.

"Bird," he said, "can you get the chicken out of the oven?"

Bird plated the breaded chicken breasts, which were stuffed with prosciutto and fontina. Dante added the fettuccini and the sprouts.

When Dante and Bird sat down, Charly held up her wine glass. "To Pane Rubato. May it surpass all your dreams."

Chapter 9

The next morning, Dante sat at his dining table with a blank card in front of him. The cover of the card was an impressionistic rendering of a field of daffodils, Abby's favorite flower. Her birthday was next Tuesday. He had bought the card weeks ago and wasn't sure he would send it. But what was the worst that could happen? She'd see the return address and toss the envelope away without ever opening it? At least she'd know he was still thinking of her.

He opened the card and penned, simply, "Happy birthday. I hope you and Zoe are well." He hesitated before signing it. "Love, Dante."

He'd Googled Abby, and came across a people search website where he paid fifteen bucks to get a report on an A. Drivakis who now lived in Manhattan and had previous addresses in San Francisco and New York. Interestingly, this same person also had an address in Nashville, and Abby had never mentioned living there. So the Tennessee connection notwithstanding, Dante was fairly certain he'd found the right address for Abby. And if he hadn't, well, she wouldn't get the card, and all would be as she intended when she left. He sealed the envelope and walked down to the corner mailbox. What if she thought his finding her address stalkerish? This card might even do more damage.

How could I possibly do more damage? I couldn't be any less with Abby than I am now.

His hands shook as he dropped the card into the box.

He then went to Pane Rubato and got to work on some final details before the grand opening the following weekend. Sal was interviewing wait staff and Bird and Dante were interviewing for the kitchen.

"Yo, D," Bird said. "You look like Dante of the Dead. You okay?"

"I've got a nasty headache and I'm not looking forward to interviewing people all day. But I'll be fine."

"I hope we get someone better than Darryl. He's alright for kitchen help, but I'd really like to slap the cocky out of him."

"I'm sure a lot of people said the same about you and me when we first started out."

"I can see that about you, but *I* was never cocky." He grinned.

A white guy with dreadlocks in a Bob Marley T-shirt and blue jeans walked in the front door, and said, "Sign says you're doing job interviews."

"Yep," Dante said. "You here for kitchen or wait staff?"

"Either, I guess."

Bird and Dante looked at each other as if to say, *you're kidding*.

Then Dante said, "Well, come on back."

And so the parade of people seeking employment at Pane Rubato started. After the first two hours, Dante and Bird needed a break. The last applicant had never worked in a restaurant before, had only seen the ad on craigslist that morning, and had decided to come down because he'd worked as a tech support rep for a software company and "how hard can it be to become a cook?"

After he left, Dante looked at Bird and said, "If the rest of the day goes like this, it's only going to be you, Darryl, and me in this kitchen and I'm going to quit."

There hadn't been a single applicant from any restaurant either Bird or Dante had ever heard of other than In-N-Out Burger (and that woman had only ever worked the cash register). Most of them didn't even have a list of places they'd worked, let alone a resume. And references? Forget it.

"Is the market for kitchen people that tough?" Dante said.

Sal, however, reported much better results. He'd hired three wait staffers, two he'd known from other restaurants. So at least there'd be people to serve the crap food coming out of the inexperienced kitchen.

The next person to walk into the kitchen was a woman with dark hair, darker eyes, and tattoos on the copious amounts of skin she displayed. She looked more suited to building custom choppers than to preparing a plate of tuna alla Siciliana. She smiled wide when her eyes met Dante's.

Dante and Bird said, "You're hired," at the same time.

Her name was Amaya, and she had worked the sauté station at Santino's, but only briefly with Dante and Bird, before she moved to Phoenix. They definitely remembered her. Dante always said she was like an eight-armed Hindu goddess, the way she kept seventy-two things going at once, all of which came out looking incredible. She'd been back in San Francisco for a year and was working at Delfina in the Mission.

"I work with Peanut over there," she said. Peanut, whose real name was Dario, was one of the best pizza guys in the city, and had worked with Dante at Napoleon's. He always said his professional wrestling name would be the Salvadoran Slayer. But at five-foot-five, Peanut was the name that stuck in the restaurant world. "Sal told him you were opening a place."

"Peanut?" Dante said, "How's he doing?"

"He's good. I brought him with me."

"Tell him to come in here. He's hired, too."

The signing on of Amaya and Peanut seemed to open things up, and by the end of the day, Dante felt like he and Bird had assembled a top-notch kitchen crew. Sal was equally happy with the front of the house staff.

After the last applicant was gone, Dante poured a glass of Scotch for Sal, Bird, and himself. "Well done," he said as they clinked glasses. "Both of you."

"This place is going to kick ass, D."

Sal nodded. "I got a good feeling about this."

On the Friday morning before the grand opening party, Dante was in the kitchen at Pane Rubato using the tip of a paring knife to punch a new hole in his belt.

"What the hell are you doing, D?"

"What's it look like?"

"Looks like you've been living in a prison labor camp."

Dante shook his head. "How's everything looking for tonight?"

"We're in good shape."

Pane Rubato had opened unofficially Wednesday and Thursday to work out the kinks, and everything had gone as well as Dante could have hoped. Sure there were some glitches with the point of sale system, like the one that sent an order for forty-two fettuccine alfredos, but nothing they couldn't figure out. The staff was coming together and Dante felt confident that they'd put together great service after great service.

Later that afternoon, he received a delivery of a case of Pertimali Brunello Reserva '01 from his cousin, Marcello, in Rome. The note read, "Congratulations. I couldn't be more proud. This is for you, not your customers..." He popped the cork on one of the bottles to let it breathe.

An hour later, Dante poured a glass of the Brunello for Bird and one for himself.

"Cheers, D," Bird said. "Here's to a packed dining room every night of the week."

He tasted the wine. "That is nice."

Dante nodded.

Bird furrowed his brow. "You okay?"

"Oh, yeah." He smiled. "So are you bringing Damika tonight?"

"I'm bringing Nyah. Damika was the last one."

"That was just last week."

"I know. I was there."

"But she seemed great. Smart, nice, gorgeous."

"She didn't own a TV, didn't know a home run from a touchdown, and spoke fluent German."

"That *bitch*."

"You know what I mean. I prefer it when a woman likes the same things I like. Nyah is a Niner and Giants fan. Plus she's hot." He winked, then sipped his wine again. "D, I just want you to know how much I appreciate you making me chef du cuisine. Especially knowing other people don't think I should be."

"Other people don't know a damn thing about the restaurant business, and even less about you."

At home changing into party attire, Dante flipped through his wardrobe, every piece of decent clothing reminding him of nights with Abby. But he got himself dressed and back to Pane Rubato. Gloria and John were already there. He grabbed a glass of champagne and headed over to them.

John smiled and held up his glass of champagne. "Congratulations, Dante. Very impressive what you've done here."

"Congratulations to both of you, too," Dante said. "We wouldn't be here tonight without you. Thank you."

Val and Lisa, the dancers from down the street, walked up. "Hi guys," Lisa said, placing her hand on John's shoulder. "Welcome to the neighborhood, officially." The cut of her sapphire cocktail dress revealed a tattoo on her hip of a heart with a dagger through it.

"You guys clean up pretty good," Val said. Her straight dark hair was pulled back in a ponytail and there was clearly nothing coming between her and her painted-on lavender dress.

Gloria looked as though someone held manure under her nose.

The young women excused themselves and Dante thought Gloria's glare would burn a hole in John's head.

Fortunately, one of the waitresses, Lexi, called Dante away to the kitchen.

"You looked like you needed an excuse to escape," she said.

"Thanks, Lexi," Dante said. "I can already tell you're going to be very valuable around here."

Dante ducked into the kitchen for a few minutes, then headed back out to the dining room where he saw John's assistant, Lauren.

"I'm glad you could come tonight," Dante said. She was maybe in her mid-forties, more the rocker mom than soccer mom. John always said that without her, his company would fall apart.

"John has been so excited about this," Lauren said. "He thinks God lives in your pizza oven, you know." She excused herself when her cell phone rang, saying, "The kids probably blew up the house. Or worse—the neighbor's."

A few minutes later, Bird arrived with Nyah. "Hot" wasn't an adequate description. She was Beyoncé and Lucy Lu in one. She turned the heads of the men *and* the women in the restaurant.

"D, this is Nyah."

"Nice to meet you, Nyah." Dante shook her hand. "Dante."

"Congratulations on your new place, Dante," she said. "It looks great."

"Thanks." It did look great. Dante hadn't really noticed until now. Sure, he was pleased with how everything turned out from his chef/owner eye, but he'd forgotten to look at the place from a guest perspective. The lighting was subtle but not too dark. The dining room and bar exuded relaxation with just a touch of hip, enough to be chic without pandering to the poseurs and the tragically trendoid.

Charly arrived with the mayor. She saw Dante and waved as she walked over.

"Hey, Charly" Dante said. "Mayor, good to see you again."

"Why is it I have to tell you every time to call me Jack?" Mayor Jack Bailey, with his movie star looks, was the media's golden boy, so having him here at the opening party would certainly be good PR.

"Sorry, Jack," Dante said.

Charly pulled Dante aside. "How're you doing, sunshine?"

Dante raised his eyebrows and blew out a long breath.

"That good?"

"I'm alright. As long as I keep busy."

When his friend, Martin, a jazz guitarist, who he'd booked to play for the party, walked in, Dante said to Charly, "Go get something to drink and eat. I'd better go help Martin get set up."

Throughout the evening, Dante played host with a smile on his face. For anyone who didn't know him well, he appeared to be excited and enthusiastic. He told stories of how he started cooking.

"My Nonna taught me to make marinara sauce when I was five years old. I was crushing the tomatoes by hand and apparently not doing a very good job because she said not to squeeze them like they were my little wiener."

The most difficult moment of the night happened while Dante was in the middle of a conversation with Lauren about how Gloria "helps" at John's office.

"She certainly has opinions about things" Lauren said.

"Don't I know it."

That's when Martin strummed a few bars of a familiar song. And when Dante recognized the tune, the notes wrapped around his heart and squeezed. "That's All." The song the street musician had played while Abby broke up with him.

Martin crooned, "I can only give you love that lasts forever . . ."

"You okay?" Lauren said.

Dante swallowed hard and said, "Think I'm going to get some fresh air," then he got up and went out to the back alley. Amaya and Peanut leaned against the building, smoking. Peanut recounted a fight he'd been in.

"You should have seen this guy." He sucked on his cigarette then blew the smoke out. "Greasy, gristly motherfucker. He bumps into me, gets all in my face. But I'm cool, trying to leave this crazy asshole alone and walk away, then he takes a swing at me. So I drill the motherfucker. Catch him right under the chin and knock him clean fucking out." Peanut grinned. "Probably didn't think I could do any damage."

Amaya laughed. "Don't fuck with the Peanut."

The air may not have been fresh out there with the cigarettes and the dumpsters, but Dante smiled and went back inside with a little more fizz in his soda. He endured the remaining hours of the party, and at the end of the night, dragged himself home.

He didn't even have the energy to pour a Bowmore, and went straight to bed. Without a thought catching his attention, the physical world dissolved away.

The next morning Dante stood on his small back deck and sipped espresso. The sky was the color of a headache—not throbbing, but constant, steady. The air felt like a cold sweat.

The phone.

It's not Abby.

"Hey, D," his brother, Frank said. "Guess who I saw the other day?"

"Idi Amin."

"What? No. I saw Michelle."

"Michelle?"

"Yeah, your Michelle. Who broke up with you to go to Los Angeles to be an actress."

"I don't have a Michelle that—"

"Shut up, D. You know who I'm talking about. She has a salon down on Ingersol."

"Oh yeah?"

"She still looks damn good."

Fortunately, a loud crash on Frank's end of the phone diverted his attention.

"Hold on a sec." Sounded like Little Frankie, his brother's third and youngest kid screaming in the background.

Frank returned to the phone. "Little mister crash and burn. He's getting so big. The other day, he even tried to take a drink of my beer." His brother chuckled in that proud papa way.

When Dante talked to Frank, he always got the lowdown on every minute detail of his family life. Ever since his daughter, Chelsea, was born six years ago, he'd call with endless stories of everything from public poo incidents to open houses at school, to his middle child, Chloe's, swimming lessons. Even his wife, Holly, would roll her eyes at him.

Frank was the oldest. Then Dante. Then their little sister, Carolyn, a banker. Married to Dave, pharmacist. She never told Dante anything about the messes her two kids made in their diapers.

"When're you coming home?" Frank said.

Holly, in the background, said, "Yeah, tell him it's been too long."

"It's been a year, hasn't it?" Frank said. "The kids would love to see their Uncle D. And you know Ma."

"I know, I know. I need to get back. It's just crazy right now with the restaurant. Maybe you all should come out here."

"Two-year-old on a plane? No thanks."

They talked for a few more minutes about Frank's bike shop, Dante's restaurant, the Yankees pitching, and rubs for beef brisket.

"If you let it sit overnight in the fridge," Dante said, "The rub really gets a chance to get into the meat and it'll taste much better."

"I'll give it a try." In the background, Dante heard another toddler wail. "I'd better get going before Frankie cracks his head open. Then Holly'll crack mine open for not watching him. Take care."

"You, too. Give my love to Holly and the rugrats."

That night, Pane Rubato was packed and the kitchen was getting behind.

"Darryl," Bird yelled, "I need that filet for Lexi. You have three all day."

Darryl, in one of the wooden-headed moments he would become known for, handed Bird a grilled chicken breast sandwich.

"What the hell's this?" Bird looked over the orders, which continued to pour in. "Whose is this? I need Lexi's steak, Darryl. You know, *beef*."

Kerry, a waiter, strolled in, singing, "It's raining men..."

Followed by another waiter, Kelly, singing, "Hallelujah!"

Darryl looked over his shoulder and muttered something in disgust.

Dante grabbed an apron and shuffled behind the line.

"Darryl, you're already in the weeds. So maybe you shouldn't worry about what the waiters are saying." Dante nodded for Darryl to give up the tongs and his spot on the grill. "Go get me some chicken breasts from the walk-in, then help Peanut on the ovens."

Sal walked through and shot Kerry and Kelly a searing look, and the two waiters lowered their heads like pups who had been yelled at for piddling on the floor, grabbed their plates, and slinked back out to the dining room.

Sammy, the dishwasher, dropped a stack of clean plates into the dispenser. His face and balding head shone with sweat, but he smiled and hummed a happy little tune anyway.

"Sammy," Dante said, "You are kicking ass tonight."

"I like working," Sammy said. "And I like being around you guys. It's fun. I like it here. My dad will pick me up at midnight."

When Darryl came back with the chicken, he looked at Sammy like he was sub-human which made Dante want to throw a spatula at Darryl's head.

"Darryl," Dante shouted, "get those over here and get on the ovens."

Dante got home around one that night. 4:00 A.M. in New York. Abby would be long asleep. He pictured her in bed, asleep on her stomach with one leg bent. The first time he saw her like that was in Las Vegas, naked on the bed after they'd spent the entire morning making love. He watched her breathe, quietly, steadily and thought there was nothing more beautiful. Now he longed to lay beside her, his arm around her, their bodies pressed together. Smelling her hair and skin when he kissed her bare shoulder.

Chapter 10

For the week following the grand opening of the restaurant, Dante felt as though his body was weighted down by iron chains, and that he was on the verge of breaking down. Every night, he dreamt of Abby.

That Saturday night, Bird came into the office at Pane Rubato. "D, you have got to get out of this funk."

"What funk?"

"This *poor me* funk. You and Abby broke up over three months ago."

"And?"

"Can I ask you something?"

"No."

"I'm going to anyway."

"Suit yourself."

"I'm not trying to be a dick, but you seem more messed up than I've ever seen you about anything. What did you see in Abby that's making this so hard for you?"

Dante rubbed his eyes. He didn't even have to think about it. "I was sure she would be my wife. I was sure we'd have a family together." He swallowed hard. "It never even occurred to me that she didn't want the same thing. So when she broke up with me, my truth, my reality dropped out from under me. And I feel like I've been in a free fall ever since."

Bird nodded. "You two ever talk about marriage?"

"Not specifically. But we talked about the future. And not just next week or next month. But obviously there was a lot about our relationship I missed, or misunderstood." Dante closed his eyes and shook his head.

"Come out with me tonight," Bird said.

"One of us has to be here."

"It's slow, and I already talked to Sal. He's going to close. Amaya's got the kitchen covered."

"Well, maybe I just don't feel like going out tonight."

"You know, D, you need to get out and date. The human willie needs attention from someone other than its owner, or the brain starts to shut down. It's a scientific fact."

"You read this in the *New England Journal of Medicine*?"

"No, *Big Round Booties.* I'll lend you the issue."

Dante rolled his eyes.

"Remember those two blondes from last night?" Bird said.

"No." He did remember them. He'd visited their table. They were maybe in their early thirties, in town from Denver for a tradeshow and had decided to stay the weekend to explore San Francisco. They had gushed over their dinners. When Dante came back to the kitchen, Bird said something about playing reverse Oreo with them.

"The one with the glasses was checking you out big time."

"She was not." *The one with the glasses? She was so cute.*

"I invited them to come back tonight and told them we'd give them a little tour of North Beach."

"Sorry, not interested."

He left the office, but Bird followed.

"I wasn't asking, D. You're coming." He took Dante by the elbow and turned him toward the bar where the aforementioned women sat, mojitos in hand, smiling at them. "Dante, you remember a couple of friends of mine. Julia and Vanessa."

Each wore jeans and a sweater. Julia, the one with the glasses, was in navy. Vanessa was in black.

Julia bit her lip and blushed a little. "Hi," she said. She couldn't have been more than five feet tall, with a slender, but muscular build. Very cute dimpled smile, and a shyness in her eyes.

"Hi," Dante said, and forced a smile.

"Thanks for inviting us out," Vanessa said.

"Always happy to show a couple of beautiful women around the neighborhood. So give us just a few minutes and we'll be right out."

Again Bird lead Dante by the elbow toward the office.

"I don't want to go out," Dante said.

"That's why I'm making you. You need this."

"What? To play tour guide?"

"To have fun. And maybe if you're lucky to get some affection from a beautiful woman."

They stepped into the office.

"This is about sex?"

"No, it's not *about* sex." Bird placed his hand over his heart. "For me it's just a beautiful connection between two souls making the most of their time together." He smiled and Dante shook his head. "For you, I'll be happy if you hold her hand, maybe a little goodnight kiss."

"Alright, then." He grabbed his coat. "Let's go."

When they got back to Julia and Vanessa, Julia, uneasy-eyed, said to Dante. "If you have to stay and work, or you don't want to . . ."

Dante smiled.

You are such a sucker for the eyes.

"We don't have to work," he said. "And of course we want to." He held out his arm to her. "Shall we go?"

Julia's eyes relaxed. Then she smiled and took his arm.

Their first stop was City Lights where they negotiated the cramped aisles, stairway, and nooks of one of the most famous bookstores in the country.

"Lawrence Ferlinghetti founded this store in 1953," Bird said. "They originally published Allen Ginsberg's *Howl* in 1956 and were tried on obscenity charges for it."

Dante arched an eyebrow at tour-guide Bird.

"I saw Ferlinghetti walking around in here one day."

"I love the Beat poets," Julia said. She picked up a copy of *Howl*, and flipped through the pages, stopping to read here and there. "This looks really interesting. I've never seen this edition."

"Mind if I take a look?' Dante said. Julia handed the book over. It was subtitled *Original Draft Facsimile, Transcript, and Variant Versions, Fully Annotated by Author, with Contemporaneous Correspondence, Account of First Public Reading, Legal Skirmishes, Pres.*

He tucked the book into the crook of his arm and walked to the front checkout. He handed the book and his debit card to the clerk. When the transaction was complete, he handed the book back to Julia.

"A little memento for tonight."

"That is so sweet."

Next, they moved on to Vesuvio. "Opened in 1949," Bird said as they walked in.

"You know a lot about this area," Vanessa said.

Bird smiled. "This is my town, and I love her like no other."

They all crowded into a little table up front.

"Bird and I were sitting at this table one night," Dante said. "Like a Tuesday. Really slow. And this homeless guy comes in, sits down at our table and asks if we can by him a drink. We both look at him, probably with a little shock on our faces, then he says, 'Relax, I'm a Judean Indian.' So I say, 'In that case, what're you having?' The guy asks for a Jack Kerouac, then proceeds to tell us how he grew up on the Judean reservation in North Dakota, and moved out to California in 1975 when the Great Dakota Drought nearly killed off all of his people."

Bird shook his head. "The guy finishes his drink, then says something, supposed to be some kind of blessing in Judean Indian—oh what was it?"

"Get this," Dante said. "Mele Kalikimaka.The Hawaiian Christmas greeting."

They all laughed.

"The guy was great," Bird said. "Too bad we never saw him again."

"This is such a fun, funky bar," Vanessa said.

She glanced up toward the gaslight chandelier. "It's like a time capsule," she said. "I love these pictures, Kerouac, Ginsberg, Dylan Thomas, and to know they hung out here. So cool. It's still got that 1958 vibe, like the whole Beat Generation exploded in here. I think it may be one of the coolest bars I've ever been in."

As they talked, Julia put her hand on Dante's shoulder. On his leg. She looked into his eyes when she talked to him.

Had this been Abby, he thought, she would have taken his hand and intentionally slid it up her thigh.

"Shall we continue our tour?" Bird said

"Actually," Vanessa said, "I'm having such a good time here. And it looks cold out there. How does everyone feel about staying?"

"Yeah," Julia said. "Let's stay."

"Works for me," Dante said.

"Alright, but you're going to miss the place where Joe DiMaggio grew up, and where he and Marilyn Monroe got their pictures taken after they got married, and Washington Square Park . . ."

Dante's mind drifted to the hundreds, if not thousands of times he and Abby had kissed in Washington Square Park. They even had sex there at 3:00 A.M. one night after a visit to the clubs on Broadway.

Dante's heart started to feel cold, and he had the strong desire to run out of Vesuvio, and just keep running. Running until his heart exploded.

Julia put her hand on his leg. "You okay?"

Dante managed a smile and nodded.

She put her hand on his cheek. "You have the most beautiful hazel eyes," she said. "I noticed them the second you walked up to our table last night."

Dante leaned in and kissed her. When they broke off their kiss several seconds later, Dante looked over to see Bird and Vanessa lip-locked.

The rest of the night was lots of laughing, talking, and drinking. After Vesuvio closed, they stood out on the sidewalk.

"I think I need a little walk in the fresh air," Dante said. "Anyone care to join me?"

"I'd love to," Julia said. "I could use the fresh air, too."

"I think I'm ready to go back to the hotel," Vanessa said.

Bird hailed a cab. "I'll drop you there," he said.

Julia and Dante headed up Columbus Avenue, arm in arm. They were quiet for several minutes.

Dante and Abby had made this walk to his house so many times. Sometimes they'd be jabbering away, other times not a single word. At times like that he'd feel the glow in his heart reaching beyond his body to hers, to everything around him.

Now, his stomach tightened, and he clenched his jaw, trying to suppress the tears that seemed to be coming up from a cold stone in his chest.

Julia finally said, "Tonight has been great. Thank you."

Again, Dante managed a smile. "You're welcome."

She rubbed his arm. "Is everything okay? You seem a little sad. I mean, you've been so much fun all night, but every once in a while, I see that sadness, like just now."

"Who could be sad with such a beautiful woman on his arm like this?"

They eventually ended up at Washington Square Park, and Dante said, "I live just a few blocks away. Do you want to come over for a nightcap to warm you up a bit?"

"That sounds lovely."

When they got into the house, Dante poured a couple of Rémy Martins, and put on some Red Garland. He sat next to Julia on the couch.

She held up her glass. "To a wonderful night."

"To a wonderful night." They touched glasses and each took a sip.

Julia put her drink on the coffee table, then leaned over and kissed Dante. She slipped her tongue into his mouth. Then she slid her hand high up on his leg.

After several minutes of making out, Dante said, "Let's move this to the bedroom."

Once there, they continued kissing on the bed.

Abby.

Dante froze.

"Dante, are you okay?" Julia said.

"Yeah, yeah."

He went back to kissing her.

Abby, Abby, Abby.

"Julia," he said into her ear. She shuddered.

Dante managed to put Abby out his mind enough to focus on the woman in his bed, and soon had Julia undressed. As he caressed her naked body, he said, "You are a beautiful woman."

She pulled him to her.

Three positions later, Dante collapsed on top of her. Their damp skin slipping and sliding as she reached up to caress his face. "Mmm. That was amazing," she said.

Dante's chest pounded. He tried to catch his breath and could only make whewing and wowing sounds. He rolled onto his back and Julia snuggled under his arm. He kissed her head and smelled the sweet coconut scent of her hair. Not long after, he drifted off to sleep.

Dante woke up a little after five in the morning, crying. Next to Julia. Fortunately she was asleep. He'd had a terrible Abby dream. His dad, who had been dead fifteen years, was there. In the dream Dante couldn't get within about ten feet of his dad. And he couldn't get a good look at him. His dad was amorphous, shadow-like. But he seemed to know Dante was upset.

His dad said, "You'll be okay."

Then he indicated that Dante should follow him down a hallway that morphed into one of the schools his dad had worked at. He was a janitor. Then he said he wanted Dante to meet someone. He opened the door to one of the classrooms and Abby was inside, though she didn't see Dante out in the hall. When Dante looked at his dad, obviously confused, his dad smiled. Then he nodded toward her as if to tell Dante to get in there. As soon as he walked through the door, Abby turned and smiled. She came over and put her hand on his face.

"I've been waiting for you," she said. "And I'm not going to let you go this time." Dante began to cry and she pulled him to her. Then he woke up.

He collected himself and went to the bathroom. When he crawled back into bed, Julia stirred. He could feel her ribs as he slid his arm under hers to spoon her. Her warm, soft nakedness aroused him. She pressed against him. He pulled her hip to bring her closer.

Julia let out a slight moan and said, "Good morning. You're up early."

They made love again, then slept a few more hours. Once they were awake, Dante made breakfast. Afterwards, he drove her back to the hotel.

She kissed him one more time, then looked into his eyes. "So much sweetness and pain in those eyes. You have an amazing heart. I can feel it. But someone did quite a number on you, didn't she?"

Dante smiled.

"Take good care of yourself, Dante." She handed him her business card. "And if you're ever in Denver, give me a call."

Chapter 11

For the next few months, the going at Pane Rubato was slow. By all accounts, the food was excellent, the service first-class. But word that a new restaurant had opened seemed corrosively slow in getting to North Beach habitués. If it was true that his food healed broken hearts, Dante had little evidence. And how would he even know such a thing? A survey? *Were you heartbroken when you came into Pane Rubato? If so, how did you feel after you left?*

Weekends at the restaurant were generally steady, but most weeknights were like the midnight shift at a funeral home.

"It's this location," Gloria said. She stood over Dante's desk, refusing his offer to sit. "The only people who walk by are degenerates out to visit the debauched neighbors."

"I'll grant you the location argument in one sense," Dante said. "Vinny's served such tourist trap crap that even the tourists knew better than to come down this way."

"Well then, what do you intend to do about it?"

"I'll figure something out."

"Perhaps I should take a more active role here."

"Look, it's been a wet winter. People don't like to go out in the rain. I'm sure when things dry out, business will pick up."

"It's only January. The rainy season doesn't end until April and we can't—"

"I'll figure something out."

"You had better." She steamed off, practically running over Bird at the office door.

"What was that all about, D?"

Dante rolled his eyes. "Nothing. What's up?"

"I think Darryl's stealing steaks. Inventory doesn't match sales. Hasn't for weeks. And last night, I saw him come out of the walk-in with his coat on. I'd seen him do it before, but didn't think anything of it. So I think we need to put him on the secret miscreant-surveillance-buddy program. After his shifts, one of us hangs around near enough to him that he can't get into the walk-in to smuggle anything out."

A few weeks ago, Sal had called Darryl "a stain" which was widely regarded as the perfect description.

"Works for me. And maybe I should tell Gloria so she can get off my back."

"Why's she on your back?"

"I guess she expects us to be packed every night."

"Don't you? Isn't that what we all want?"

"I guess."

"What's with you? There shouldn't be any 'guessing' about it."

Dante tried to glare him off.

"Look, D, you've been walking around this place like death's depressed brother for three months. What have you lost, thirty pounds?"

"Twenty-five."

"Oh, well excuse me. Twenty-five." He shook his head. "What are you waiting for? This is the shot you've wanted all your life. We've got everything in place to be one of the best restaurants in one of the greatest cities in the world. All we need is you. Your fire, your passion. We need that kid who came to San Francisco and *knew* he could cook with anyone, *knew* he'd make it. It's time to do this."

Dante just sat straight-faced and began to slowly clap.

"Fuck you, D." Bird turned and walked out.

Maybe Dante had made a mistake opening this restaurant. While he was off making his so-called dream come true, Abby was planning her exit from his life. Maybe it was because she knew that once this damn place opened, she'd see even less of him, and decided she needed more support, the kind of support only a family could give. She knew what he'd be up against opening his own restaurant, and that's why she made her plans without him in them. Pane Rubato had basically cost Dante the chance, maybe his last, at a family.

When Dante got home that night, he put Miles Davis' *The Complete Bitches Brew Sessions* on the stereo. He poured himself a triple shot of Bowmore and sat in his favorite chair. He sipped the smoky Scotch whiskey and leaned back. The first tune, "Pharaoh's Dance," was an expansive, snaky, twenty-minute rendition of pure heroin. The congas sneaking in and out. The layering of guitar, electric piano, trumpet. The pulsing drums and bass. By the time it was over, Dante had finished his drink and poured another. The spectral, echoic "Bitches Brew" came next. Dante leaned back in his chair and closed his eyes. The whiskey numbed his body as the music lulled him into a trance-like state.

A pan clanged the kitchen. He listened to rolling thuds as drawers opened and closed. Then the singing started. "*Ciuri, ciuri, ciuri di tuttu l'annu, l'amuri ca, mi dasti ti lu tornu . . . Lah lah la-la la, la la, la la, la lah.*"

"Hello?"

Clinking cutlery and more singing answered. Dante went to the kitchen where Nonna stood at the stove, stirring a pot and smiling.

"It's done," she said. "*Siediti.*"

Dante sat at the kitchen table and Nonna set a bowl of minestrone in front of him. Dark green chard and white cannellini beans. Red tomato and orange carrot. He breathed in the aroma of the soup. The spiciness of the sausage filled his nose first, followed by garlic, thyme, and parsley.

She ran her hand over his head, then sat across the table from him. "What are you doing to your heart?"

"I'm hoping to win back the heart of my true love. Didn't you say I had to bring hope back into my heart?"

"Eat your soup and let me tell you a story."

"I'm not hungry, Nonna."

"*Mangia.*"

She waited for him to take a bite. When he did, the taste brought him back to the cold winter evenings of his childhood when Nonna would make this soup and serve it with her fresh bread, still warm from the oven.

"I always forget that you'd use your own spicy fennel sausage. It's perfect."

"You'll have no color if you eat no spice."

Nonna sat at the table with that smile in her eyes whenever she told a story. That playfulness of a five-year-old as well as immense wisdom, kindness, and understanding.

"*Ascolta,*" she said, and Dante settled in for her story. "*C'era una volta un principe chiamato Desiderio . . .*"

Once upon a time, there was a prince named Desiderio. On the day before his wedding, he decided to go out hunting to calm his nerves. Upon hearing this, his fiancée, Persamora, said she wanted to come, too. "The forest," Desiderio said, "is no place for a woman."

Persamora glared at the prince. "The only place not for a woman will be your bed if you ever tell me that again."

Desiderio knew better than to refuse Persamora. Once out in the forest, they came across a hideous ogre. Desiderio shouted for Persamora to ride home as fast as she could, but she would not go. "If I leave you," she said, "you will surely die. If I stay, we can defeat the monster together."

But they were no match for the giant. Desiderio was beaten senseless and when he awoke several days later, his mother, the queen, told him that when he and Persamora had not returned, the king sent out a search party. They found Desiderio, bloodied and in the angel of death's grip, but no sign of Persamora. The king's army was scouring the countryside for the princess-to-be. His mother said, "We fear she is lost forever."

"Then you should have let me die," he said.

After a month, the prince's body made a full recovery, but his heart remained crippled. The king and queen hoped that with time Desiderio's heart would heal and he would find a new love and produce an heir to the throne. But the prince did not get better. He wasted away until he looked like a skeleton in clothes.

Nonna touched Dante's face. "*Come te*," she said—Like you. She nodded toward the bowl, indicating he should finish the soup.

After several months, the king and queen became very worried. Every day, the prince would withdraw to the woods. He would sit on a stump, and Grief would come to visit him. Desiderio would cry and Grief would say, "There, there. As long as I am here, Persamora remains in your heart. For without me, your love will be lost forever. And you don't want that. I will visit you every day and keep your love alive."

One day, after one of Grief's visits, the prince sat on his stump with his head in his hands. A woman's melodic voice said, "Why does Grief come to you every day?"

Desiderio looked up to see a white fox. "Because my love was taken from me and Grief keeps her alive in my heart."

"Grief does not keep your love alive. Your heart keeps her alive with warm memories. Grief only gives you cold reminders. You must send Grief away."

Nonna took Dante's hand and repeated the words. "*Devi mandare via Dolore.*" You must send Grief away.

"You seem very wise, fox." Desiderio said. "Tomorrow when Grief comes, I will tell him to leave."

The next day when Grief visited the prince in the woods, Desiderio said, "Grief, I no longer wish for your company. Please go."

Grief's eyes grew wide. "But why? Do you wish to let go of the love in your heart?"

"The fox said you do not keep my love in my heart."

"Did the fox tell you that when I go I will take your love with me?" Then Grief reached into Desiderio's chest and his frozen hand took hold of

the prince's heart.

Poor Desiderio wailed and moaned. Then he summoned all his strength and pushed. "Go, and release my heart from your icy clutch!"

Grief fell to the ground. Tears streamed from the prince's eyes. "Leave me."

Grief slunk away.

Finally, after a year, the prince's strength returned. He rode out to the forest to mark the spot where he had lost his love. As he approached, he saw the ogre trudging through the trees. Desiderio followed the giant until he came to the cave where the ogre lived. Then he sprang from the shadows and raised his sword. "Foul beast!" he shouted, "now I shall avenge my beloved's death."

The ogre looked at Desiderio and said, "I should have eaten you when I had my chance. Your beloved is not dead. I took her for my own wife."

The ogre swung his tree-trunk arm, knocking the sword from the prince's hand and throwing him into the mountain wall where Desiderio fell unconscious. The brute bent to devour his victim.

Persamora, who had been watching from the cave, ran behind the monster and recovered the dropped sword. She snuck up behind the ogre and just as he was about to bite into her prince, she swung the blade with all her might at the giant's neck. The steel sliced straight through his gristly skin and took the ogre's head clean off.

Persamora revived Desiderio and said, "My love, I knew you would come for me. I knew you would not abandon my heart."

They rode back to the castle and the next day they were married. The wedding celebration lasted a full three days. Desiderio and Persamora then lived the rest of their days rich and consoled.

Dante looked at his Nonna. "So you're saying I need to master my grief?"

Nonna rolled her eyes and shook her head. "No, I'm telling you to go out into the forest and cut off an ogre's head." She crossed her eyes, and made the motion of slicing her hand across her throat, then smiled. She stood and placed her hand on his cheek, then faded away.

"But wait! I have a question! How do I know if I'm healing hearts?"

Nonna, however, did not reappear.

"Damn it."

If she was going to make a habit of appearing, he should make a list of things to ask her.

Chapter 12

The next morning, Dante awoke with more energy than he'd had in weeks. Nonna's message made complete sense. He was letting his grief get the best of him at the expense of everything else. Today, he would turn that around. Bird—oh boy, he owed Bird a big apology—was right.

The phone rang.

"Hi, honey," his mother said. She had a Calabrese accent, and the voice of a woman who could have sung opera.

"Hey Ma."

He shouldn't have picked up the phone. Not that he didn't love his mother, but she had a one-track mind of late.

"You meet any girls?" she said.

"Well, there's this eighteen-year-old Ukrainian girl from the Internet—"

"Dante!"

"Why do you ask if you don't want to know?"

"I wasn't asking for jokes. No girls, then?"

"No, Ma."

"All those pretty women in San Francisco and you don't want any of them?"

"It's not about me not wanting them," he said. "What makes you think they want *me*?"

"What about that Charly? She seems to like you."

"Most of my friends do tend to like me."

"She likes you for more than a friend."

Okay, I need an excuse to get the hell out of this.

"She does not. She has a boyfriend."

"I've seen the way she looks at you."

"Ma."

"I've seen the way you look at her."

"Ma!"

How about telling her I sliced open my hand with the bread knife?

"Oh, alright. You just keep ignoring the truth. I just want you to be happy. I want you to find love. My heart breaks to think of you all alone."

"I've got a great life. I don't need someone else to make me happy."

"But love *will* make you happy. Look at Frank. Look at Carolyn. They have everything you have and they have families. Until your father died, I couldn't have been happier. I want that for you. I want there to be someone to share your great life with."

Where is that knife?

Finally she said her friend, Rufina, showed up at her house. Dante was off the hook and free to have his breakfast of espresso and toast.

When he arrived at Pane Rubato an hour later, Bird was already in the kitchen making a batch of marinara. Dante stood for a moment, but Bird didn't look up.

Finally Dante said, "Dude, I'm sorry about yesterday. I was an ass."

"Yes you were."

"You were right. I've been blowing it here. If I ever act like that again when you're trying to help, you can punch me dead in the face."

"Don't think I won't."

"I wanted to talk to you about some ideas I have to get people in here, too."

Dante had been thinking about his nonna's visits on the walk into work that morning. The first time she showed up, she told him he was now a heart healer. Valentine's Day wasn't too far off and he needed something to help him feel better.

"What do you think of a Feast of the Broken Hearts at Pane Rubato on Valentine's Day? You know, food to heal the heartsick soul?"

"I love it," Bird said.

"Yeah? I was thinking the promotion would be something like, 'Don't spend your Valentine's Day broken-hearted and alone. Join us for The Feast of the Broken Hearts. Using his nonna's special recipes, our own broken-hearted chef will prepare a meal sure to make you forget your heartache.'"

Bird smiled and nodded.

Dante continued. "And from now on, I'm going to see to it personally that everyone who comes in here has a great experience. I'm going to come out and talk to people and let them know how much I appreciate their business. I'm going to make them want to come back and to bring their friends." He smiled.

To give people another reason to come in, Dante booked his guitarist friend, Martin, to play solo guitar during the week, and his trio for the weekends. That night Martin played his renditions of songs like "Angel Eyes" and "Stella By Starlight" and "Waltz For Debby." Dante made the rounds through the dining room. He stopped at each table and asked the guests how their dinners were and offered them another glass of wine, a shot of grappa, or a cup of coffee on him. In some cases, he told them the story of their entrée.

"The *pasta con le sarde* was one of my nonna's favorites, especially on Fridays during Lent. Me, my brother and sister would all say, 'No, we're not going to eat *sardines*.' Then one day I actually tasted it, and of course I loved it. The sardines aren't nearly as fishy as you might think. When I saw the wild fennel at the farmer's market this morning, I knew I had to put this on the menu tonight. I love the texture of sardines and anchovies along with the fennel, pine nuts, and currants. And isn't the color beautiful with the saffron and the tomatoes?"

Between sets, Martin sat with Dante at the bar.

"Thanks for giving me the gig," Martin said. "And the food. Getting paid and fed goes a long way for a jazz musician."

"I'm just glad you were available."

"Me too. I haven't seen you since the opening." He looked Dante up and down. "You didn't look too good then and you don't look so good now. You alright?"

"Broken heart diet."

"Broken heart diet? Doesn't look like there's any food on that diet."

Dante chuckled. "Not a lot, no."

Martin held up his glass of Maker's Mark. "Well, here's to getting fat and happy."

When Martin went back to play his last set, Bird came over to the bar. "D, I have a friend I want you to meet tonight."

"Friend?"

"Yes. I think you'll like her."

Dante shook his head. "Look, I appreciate that you want to help, but this isn't my thing. I don't know how you do it."

"Have sex?" Bird grinned. "Well, you take your penis and you put it in the woman's vagina."

"Funny." Dante didn't smile. "Sex doesn't cure everything."

"It isn't all sex. I truly love to make a woman feel special. I love to look them in the eye. I love to listen when they're talking. I really try to absorb them."

"Seems you only ever absorb them for a week or two at a time."

"Maybe I'm just looking for the one who will absorb me back."

Over the next two weeks, Dante worked hard at sending Grief on his way every day. Positive online reviews of the restaurant, some of them glowing, appeared almost daily, which helped his mood. And his food was better than ever. He focused on simple and rustic, which seemed to be working.

He had also spread the word about The Feast of the Broken Hearts. One of his favorite local artists, Haley Behrens, agreed to do the event poster. She painted San Francisco at sunset from a distance, between the Golden Gate and Bay Bridge. The dark blue sky streaked with clouds of pink, orange and yellow. What appeared at first to be another swirling line of clouds was actually a procession of hearts streaming into the city. *First Annual Feast of the Broken Hearts* and all the pertinent text floated above the skyline. He was now waiting for the poster and postcards to come from the printer.

Most people who heard about it liked the idea of the Valentine's feast. John, who came into the restaurant at least once a week, had said it was the single most brilliant idea he'd ever heard for Valentine's Day.

"This," he said, "is going to give so many depressed people who would otherwise be left out a chance to celebrate."

Gloria, however, was not impressed. She was at Pane Rubato for one of her random botherations when she brought up the feast. "John tells me you're having some sort of feast for the blackhearts."

Kerry delivered her San Pellegrino, setting the bottle on the table with a ballerinaesque bow. He wore mini loop earrings and his shirt clung to his protruding pectorals. He also sported eyeliner and a bit of lip gloss. He fluttered his eyes at Gloria, then pirouetted and left.

Gloria rolled her eyes. "Does he have to be so flamboyant?"

"Yes."

She gave a tiffy pop of her lips, then sipped her water. "Now, this blackheart feast of yours is a mockery. Are you planning to place a burnt rose on every table?"

"We're not making fun of Valentine's Day. You know, not everyone is in a relationship or has someone to spend Valentine's Day with. Maybe they recently broke up or just can't seem to find the right person. So we're asking people not to stay home alone. Come out and spend the evening with us. And here's the best part." Dante clapped his hands. "We aren't going to have individual tables. We're bringing in a bunch of long tables so everyone sits together family style. No one eats alone. It's perfect."

Gloria just shook her head. The feast was just the latest effrontery, coming on the heels of Pane Rubato getting a catering gig for a Gina Farello fundraiser. "My husband and I have given a lot of money to try to get that woman out of office over the years. I certainly don't want to participate in *raising* funds for her."

Unfortunately for her, Dante controlled catering decisions. "Well, it's raising funds for us, too. And we need them more than you need to make a political statement."

When he got home that night, he grabbed the day's mail. Mostly junk. Then his eyes caught a hand-addressed gray envelope. The handwriting and return address, A. Drivakis, registered at the same moment. The blood sped away from Dante's head and he sat down. He stared at the envelope for several seconds.

This had to be good, right? If she wanted nothing more to do with him, she would have flat ignored his card, wouldn't she? Or maybe she would send a letter telling him as clearly as possible that he was to leave her alone: no cards, letters, e-mails, phone calls, text messages, carrier pigeons, nothing. And if he contacted her again, she would consider it harassment and seek legal action.

But if it were that kind of letter, she probably wouldn't have addressed the envelope by hand. In fact, she would probably just go straight for the lawyer to begin with.

He sniffed the envelope. Why, he wasn't sure. But he thought he caught the faintest scent of Abby in the paper. Then he realized he was biting his lip so hard he tasted blood.

Okay, freakboy, just open the damn thing, will you?

He pulled up the corner of the flap until the paper tore. Then he slowly slipped his index finger down and opened along the short side of the envelope. He slid the letter out, carefully unfolded it, and began to read the handwritten note.

Dear Dante,

Thank you for the birthday card. It was nice of you to remember and take the time to look up my address and send a card.

I also want to apologize to you for the way I handled my leaving. You were an important part of my life and deserved better than the way I treated you at the end.

I've thought about calling or sending an e-mail just to see how you're doing, but after leaving the way I did, I didn't feel I had the right to contact you. When I got your card, I knew I could take the opportunity to apologize and find out how things are for you. So if you want to call or e-mail, whatever, I'd love to hear from you again.

Take care,

Abby

Her card with her new contact info was in the envelope. On the back of the card, she wrote in her home and cell phone numbers. Next to her cell number, she wrote "in case you forgot" and a smiley face.

Dante set the note and card on the table. She'd love to hear from him again. *Love* to hear from him. Love.

Hey, let's not get too carried away there, chief. She'd love to hear from you but signed the letter, "Take care."

Still, it was a nice apology. And she opened the door, *at least* to being contacted.

Or at most *to being contacted.*

Chapter 13

Dante wanted to call Abby right after he read her note. He wanted to call her the next morning. The next afternoon. The next evening. And practically every minute from the moment he had finished the note until one afternoon a week later. He didn't have to dial: her cell number was still stored in his contacts.

She didn't answer. Hopefully not on purpose. He left a well-rehearsed message. "Hi Abby, it's Dante. Just called to see how you and Zoe are doing. Hope all is well."

Simple, not too desperate-sounding. He didn't ask her to call back so he wouldn't come off as begging. All in all, he was pleased with how the voicemail turned out. It said, "I get along without you just fine, but I care enough to wish you well." That was almost three weeks ago and she still hadn't returned the call.

Maybe he overestimated her desire to talk to him just a little. *What did you expect to happen, anyway? Her to call back the second she got your voicemail and say she wanted to get married?*

But the previous three weeks hadn't been *all* about Abby. The Feast of the Broken Hearts was tonight and every indication was that it was going to be big. Dante got it listed on all the various event calendars in San Francisco and when a popular morning radio show announcer, who had recently gone through a divorce, heard about The Feast, she brought Dante on the show to plug it.

On the air, Dante said, "I know a lot of people don't like to go out to eat by themselves. But I want to make sure everyone understands that you don't need to come to The Feast of the Broken Hearts with a group of friends. That's great, too. But if all your friends have plans and you're alone for Valentine's night, please join us. The whole reason I came up with this event was so I didn't have to be alone myself. So come out and keep me company." After that, the restaurant got scads of reservations.

Whether or not the buzz around The Feast of the Broken Hearts was responsible, Pane Rubato saw a slight, but noticeable uptick in nightly revenue the week before Valentine's Day. Even if Gloria said, "When we double that on the weeknights and quadruple it on the weekends, I'll be satisfied," Dante knew the restaurant was on its way to success.

Just before opening the doors for the celebration, Dante stood in the dining room and took in the atmosphere. It was decorated with hearts of all shapes and colors. A disco ball slowly spun stars around while Martin and the trio warmed up with a jazzy, bluesy arrangement of "Sergeant Pepper's Lonely Hearts Club Band."

Dante smiled. "You're going to be playing that one all night long."

When he opened the doors, two men and two women were already waiting to get in. "Welcome," Dante said. "And thanks so much for coming in tonight. Did you all come together?"

A diminutive woman with shiny blonde hair said, "No, we all just met outside."

It was probably his imagination, but Dante got the feeling smiling wasn't something this woman had done a lot of lately. The stout fellow in a too-small blazer couldn't keep his eyes off her.

Dante guided the group to a row of tables and said, "As you probably know, we have a Prix Fixe menu tonight." He handed menus to the guests. "Can I start you off with a complimentary aperitif?"

And so it went all night. By 7:00, the place was packed with smiling faces, laughter, and music.

Dante took Martin's mic and got everyone's attention. For the last week, he'd been preparing to tell the story of how he started cooking and how it related to his first broken heart.

"Thank you all for coming out and keeping me company tonight. The journey that brought me to this night started when I was five years old. My nonna told me a fairytale about a king who had searched all his life for his true love. In the story, the king trades his entire kingdom for a beautiful wife, but because his heart is full of pure love, he not only wins the heart of his beloved, he retains his kingdom. After Nonna finished, I announced that I too wanted a beautiful wife. I told my mom and dad. My older brother and little sister. Everyone laughed. But that night at dinner, I said, just like the king said when asked why he would trade all of his riches for a woman, 'To have a beautiful wife is to have the world.'

"The next day, while my kindergarten class was at recess and I saw my love, my future beautiful wife, Tammy Birch standing alone. I walked straight up to her and said, 'You are the most beautiful girl in the world.'

"She sneered and said, 'You're gross! Get away from me.' Then punched me right in the eye. Nailed me. Knocked me flat on my bony little butt.

"When I got home from school that day with a black eye and a bruised heart, Nonna asked what happened. I told her how Tammy Birch called me gross and punched me in the eye for saying I liked her.

"Nonna said 'That's why you must look for not just the pretty girl, but the one whose beauty shines through from her heart.' And asked if I would come and help her cook.

"We went to the kitchen and made homemade pasta with meatballs and marinara sauce for the family dinner. While I kneaded the pasta dough, Nonna said the most important thing to know about cooking was that it, like life, was all about love. 'As long as you cook with real love,' she said, 'people will love your food. And when it comes to your heart, sometimes it will break. But never lose hope. If you give your love honestly, your heart will heal. And someday you will find the person who will accept your love honestly.'

"And so here we are. I hope you love the food, and that you enjoy yourselves tonight."

As the night progressed, total strangers toasted each other and perhaps would become friends for the rest of their lives. Not only was the event clearly headed for financial success, Dante knew the people in his restaurant would always remember the very first Feast of the Broken Hearts.

The shiny blonde woman hugged Dante when she left. And again, it may have been his imagination, but he would have sworn she looked different. She looked at peace. She looked happy.

She wasn't the only person transformed. One guy came in dressed in a stylish blue suit and tie of coral, azure and canary but he himself looked cadaverous. He didn't smile when he was greeted. Not so much as a smirk when he was seated. But after one bite of spinach and prosciutto lasagna, he became positively rosy. Before he left, he asked to see Dante.

"I came here tonight," he said, "to call you out as a phony. The piece I plan to write now will be about how I came to your restaurant expecting the cold and cynical world I've grown accustomed to and found warmth, sincerity, and hope." He paused, then half-chuckled. "And the best lasagna I've ever tasted. Thank you."

He handed Dante his card: Tim Jorgensen, *San Francisco Chronicle*.

Later that evening, Charly showed up.

"You're too skinny," she said. "But at least you're smiling. I don't see you for over a month and you turn to skin and bones. How much weight have you lost, anyway?"

"I'm still trying to get that last ten off." He grinned. "Where's the mayor tonight?"

"Sacramento, meeting with the governor."

"I guess politics knows no romance."

"We celebrated Valentine's last night."

"Have a seat at the bar and I'll bring you some food."

"That sounds fab. I'm starving."

Dante brought her the three-cheese medallions, two four-ounce beef tenderloin medallions, wood-grilled and topped with gorgonzola, asiago, and parmesan cheese. Fresh veggies and a mound of fettuccini alfredo crowded the plate.

"How am I supposed to eat all of this?"

"I'd go with the knife and fork, myself."

Charly did, in fact, eat all of her dinner ("Hey I ran eight miles this morning"), then stayed after the restaurant closed to have a few drinks with Dante and Bird.

They kidded her about finishing the huge plate of food and said maybe if she cooked at home once in a while instead of eating her protein bars and energy shakes, she wouldn't always be so hungry.

"Even you," Dante said, "could make the fettuccini alfredo."

Charly shrugged it off. "It's not so much that I can't cook, it's that I don't like to."

"But there can be so much joy in making a meal."

"I think there are bigger problems in the world than whether your fettuccini is perfect."

"Good lord, don't give me the 'big bad serious world' speech."

"But it's true. We're still recovering from the last president whose idea of a foreign policy threatened the stability and security of the entire planet. In a hundred years, your restaurant here may be under water because of global warming. There's homelessness and hunger and—"

"Okay, okay, okay. But what does that have to do with cooking?"

"Food isn't exactly a noble cause, is it?"

Dante made a mocking face. "Well, maybe I don't run the operations of the home district of the Speaker of the House of the United States House of Representatives. Maybe I occasionally have to remind my staff to keep their dicks out of the food. But really the only difference in what we do is scale. You take care of the big, societal problems and I take care of the individual pleasures. What good is a life if you can't enjoy yourself a little?"

"Prostitutes specialize in individual pleasures."

Dante shook his head. "Is there no room in your world for a handmade Tagliatelle alla Bolognese with a glass of Chianti Reserva?"

"There's room in my world for satisfying and nutritious."

"Then why do you even come in here?"

"Because I don't cook and I'm a creature of habit. You're close."

"Way to make me feel special."

"*And* I like it here. When I find a place I like, I go there a lot. I go to the taqueria around the corner from my house once a week, if not more, because it does its job of filling me up with food that's not complicated and not too bad for me. Why does it need to be more than that?"

"Why did Maria Callas sing anything beyond folk songs? Why did Brunelleschi design a dome instead of a sturdy box? Why did Michelangelo paint the ceiling of a chapel anything other than white?"

"Are you putting your pasta on the same level as the Sistine Chapel?"

"Are they not both proof of the existence of God?"

Charly smiled. "They're proof that you're a loony."

"Tell me you don't love to have my Cannelloni in your mouth."

Bird jumped in. "Alright, this is getting pornographic. So unless you want to get me all horny, shut up and have another drink."

When he got home that night, Dante sat at his dining room table. What a night. The event surpassed his expectations on every level. All those people had such a good time. A lot of them probably desperately needed a night like that, himself included. Without The Feast, he would have slow-roasted in thoughts of what Abby was doing.

Maybe she went on a date tonight. Maybe she was seeing someone now and that's why she hadn't called back. She and her beau might have gone to some romantic Manhattan restaurant where the candlelight, the music, the wine would have put a dreamy shimmer on the world. Maybe tonight her new relationship took a turn. Maybe someone had admitted to being in love. She might be with him right now, his arm around her while they slept.

Dante lowered his head to the crook of his elbow on the table. And no matter how many deep breaths he took, his heart barely continued to beat.

He finally got up to go to bed, stopping in the bathroom to brush his teeth. In the mirror, his eyes looked bloodshot and darkened with fatigue. "Maybe you'll never heal," he said to his reflection. He closed his eyes and took a deep breath.

In bed, as he started to fall asleep, he heard a little bump coming from the direction of the kitchen, then someone singing, "*Ciuri, ciuri, ciuri di tuttu l'annu, l'amuri ca, mi dasti ti lu tornu . . . Lah lah la-la la, la la, la la, la lah . . .*"

He called out, "Nonna?"

When he got to the kitchen, Nonna stood at the counter sautéing mustard greens with garlic and red pepper flakes. A fresh loaf of bread rested on the counter next to her. Nonna looked up and smiled. "*Ciao*, Dantelino."

"*Perché sei venuto stasera*?"—why did you come tonight?

"You're trying too hard to make your heart heal. Try less."

Dante arched an eyebrow. "Try less?"

"Exactly."

Dante rubbed his eyes. Nothing he heard or even saw made any sense to him.

"Are you sure I'm not going crazy?" he said.

"Are you asking *me*?"

"Well, I guess if you said I wasn't crazy, how would I know for sure? I mean if I'm making you up in my head, then anything you said that I believed would just prove I'm crazy."

"*Mi stai confondendo*"—You're confusing me. "I'm not in your head." She put the greens on a plate and cut a couple of slices of bread.

"If I took a picture of you, would it come out?"

Nonna shook her head. "That's your problem—you try to figure everything out in your head. What does your heart tell you?"

Dante tried to think what his heart was telling him.

"Stop using your head to tell you what your heart is saying! Just listen. Use your intuition, like you do with cooking. Trust that you will heal, and bring yourself to truly believe it."

Nonna handed the plate of greens to Dante. "I have to go. Remember—try less, and trust more."

She smiled, then faded away.

"Try less, trust more," Dante said. "How do you try less?" He sat for a moment and thought about it. Then said, "Maybe not asking that question in the first place is a step in the right direction."

Chapter 14

Dante's heart had a ways to go before it healed, but over the passing days something was going on for others who had eaten his food. The *Chronicle* writer, Tim Jorgensen, called Dante for an interview about The Feast of the Broken Hearts. In the piece, which came out a couple of days later, Dante was quoted as saying, "Shunryu Suzuki Roshi, the Zen master who founded the San Francisco Zen Center, said, 'When you cook, you are not just working on food, you are working on yourself, you are working on others.' The Feast of the Broken Hearts follows that idea. Maybe by having people get together, they'll realize they're not alone in how they feel. It may be a little sappy, sentimental, but I think when you're dealing with a broken heart, that's exactly what you need."

Jorgensen himself wrote, "It was hand's down the best Valentine's evening I ever spent, including times when I was in a relationship—which may say a lot about how I ended up at this event to begin with." He went on to say that The Feast of the Broken Hearts was destined to become a North Beach annual event.

And for weeks, it didn't let up. "It's been crazy," Sal said. "We're still getting calls from people saying we actually cured their broken hearts."

Just that afternoon, a woman came up to Dante at the restaurant and said, "I don't know what you put in your food at that party, but I went from wanting to jump off the Transamerica Building to being as at peace as I've ever been. You are truly some kind of angel."

Dante smiled. What Nonna had said was true. And it felt incredible to know he really was curing broken hearts.

Rumors of Charly having been at The Feast of the Broken Hearts also sparked speculation that she and the mayor were on the outs. Tabloids reported that she had also been seen being "rather chummy" with a certain chef.

One night when Charly was in the restaurant, she said, "I realize it comes with the territory, but it still annoys the hell out of me. As if dating the mayor of a major city doesn't come with enough of its own pressure. The guy works all the time, which is fine with me. He's got a job to do. So do I. I'm in Washington practically every other week. So of course we're not going to see each other every night. If I go out with some friends when he's out of town, why does it have to be news?"

Dante smiled. "Because he's the hunky mayor of San Francisco. He's a celebrity."

"I just wish everybody would stay out of our business."

Dante wondered if Abby was dating some studly TV star in New York. They must be all over the place at her office at Cook Network.

He took a deep breath.

Charly touched his hand. "How are you doing, by the way?"

Dante shrugged. "I'm trying to let things go."

"How's that going?"

"I could use some distraction. You around this weekend?"

"Yeah, let's go do something. How about Sonoma on Sunday, a little wine tasting?"

"I love that idea."

They arrived in Sonoma Sunday morning and went to wineries where Dante knew people, so they got to taste the good stuff. An '09 Ferelli Chardonnay: pear, white peach and black pepper flavors with an almost oily texture. A '03 Cabernet from Sable Horse: silky, spicy with robust blackberry, very lush.

At a little winery, DeLeo, named after the family that founded it in the early 1900s, Dante's friend, Carlo, had some great stories. "I was a kid when I first started working here in 1971," he said. "Fresh off the boat from Torino. And you see right out that door that the vines start?" He pointed a dark, hairy arm toward the French doors where, outside, rows of grapes reached into the distance. "This couple, they go down one of the rows when they think no one is looking. I tell Lina, the owner, rest her soul. She laughs and tells me to go after them and get them out. As I'm walking along, all of a sudden I see the man's hairy ass bouncing up and down on his wife right there on the ground."

Charly nearly blew wine out her nose laughing.

"Of course," Carlo said, "my virgin eyes are shocked and I go running back. Lina's waiting at the end of the row laughing her head off because she already knew what I'd find. She told me it had been going on since the fifties. And even now, every summer a few couples, maybe more, go in there."

Charly finally recovered enough to ask, "And they don't do any damage?"

"No, not really. That's why Lina never put a stop to it, and why now most of us turn the other way."

When Carlo excused himself to get a bottle of Brunello, Charly reached for a glass of water that was on the other side of Dante. She put her hand on his shoulder for balance, but pressed her entire body next to his, long enough for him to feel all the important contours. And for a second, he thought Charly might actually kiss him. But then Carlo returned.

After that, they had an early dinner at Ciel Bleu, Dante's friend Luc's place. He served them lobster-toasted garlic quesadillas with brie and chipotle jam as an appetizer. Dante had seared calamari with white beans and chorizo and Charly had spicy wok-stirred blue mussels with rhubarb-birch syrup.

Afterwards, they walked around the square.

"I have that 'Sonoma glow,'" Charly said.

Dante stood in front of her and playfully looked her up and down. Then his expression turned serious. "Have you always been so beautiful or is this your Sonoma Glow look?"

Her face flushed. "It's the wine talking."

"I'm not hitting on you—you have the mayor. And me, well, I just have emotional problems." He smiled. "I'm just saying you're a beautiful woman. That's all."

Charly smiled. "Thank you."

"Okay," Dante said, "We'd better go get some coffee and let the wine wear off before we go home."

They headed over to Blue Dog Diner where they talked and drank coffee until the place closed at 11:00. When they got back to San Francisco, Dante dropped Charly off.

"Thank you Charly," he said. "You are an amazing friend to spend the day with me like this."

"You're welcome, sunshine. It was a lot of fun." She got out of the car, and Dante watched her until she got into her house.

The next morning, the phone rang as Dante dragged from the bathroom to the kitchen to make his espresso. He was definitely slogging through a melancholy mud bog. He reached the phone on the fourth ring.

"Hello," he croaked.

"Hi Dante, it's Abby."

It's Abby? On the phone? Right now?

"I hope I didn't wake you," she said.

"No, not at all."

"I just had a meeting cancel and I thought I'd try to get a hold of you before something else came up."

"I'm glad you did. It's great to hear your voice. How are you?"

"I've been really busy at work. But you know, I never knew I could love a job this much." Dante could hear the grin in her voice. She also said Zoe was a natural New Yorker. "Even winter was fun. I actually enjoyed the snow."

"It sounds like you're doing great. I'm really happy for you."

"Thanks. That's nice to hear." She paused then said, "I was thinking about you the other night. That time at Ocean Beach with the dog . . ."

They had gone to Ocean Beach one surprisingly-warm-for-Ocean-Beach evening and arrived as the sun was setting. They brought a fake firelog, a bottle of Cabernet, and a couple of blankets. He had kissed her lightly at first. But as their lips melded, and their tongues merged, Abby shivered. She drew back and narrowed her eyes. "What did you do?"

"I don't know." He pulled her closer. "But let's see if we can do it again."

When it was over, they lay half naked, spooning under the blanket. The ocean breeze flicked the flames over the log.

"Dante," Abby said.

"Yes?"

"There's a dog sniffing at our feet."

A lanky chocolate lab stood smiling at the two of them. An effeminate man's voice called over the dune. "Ipanema, you come here right now."

Abby's eyes grew wide. "Oh shit!" she whispered. She and Dante scrambled to get their pants, which Ipanema took to mean they wanted to play. The dog grabbed the blanket and pulled, exposing their unclad butts to the fire-lit night and the two men who had come over the dune.

The first guy's jaw flew open and he gasped. "Oh, Jesus, Ipanema, No!"

The other one tried to grab hold of the dog while covering his eyes. "Come here right now! Oh God, I'm so sorry." Ipanema thought it was much more fun now that his people were involved. He romped about, tugging the blanket, staying out of reach of his owners. At one point, a cold wet dog nose planted itself squarely on the left cheek of Dante's bare ass.

One of the guys finally caught Ipanema's collar and they apologetically dragged the dog out of sight.

"That was quite a night," Dante said.

"It was . . . Okay, I better, uhm, stop thinking about it or I'm going to get myself into trouble."

"Nothing wrong with a little trouble, is there?"

There was a long pause and Dante started to tingle with the thought of what Abby might say. Then she said, "So anyway, how's the restaurant?"

They talked for about a half hour more.

"It sounds like you're doing great," Dante said. "I'm really happy for you."

"Thanks. It was really nice talking to you."

When Dante hung up, he cried: that was the Abby he fell in love with in Las Vegas. He sat in his bedroom, looking at the engagement ring he bought for her. Was it being back in New York that made her happy again? Did she feel more connected to her family? Could she be happy with *him* in New York? The pain of her leaving felt as fresh and strong as the day they broke up. Maybe Abby was his fate and he should go to New York and ask her to marry him.

A couple of weeks later, Abby called again. It was near ten and Dante had just gotten home.

"I finally finished my work tonight," she said, "and Zoe's asleep, so I thought I'd say hello."

"I'm glad you did. I've been thinking a lot about you." Dante cringed. That last part slipped out.

"You have? In what way?" The lubricity of her voice caught Dante off guard. But he was able to come back quickly.

"In what way would you like?"

"I'd better not say." She almost cooed.

"I think you should." A flash of heat ran between Dante's legs as he settled onto the couch.

"Okay." She cleared her throat. "I want you to have thought about me . . . completely naked."

Dante bit his lip.

She took a few guttural breaths.

"Hang on, I'm going to close my door."

Dante heard the door click, then some rustling.

"Okay, I'm back." She breathed heavily again. "I'm on the bed. On my stomach. I'm not wearing anything."

"Oh my god."

Abby went on to describe a fantasy of the two of them on a tropical beach in the hot night air, their bodies illuminated by moonlight.

When it was over, Dante was pantsless and breathless.

Abby, still catching her breath, said, "That was amazing."

"No kidding."

She laughed. "I really did just call to say hi."

"Well, hi then."

Once their breathing was back to semi-normal, the conversation turned to the ordinary, mostly about how hectic their lives were.

"The restaurant must be keeping you busy," Abby said.

"It's just been crazy busy. We can barely keep up. I'm usually not home until after midnight."

"Speaking of which," Abby said, "I should probably get to sleep." She paused and sighed. "Goodnight." The way she said "goodnight" reminded him of so many times when, after they'd made love at his house, he took her home to Zoe, and they'd stand on her doorstep, her eyes gleaming with love. How he'd kiss her and practically float all the way home.

He had to catch himself when he almost said "I love you" into the phone. "Goodnight to you, too." When he hung up, he leaned back on the couch and thought how much he wanted to hold her, caress her, fall asleep with her in his arms. And how much he wanted her back.

Chapter 15

Over the next several weeks, though he didn't have a repeat phonegasm with Abby, she did call and e-mail regularly. In her last e-mail, along with the normal update on her busy life and Zoe, who had a Spring play in which she played the part of a lily, Abby said she had a kind of naughty dream about Dante the other night. "I really need to stop bringing that stuff up, don't I? Especially since we're on different coasts."

Dante kept reading that line over and over. Was she trying to tell him something? Would she take him back if he was in New York? He tried not to get his hopes up, but it all seemed to be a positive development.

One night, Dante got home from work late, and saw the message light on his home phone blinking.

"Hi Dante, it's Abby. You're probably still at work." Her words sounded a little slurred. "Victor has Zoe this week so I went out with a few of the girls tonight. I guess I shouldn't tell you this, but your name came up." She cleared her throat. "When my friend Melissa asked us to name our all-time greatest lover. They wanted details, but I explained that a lady never tells." She half laughed. "And I guess I must've been going on and on about you because Melissa finally said it sounded like you were the one that got away." She let out a long sigh. "Anyway, I'm home now. And I probably shouldn't tell you this, either—I probably shouldn't even be calling you—but I wish you were here right now. Holding me like you used to. And those incredible kisses. I wish you were here in my bed." Her voice trailed off, then returned. "Maybe you *are* the one that got away." Another long sigh. "Okay, I'm going to stop talking now."

After Dante heard the message, he melted. The one that got away? Drunk dial or not, she clearly still had feelings for him. And he knew he still loved her. Maybe it was time to actually ask her to marry him.

But that would be crazy. How could he leave everything behind in San Francisco and make a change of that magnitude?

Pane Rubato was going well. The heart healing brought in a lot of new people, but droves of happy people were coming in, too. It was all exciting and fun. But if he took stock of the times he felt genuinely happy, he'd have to say most of those times related to contact with Abby. Whenever he saw her name in his e-mail inbox and especially when he heard her voice, it was like a shot of pure euphoria. And even now, thinking of waking up next to her every morning, his heart pounded. Maybe she was worth leaving San Francisco behind to get everything he'd ever wanted in New York.

From a career perspective, he could probably get re-established in New York. He could find a place to open a restaurant. Even just a fifteen- or twenty-seater. So moving wouldn't necessarily be career suicide. And it wouldn't mean he'd have to give up Pane Rubato completely. He would still own half of it. He trusted Bird and Sal to run the place. So really it was just a matter of moving cross country. The rest, he was sure, would take care of itself.

And if he didn't ask Abby to marry him, he'd always wonder. They had something great once and circumstances got in the way. If he did ask, she wouldn't say no. He knew it.

So Dante went to his laptop and booked a flight to New York for the weekend.

The next morning, fully sober, he still had no question about making a trip to New York for Abby. He told Bird he'd be taking the weekend off because he was meeting his brother in L.A. who was down there for a bicycling race.

"What race?" Bird said. "When did this come up?"

"What are you, a cop? I'll see you Monday."

When he got to New York that Saturday, as he held the box containing the engagement ring in his blazer pocket, he knew that no matter how the situation had come about, he was meant to be here now.

He stood in line for a cab at Kennedy Airport. Car exhaust filled the warm air. The nice day was a good omen. The woman in line in front of him wore Bijan, Abby's perfume. Another good omen.

Dante's plan was simple. After he arrived at the hotel near Abby's place in the West Village, he'd go pick up a dozen roses. He'd ring her doorbell and hold the bouquet in front of his face. When she answered, he'd reveal himself. He would ask her to marry him right there on her front stoop.

He barely remembered the ride from the airport. He checked into his hotel, Abingdon Guest House, and found a flower shop across the street. He bought a bouquet of red roses specked throughout with tiny white baby's breath blossoms.

As he walked up to Abby's place, a two story brownstone, his hands shook. His heart bruised his sternum. He was seconds away from seeing those eyes he missed so much. That smile. He could almost feel her lips on his. And when they kissed, he would have to do his best not to fall apart right there on her doorstep.

He took a deep breath and rang the doorbell, holding the flowers in front of his face. When the door opened, he lowered the roses and his eyes met Abby's. They lit up with recognition and she smiled. A big, bright, happy smile.

That was what he came for. He knew she loved him. He knew she was his and they'd be together for the rest of their lives.

"Dante, what are you doing here?" She covered her mouth as he handed her the roses.

Behind Abby, a little girl squealed. "Dante!" Zoe ran up and practically jumped into Dante's arms.

"Hi there, sweetie," he said.

She hugged him, nearly cutting off the circulation to his brain.

"Come in, come in," Abby said.

They walked into the living room where Dante sat on the couch as Abby put the roses in a vase.

Zoe hopped off Dante's lap. "My dad's taking me to the Yankee game tomorrow. Do you want to come?"

"I think your dad will want to spend the time with you."

"Maybe another time," Abby said, "the three of us can go to a game."

See, she's already thinking of us like a family.

Zoe smiled. "Okay!"

"I'm just so shocked you're here," Abby said. "What are you doing in town?"

"I came to see you."

"Zoe, sweetheart, can you let me talk to Dante alone for a few minutes?"

The little girl nodded then left the room.

Abby sat next to Dante and put her hand on his leg. She looked into his eyes and smiled, then bit her lower lip. "Maybe I can get my mom to watch Zoe tonight." She ran her hand up his thigh. "Since you came all this way, I want to make it worth your while."

"Well, actually, I have a good idea how you can do that."

That salacious smile came across her face. "Ooh, I'm sure you do. And I can't wait to hear about it." She kissed him, slipping her tongue in his mouth. "And I want you to tell me all about it tonight. Right now I need to make the arrangement for Zoe. Pick me up at 7:00?"

Dante swallowed his frustration. "Sure."

So he'd have to wait a few more hours. He'd waited this long.

That night, when he showed up at Abby's house, she was in a little black dress that brought out all of her curves, and showed just enough skin to make you want to see more.

When Dante saw her, he said, "That must be the sexiest black dress in existence."

Abby smiled. "Glad you like it. It's just a hint of what's to come tonight."

They went to Le Bernardin for dinner. Dante planned to propose at some point during dinner when the moment seemed right.

"How'd you get us in here?" Dante said. "This is one of the hottest restaurants in New York."

Abby shrugged. "I know a guy."

They had a couple of cocktails at the bar while waiting for their table. By the time they were seated, Abby's smile had become wickedly playful.

Abby said, "I'm glad you're here. I have to admit I've really been missing you lately,"

Dante reached into his jacket pocket and took hold of the ring box.

Abby continued. "I miss the way we were together."

"It's so nice to hear you say that." Dante's heart raced. This was the moment.

Abby leaned in. "I can't wait to get you home and do some very naughty things to you."

His heart sank a little, but he managed a smile.

After dinner, they went back to her place. As soon as they got in the door Abby started to undress Dante.

"I want you naked." She unbuttoned his shirt and nearly tore it off. She unbuckled his belt and started to pull his pants off.

Dante looked over toward the window. "The curtains are open."

"I don't care." She took his pants and boxers at the same time and pulled them to the floor.

As he stood naked, she kissed him long and hard. Then she took his hand and led him to the bedroom. She pushed him onto the bed. She stripped and said, "You've been away from my bed for too long."

She crawled on top of him. With her hair flowing around her face, she looked into his eyes. "I've got some making up to do."

The next morning, Dante awoke to Abby kissing his neck and rubbing his chest.

"Good morning," she said.

They made love again, and afterwards, Abby said, "I forgot just how good we are together."

They cuddled for the next hour, and made plans to grab breakfast, then pick up Zoe and go to the Central Park zoo.

"I'm so glad you're here," Abby said.

Dante felt his heart connect with her on a level he hadn't thought possible, and he knew now that they were going to be married. He would finally have the fairytale life he imagined when he was five.

When Abby got up to go to the bathroom, Dante leaned over and pulled the ring box from his jacket pocket.

Abby returned and sat next to him in the bed. Dante couldn't help grinning.

She smiled and said, "What're you doing?"

"I still love you and I know I'm supposed to spend the rest of my life with you. I'm ready to move to New York to be with you." He took the ring from under the sheet. "Will you marry me?"

Abby just stared at the ring for a long time. No joy came to her eyes. Her expression wasn't full of elation.

Finally, she said, "I can't ask you to give up everything in San Francisco for me."

"But I really—"

She held up her hand to stop him. "It's too much pressure. And I don't want that kind of pressure in a relationship."

"But I wouldn't be giving up anything. I'd just be doing it in a different place."

She shook her head. "I have Zoe to think about."

"And I'd be here to help with her."

"You'd be in New York but you wouldn't be *here*. You'd be trying to keep your restaurant open."

Abby stopped and looked into his eyes. Dante tried to speak, but no words would come.

She took a deep breath. "I'm sorry. I know this isn't how you wanted all this to go. And I do miss you." She opened her arms as if to offer her naked body as evidence. "Obviously. But I don't think you understand just what a move like this would be like."

"I've lived in Rome and San Francisco. I'll be fine in New York."

"That's not what I mean. It was my job that brought Victor to San Francisco. It was always a huge source of tension between us. Every problem in his life was because he'd left New York and he grew to resent me for it."

"I'm not Victor. And you just said yourself that we were so great together. Unless you only meant in bed."

"No, I didn't mean only in bed. But I just don't want to be married again. Something about the whole arrangement ruins relationships. I love my life right now. And maybe I got a little carried away with seeing you."

Dante sighed. "When you broke up with me, you said it was because you had to come back to New York to be near your family. Okay, I get that. When I offered to come to New York with you, you said it was about Zoe. Now you say it's about marriage. But it seems to me the truth of the matter is that you just don't want to be in a relationship with me."

"I feel like you're putting me on the spot."

"I guess I am. If you don't want a relationship with me, I should know that so I stop holding onto some stupid idea that maybe you do."

Abby stared out the window for several seconds then turned and looked Dante in the eye. "I'm sorry."

He sat for several seconds while his mind silently screamed to explain. She was making a mistake. They could be together, be a family. If she would give him a chance. Why couldn't she see? Why couldn't she open her heart to true love instead of hiding behind all these false excuses?

But all he said was, "I will always love you."

He got out of bed and put on his clothes and walked out of her house. The bright morning sky may have been clouded over with noxious gas for all he knew or cared. He wandered a few blocks, maybe twenty. He might have just gone around the same block for hours.

At some point in the early afternoon, he ended up at the corner of Hudson and 11th Street under the White Horse Tavern sign. This place was famous, right? And even if it wasn't, they surely had beer and whiskey inside.

He walked in and sat beneath one of the two white-horse-head-adorned chandeliers. He ordered a whiskey. And another. And another. Until his eyes were barely open and finally someone said it was time he went home. He agreed.

He guided himself back to the hotel by sheer luck and crawled into the bed, fully clothed. The room whirled and he wasn't entirely sure he wouldn't be sick soon. But at least the nausea worked to keep his grief at bay. And a good retching might do a lot to help a guy forget that his one true love had rejected him.

Unfortunately, he didn't vomit. He just lay there. In the room's spin cycle. Sick to his stomach and heartbroken. Until Mercy came and knocked him senseless.

Chapter 16

Dante stood in the airport the next evening, numb, waiting on the first available flight to San Francisco. He'd spent the entire day there trying to get on a standby flight. Severe thunderstorms up and down the east coast had delayed flights for hours. Dante was lucky enough to get one that would stop in Denver before arriving in San Francisco sometime in the morning.

Then Charly called. Dante answered because he had to tell someone and he couldn't bring himself to make a call. When he saw Charly's name on the phone, he felt a little less like jumping in front of a 747.

"You're in New York?" Charly's voice was shrill through the phone. "And Abby rejected your marriage proposal?"

"Yes on both."

"First, what the hell were you thinking? Why would you go to New York?"

"I have to go." He hung up. She called right back. He pressed the Talk button, told her he was fine, and hung up again. Then he turned the phone off. And headed for the closest bar.

At Bar Avion, the bartender poured the third shot of Wild Turkey within about twenty minutes. "Okay, this is it for a little while," he said. He was petite for a man, a little frail. He had dark, curly, hair, and pale skin accentuated by the dark five o'clock shadow.

Dante threw back the shot then chased it with a sip of beer. "Okay. You're probably right. Better slow down."

The young woman next to Dante ordered a glass of chardonnay. She turned to him.

"I'm scared of flying, too."

Dante put his hand on his face. It felt rubbery. The young woman held up her glass.

"Here's to liquid courage." She had the perfect voice for a 1940s hotel switchboard operator, with a little Glenda, the Good Witch of the North thrown in.

Dante raised his beer mug to meet her toast. Her shoulder-length auburn hair was tucked behind her ear and her green eyes twinkled at him. She had a beautiful smile and a pretty face, but it was covered in too much cake batter. Her gray sweater clung tightly to her tremendous breasts.

Her name was Jan and she was heading home to Chicago. She was in New York for work. "I only fly when I absolutely have to."

Poor thing. You should comfort her.

"Actually, I'm not afraid of flying. I just got turned down on my marriage proposal."

"Oh my goodness. That's terrible." Sounded like she was from Minnesota. Maybe Wisconsin.

Dante told her his whole story: from Las Vegas to that moment. "And I never really believed that she didn't love me, too. Not until yesterday."

"Oh my." Jan put her hand on his arm. She took another sip of her wine. "That is so sad and romantic. No one has ever loved *me* like that. I don't even know if anyone has ever loved me at all." She looked into her wine glass. "I mean, I've had boyfriends and a couple have said they loved me. But, gosh, no one has ever made a"—she did the quote mark fingers in the air—"grand gesture."

"I think I'm going to refer to it as a desperate act from now on."

"Don't you dare. There aren't many romantics left in this world.

Most women I know would kill for a guy like you."

Everything seemed to be running in slow motion. Dante's head was steaming and three feet thick. Jan smiled at him and to his surprise, she started to lean in for a kiss. So he went for it.

To his equal surprise, his bottom lip smashed into the top of her forehead as she reached for her bag at the foot of the barstool.

"Owie." Her hand covered the collision spot. "Oh honey, are you alright?"

Dante removed blood-tipped fingers from his swelling lip.

Nice going. You're such a twit.

"I'm sorry," sha said. "I didn't mean to give you the wrong idea."

Everyone in the bar was looking at Dante, so he grabbed his carry-on and walked away.

Dante finally got on his flight, and arrived at home in the optimal state of inebriation: drunk enough to feel warmly numb, but not so much he couldn't perform basic physical tasks like walking or talking—though he stumbled doing both.

He dropped his carry-on bag in the middle of the living room floor. The smack of canvas against hardwood was far less satisfying than he had hoped. He stared at the bag. It was the wrong kind of material to get a good dull thud. Or a wettish *thugck*. Something that would sound like his heart hitting the floor.

How could he ever have imagined that his idiotic plan was going to work? Hey, if I just fly to New York and show up on her doorstep, of course she'll marry me. Who wouldn't?

Abby had rejected him with barely any thought. She didn't ask for a week or day, or even an hour to consider his proposal. She knew she didn't want to marry him, and that was that.

Dante took a deep, shaky breath. He filled a glass halfway with Scotch. The first taste abated the drilling in his chest. He put the glass to his mouth again, but stopped before letting the whiskey touch his lips.

He put his drink on the table and picked up the phone. He dialed Charly's number and it went straight to voicemail. "Hi, it's me. Call me when you have a chance."

Dante took another mouthful of Scotch. After he swallowed, he took another deep breath.

Why did Abby not want him? The only good explanation was the simplest one: she didn't love him. She had once. He was sure of it.

The tears flowed from his eyes. She *had* once loved him. And they were so great together.

The next morning, he woke up feeling like his brain was pushing its way out through his eye sockets. He lurched out of bed, stumbled straight to the bathroom and retched. Every muscle wrenched, trying to wring the poison from his body. In spite of the loud heaving and great effort of his stomach, not much came up.

He wiped his mouth with toilet paper. Then he looked at his reflection in the mirror. His watery eyes were bloodshot and rimmed red. His face pallid.

He called Pane Rubato on the kitchen's line. Bird answered.

"I'm not coming in today," Dante said.

"You sick?"

"I went to New York and asked Abby to marry me."

"You what? I thought you said you were going to L.A.."

"She said, 'no.'"

"D—"

He put the phone down and ran his hand through his hair. Something needed to change, he needed to change.

He grabbed his jacket and left the house. A few blocks later, he walked into Giordano Barber Shop. Pete Giordano, pushing eighty, only a few straggly hairs clinging to his age-spotted pate, peered through his thick black glasses. "Ah, Dante, have a seat."

Dante plopped into the barber chair and Pete spun him to face the mirror. "The usual?" Pete said. "Above the ears, a little off the top?"

"No, let's go Number One on the clippers."

"You sure? This head of hair?"

The front door bell clanked when Pete's friend, Tony, came in. In his seventies, he was still a walking granite boulder with a bushy mustache and overgrown hedge eyebrows. You could hear every cigar and whiskey shot in his voice. "Petey, son-of-a-bitch, the line at Trieste was too goddamn long." His eyes lit up when he saw Dante in the chair. "Dante, how are you?"

Pete said, "He wants me to shave his head."

"Oh no. Gotta be—"

Pete nodded. "Yep, that's what I thought, too."

"What?" Dante said.

"A woman," they said in unison. "Son-of-a-bitch," Tony added.

Pete looked at Dante in the mirror. "A broken heart makes you want to shave your head. Makes you think if you change how you look, it'll change how you feel."

"Don't really work that way," Tony said.

"Yeah, well, I still don't want this hair on my head." He made to get up. "So if you don't want to do it—"

Pete put his hand on his shoulder. "Alright. I just don't want you to come back to me tomorrow and say, 'What the hell did you do to me?'"

"I won't."

Pete took the clippers, adjusted the setting, and took a deep breath. He turned it on and plunged straight down the middle of Dante's head.

Dante half smiled. "No turning back now."

When the buzzing and flying hair ceased, he was left with nothing but fuzz atop his noggin. His hair hadn't been that short since his was five years old. His dad would run his hand over his little sandpaper head, saying, "Feeeel." It was less fun to do as an adult, but he did take a certain pleasure in the sensation of stubble on his head.

"Feel any better?"

"I guess we'll see."

He went home and made two slices of toast. Slightly burnt. He made coffee and spiked it with whiskey.

No messages on his home or cell phones.

He finished his coffee, then went to his bedroom. He took the ring from the drawer in his bedside table. If Abby didn't want it, why should he keep it? He could take it back to the jewelry store, or a pawn shop. But that seemed the weak way to go. Maybe burn it in the fireplace. Did diamonds burn? Even if they did, the ring's remnants would still live in his house. He couldn't crush it, and throwing it in the trash would be anticlimactic. He needed to do something ceremonial. He needed to give it over to Mother Earth. He'd drop it from the middle of the Golden Gate Bridge and let the bay and ocean fight over who got to keep it. Just the thought of watching the ring plummet toward the water buoyed him.

He parked on the San Francisco side of the bridge and walked among the sightseers until he reached mid-span. San Francisco gleamed in the late morning sun. He reached into his jacket pocket and grabbed the velvet box. He opened it and stared at the diamond, this malignant tumor in his life. There was no longer any sparkle, no shine. It may as well have been a piece of cloudy glass stuck to a hunk of lead. And he was a mere flick of the wrist away from being rid of it.

He held the ring between his thumb and forefinger, then stuck his hand through the bars. The wind howled over his hairless head.

A hand touched Dante's shoulder. "Hey buddy," a police officer said. "You're not tossing anything off my bridge." He smiled. "And I'm guessing she's not worth it, anyway."

Dante looked at him with shock, then nodded and slid his hand into his pocket. "Is it okay if I stay here a bit?"

"Long as you and everything you came with stay on the bridge."

Dante and everything he came with eventually left the bridge together. He couldn't stand the thought of going back to his house, so he drove to Ocean Beach. On the way, he stopped and bought a pint of Wild Turkey. It was early afternoon and this part of the city was clouded over and cold. He labored through the sand until he found a log to sit on.

He opened the bottle and took a long pull of Kentucky straight bourbon whiskey. He stared out at the gloomy horizon. The Marin headlands, ghostly behind the murkiness, jutted out into the Pacific. A tanker headed through the Golden Gate into San Francisco Bay. The wind whip-roared in his ears, but it wouldn't blow Abby out of his mind. The waves advanced and retreated but wouldn't take Abby away with them. He gazed out at the gray and blue wishing something, anything, would clear his head.

An hour later, the bottle was half empty and Dante was half blind. He stood and started to walk back toward his car, but after a few steps, began to have serious doubts about his ability to remain on his feet. He plunked down in the sand. Then his stomach heaved and the first wave of vomit shot up his throat and onto his shirt and pants. Somehow he got to his hands and knees and continued emptying the contents of his stomach onto the sand.

When he stopped and caught his breath, when the blood drained from his forehead, he realized that his clothes were covered in vomit, and he was struck with another brilliant idea. He had shaved his head, he had rid himself of the poison he had ingested, and now he should free himself of his clothes. He wanted to be naked to the world. He wanted to be stripped of everything. And he wanted to get the puke off himself. So he stood and dropped his pants. He hadn't removed his shoes and he tried to lift one foot while his pants were around his knees. He fell over on his side and his ear hit the sand. But he got both shoes off and his pants followed. The sweatshirt and T-shirt came off next, leaving him in boxers and socks. Finally, he yanked down his underwear and threw his arms in the air. Then he decided he needed the Pacific to cleanse him, the salty ocean water to purify him.

At that point, the beach patrol decided the public beach was no place for a drunk naked man. They tried to explain that clothing was not optional here. That perhaps Dante had confused Ocean Beach for Baker Beach. He assured the assholes he knew where he was and asked why they couldn't let him be. There were hardly any people there. He wanted to let the universe flow through him and be in a natural state. He stood his naked ground as a frigid wave washed around his calves.

"Is wearing socks part of a natural state?" one of the rangers said. Dante didn't like his tone one bit. Smug bastard.

"Okay, sir," the second ranger said. "You've had your fun. Time to go home."

"You think this is fun for me? You think I'm enjoying myself? Well, you're wrong. You're fucking wrong."

He turned and ran toward the water, which had receded about twenty feet. He stumbled after a few steps and the rangers rushed him. Dante quickly got to his feet and eluded the first one. The second one got a hand on him, but he was able to shake free. Then Dante took off down the beach, running as fast as he could. He only got about fifteen feet before both rangers tackled him and drove his chest and shoulders into the wet sand. A second later, another wave came up and the cold water hit his entire nude body and also drenched the rangers. As the water withdrew, a clarity came upon Dante. He didn't struggle. He didn't attempt escape. He simply asked if he could put on his clothes prior to his trip to the police station, a request the rangers kindly granted.

Chapter 17

When Bird showed up to take Dante home from jail, he didn't say a word, just gave him that look of distaste and disapproval usually reserved for a colossal fuck up by a rookie in the kitchen.

He took Dante home and made him a bowl of linguine with tomato and pesto sauce. "You're an adult," he said. "You know what you need to do, even if you lose your way. Now act like a man and take care of your business."

He grated pecorino cheese over the top of the pasta. "You got one more chance to get your shit straight. You're like family to me, D, and I'm not going to watch you fuck up all you have in your life." Dante glanced up. "This is the last time I see you like this, understand?"

Dante nodded.

"You take a day, a week, whatever, to figure yourself out. And get help. Professional help."

Before leaving, Bird hugged Dante then told him to shower because he reeked of moldy ass cheese. After he left, Dante sat at the kitchen table, staring at the pasta in a hangover-induced fog. His head ached. His stomach churned.

He pulled the ring from his pocket. Abby's face looked so happy when he showed up at her door. Her eyes, her smile revealed her true feelings. He saw love looking back at him. You can't fake that. So maybe his appearance and proposal were too much all at once. Maybe after she had a chance to let things settle in her mind.

He got up, walked into the living room, and poured another Scotch, emptying the bottle. He swigged the whiskey, then he crawled into a dark little crevice somewhere in the back of his mind and tried to hide from the hot sharp pieces of metal that kept piercing his heart.

Drink and exhaustion ruled the hours. With the Scotch gone, he moved onto Wild Turkey to keep the buzz going and as the day progressed, he couldn't tell which parts were dream or just dream-like. The phone may have rang a time or two and if he answered, he wasn't sure who called or what they had talked about. He was relatively sure he hadn't left the house. But he was amorphously aware of sleeping in the sun. Whether that was on the back deck or front step, he couldn't be sure.

At one point, he realized he was sitting in the dark. It felt like mildew filled his eyes. He turned on the light and looked at his watch. How did it get to be after ten? He stood on wonky legs and keeled to the kitchen. He steadied himself on the counter as the room began to spin. Maybe he'd better have something to eat. He hadn't had food since—

Fuzz filled his eyes and he had the sensation of falling.

When he opened his eyes, he was on the floor and the house was dark. Someone was at the stove, singing, "*Ciuri, ciuri, ciuri di tuttu l'annu, l'amuri ca, mi dasti ti lu tornu . . . Lah lah la-la la, la la, la la, la lah . . .*"

Nonna turned and bent down. She touched Dante's face. "*È tempo di svegliarsi*"—It's time to wake up.

Dante rolled over and got to his hands and knees. He put his hand on the counter and pulled himself up while Nonna spotted him. He steadied himself and took the few steps to the kitchen table where his tailbone hit the wood of the chair with a crack.

Nonna put a bowl of *pasta fagioli* on the table and sat down. Dante took a bite and again the taste of Nonna's food was unmistakable.

"Only you can heal your heart," she said. "But you're going about it the wrong way. And I cannot tell you who your *amore vero* is. But I can tell you that your true love is already in your heart. It was always there. Somewhere deep inside. And *Dolore* only makes it harder to understand your heart. You must clear your head so you can hear what your heart is trying to tell you."

"What happens if my true love's heart doesn't realize I'm her true love?"

"The stories you tell yourself become the stories you live. But if you listen to the story deep in your heart, the rest will be taken care of. *Ascolta*."

"But—"

"*Ascolta*!" She glared with head-slapping intensity.

"C'era una volta un giovane di nome Papireto che piangeva ogni giorno per il suo cuore infranto . . .

Once upon a time, there was a young man, Papireto, who cried every day over his broken heart. He cried day and night, for his beloved did not love him back. He cried so much that a river formed from his eyes, the River Papireto in Palermo. The people of the town were so worried he would flood them out of their homes that they tried everything to cheer him. They brought clowns and played music, but still Papireto cried.

Finally, they called upon Papierto's uncle, Frumentollo, the greatest baker in all the land and a man of renowned wisdom and calm. He was the last hope to save the town from Papireto's inundation.

The baker came from Monreale the next day and saw tear water running through the streets of Palermo. He got in a small boat and sailed along the tears until he found Papireto at the riverhead. Frumentollo tied the dinghy off on a nearby lamppost and called to his nephew. "Papireto, why do you cry?"

"My heart belongs to a woman who does not love me."

"She does not love you, that is true. But why do you cry? Will the tears turn her heart?"

"No. I cry from heartache."

"Your tears of heartache ended long ago."

Papireto scoffed. "Perhaps you have not seen the river on which you float."

"I see your tears, but these tears flowing past my boat are not from heartbreak. They are from self-pity."

At that, Papireto cried harder, sending a wave that nearly capsized Frumentello.

The baker steadied himself on the rocking boat and said, "You do not cry from loss of love, you cry from the loss of yourself, of your life. Your soul starves and you must learn to feed it."

Papireto sneered. "Then maybe you should bring me cake."

"You must bake the bread."

"Bake the bread? What kind of foolishness—"

"Yes, bake the bread. The food of life. The food of love. Bake the bread in spite of your pain. Bake the bread when you have no strength. Bake the bread, not out of anger or hurt or bitterness, but with love, with passion. Bake the bread for your heart. For others. Nurture yourself and others. Feed yourself and others. When you master the bread, you will master your life."

Papireto's tears began to slow.

His uncle continued, "The labor, the concentration, the devotion will remind you what's important so you can heal yourself. I say again, master the bread and master your life."

Now Papireto's tears ceased altogether. "Will you give me the recipe?"

Frumentollo smiled. "There is no recipe for good bread. I will tell you only this: start with yeast, water and flour. The rest is up to you. When you make it, trust your instincts, trust your touch. Feel your way through it. Listen to the ingredients, let them work for you. Let the method develop itself. Above all, be patient. Try, fail. Work and rework. Not for perfection, because that is unattainable, but for the effort itself. And one day, with one bite, you will know when you have mastered the bread."

After that day, Papireto cried no more and he set about making his bread. For weeks he did not make a loaf that was even edible. But still, he persisted and with time his bread was not bad, but still didn't resemble any bread he had ever seen or tasted before. Eventually, his bread became quite good and the townspeople lined up every morning to pick up a loaf. And though he was happy to share the bread, still, it was not quite what he wanted. He knew he had not mastered the bread.

One young woman, Nerezza, came to Papireto's bakery every day for bread. So consumed with his baking was he that he did not notice her shiny sable hair or the constant gaze of her sapphire eyes upon him.

"Your bread is better than any I have had," she said.

"Thank you. It still needs some work, but I am glad to share it with you. I hope it brings you some measure of peace and joy."

She held the warm bread close to her heart. "More than you know."

And every day, she would leave a little of her heart behind with him.

Papireto became a great baker in his own right and every day he turned out the most beautiful loaves anyone had ever seen. He too, was pleased with the fruits of his labor, but still, it was not quite right.

One day, Nerezza came for her bread as always, but this time when Papireto saw her, he fell deeply in love. He was so struck by her beauty that he could not say a word to her when he gave her the bread. Nerezza left that day, heartbroken, fearing she had done something to anger the baker.

That night, Papireto did not sleep as he worked on his recipe. The next morning, he pulled a loaf from the oven. The crust was exactly what he thought it should look like. He pulled the bread apart, watching the steam rise from its insides; it was the color and aroma he had been trying for all these years. Finally, he tasted it. He closed his eyes, and a single tear ran down his cheek. The texture and the taste were exactly as he desired. He had at long last mastered the bread.

He pulled the rest of the loaves from the oven, then took the best three he could find. He got on his horse and rode through the town to seek out Nerezza. He searched and searched until he found her on the banks of the river still named after his tears, River Papireto. When he rode up, he noticed she was crying.

Papireto hopped off his horse and approached her. When she looked up, he said, "I brought your bread." He held up the loaves.

She smiled through her tears. "You brought those for me out here?"

"I didn't want to wait until you came to the bakery."

Her smile was now brighter than the morning sun. "Why not?"

"Because I couldn't wait to see you again."

"Wh—"

"Because I love you." And with that, he kissed her.

They were married three days later. Papireto became the greatest baker in all of Sicily and he and Nerezza lived out the rest of their days happy and content.

"Nonna, I can bake bread."

"Of course you can. What kind of Palermo would you be if you couldn't?" She smiled.

"I thought you said my food couldn't heal my heart."

"And it cannot. Eating your food will not cure your broken heart. But, like with Papireto, the *lovoro*, the *concentrazione*, the *devozione* will remind you what's important so that you can heal yourself."

Chapter 18

Dante awoke early the next morning, knowing it was time to bake the bread. But before getting to work and because he still fully smelled of mold, cheese, and ass, he went straight to the shower. As the hot water hit his body, he could feel his pores unclog. As he breathed in the steam, his sinuses cleared. The soap washed away the dirt and sand and oil. He closed his eyes and let the water run over him. He thought about the bread, imagining how it should taste and feel and look. When he emerged from the shower thirty minutes later, he felt like so much of the last three days had been rinsed down the drain.

Then back to the kitchen. He went to the cupboard where he kept flour. He'd need that. What else? He tried not to think too hard about it. Yeast. Water. Salt. That should be enough to start. He dug into the back of one the lower cupboards and found his old gray ceramic mixing bowl. A gift from his mother the day he moved from Des Moines. "Your Nonna had one of these," she said, "I have one, and now so do you." Tears ran down her cheek. "A little reminder of home." It had been too long since he used it.

He set it on the counter and opened the packet of yeast. He poured it into his hand, feeling the dry granularity of it. He smelled the pungent yeastiness. "Okay, ladies, I'd like you to help me with my bread. So what do you need from me?"

A place to grow. Water. Warm water.

Still holding the yeast in his left hand, he filled the bowl with a small amount of lukewarm water, sprinkled in the yeast and stirred it with his hand until it dissolved. "And I bet you'd like a little food."

He went to the cupboard and got a bottle of honey. He returned to the bowl and squeezed the bottle. Honey drizzled into the water until he had a few tablespoons. He added a little salt and stirred it with a wooden spoon.

"Okay, let that sit for a minute or two so y'all have a chance to do your voodoo."

The doorbell rang. The front door opened and Charly called out, "Hello."

"In here."

As soon as she got into the kitchen, she laid into him with both hands to the chest and put him on his ass.

"What the hell is wrong with you?"

He looked up from the floor and decided to stay put. Her eyes shot armor-piercing bullets into his skull, sending fragments of his brain all over the kitchen.

"I know you're in pain, but Jesus Christ, get over it. What's the point of doing this to yourself?"

"Charly, I'm—"

She kicked him in the ass.

"Get up and get a grip on yourself, goddamnit. I'm shutting this pity party down."

She didn't let him get off the floor. "You have a life to take care of. Didn't you tell me that one of the things that always bothered you most about your father's death was that he had such a wonderful life and that he was taken from it? How you never understood how people could take life for granted? Aren't you wasting your life like this?"

Ouch. Nailed him with that one. Dante was ashamed for the way he'd acted, knowing his father's spirit had probably witnessed everything. Ashamed that he'd wasted even a moment of something so precious.

Charly put her hand out to help him up to the kitchen table. "You have friends and family who love you and want you in their lives. And they're concerned about you. Scared that you're in danger. You should have heard how Bird sounded when he called me. I've never heard worry like that from him before. He begged me to come over here and talk to you."

Her voice rasped and she took a minute to try, unsuccessfully, to clear her throat. She got a glass of water, but she wasn't done lecturing.

"Need I also remind you that you have a restaurant to run?"

"No, but—"

"You have all this great stuff going on in your life."

Dante pressed his palms to his eyes because if he'd have put his hands over his ears, Charly would have slapped him.

Finally, Charly sat at the table. "I don't know what it's going to take, but you have to do something. You have to get help. And I don't want to hear any of your whining. If I have to come over here every single day to kick your ass, I will. If I have to get your family involved, I will. This shit ends today." She looked around and noticed the work in progress. "What are you doing, anyway?"

"Making bread."

Seeing the perspicuous *Why*? on her face, Dante said, "It's part of healing."

"Oh." She tightened her lips and Dante knew she was trying desperately to reword all the snide comments in her head so she could say *That's stupid* in the nicest, most supportive way possible. "Interesting."

Again she paused. Finally she said, "But don't you think—well, whatever it takes to keep you from running around drunk and naked is worth a shot as far as I'm concerned."

Charly stayed with Dante for a couple of hours while he made the bread. When he put the loaves in the oven, he sat down at the kitchen table with her.

Before she left, Charly dug through her purse. "What about professional help?" She handed Dante a card. "She's an excellent therapist.

She can help you."

Dante stared at the card.

"Therapy is for whackos."

She punched his arm. "Yeah, well, who was the one flapping his wiener around Ocean Beach in nothing but his socks?"

After she left, Dante pulled his bread from the oven. It looked okay, not great. He cut through a crust; not the kind of crisp he wanted. The texture was nothing special. And the taste? Not bad. Especially considering where he had been a day earlier.

He went back to Pane Rubato that afternoon. And at home that night he went back to the kitchen. He had enough of the ingredients to make another batch of bread.

When he arrived at the restaurant the next morning, it buzzed with morning prep activity. Bird and Peanut were singing "Guantanamera" at the top of their lungs. Dante couldn't help but smile at the two of them howling like wolves at the moon.

Sal came in with a dour expression. Dante thought maybe the printout of the day's specials was wrong or one of the wait staff called in sick. "What is it, Sal?" Dante said.

"I just got a call from John Sierra's assistant. He died last night." The kitchen went silent.

Dante put his hand on his forehead and leaned against a prep table. "How?"

"Heart attack."

"Oh no." He let out a long breath and felt like he was bleeding from the chest. "I don't—I can't even—"

He blinked hard and finally said. "Let's close today. I'm sure the news is going to upset a lot of people. And out of respect, I don't want it to be business as usual. I guess I'll go over to their house this afternoon and see if there's anything I can do."

§ § §

Dante arrived at the house where Gloria sat in the living room, staring blankly.

Dante saw John's assistant, Lauren. She was pale, and her dark-circled eyes were bloodshot, but she seemed to be the one in charge.

"I can't believe this," Dante said.

"Yeah, I know. I still don't think it's registered in my mind."

"How's Gloria doing?"

"Chased her Ativan with half a bottle of Chardonay."

Dante cringed. "Ouch."

"I'm pretty sure she hasn't eaten anything at all today. But who can blame her?"

"I brought one of her favorite dishes. Maybe I can get her to eat a little."

He walked over and sat in a chair to her right. She didn't even look at him. "I'm so sorry, Gloria. John meant a lot to me, so if there's anything I can do, please let me know."

Gloria continued staring straight ahead.

"I brought some baked penne with sausage. Can I make a small plate for you?"

Still no sign from Gloria that she had even heard him. He went to the kitchen and plated some of the pasta and heated it in the microwave. He brought it back and placed it on the coffee table in front of her. Maybe the smell of the tomato sauce, the sweet Italian sausage, and the cheese would spark her appetite.

"I'll just leave this here."

The look on Gloria's face wasn't unfamiliar. His mother looked the same when his dad died. He was home from school for the summer, having just graduated from Iowa State with honors in Hotel Restaurant Management in three years (he'd also graduated from high school a year early, a month before his seventeenth birthday). That night, he was at work in the kitchen at City Grill, then went to Julio's for a few drinks with his friends. The hot new waitress from work, Carrie, went with them and she was flirting with him.

At home in his bed, he thought how great life was. A cute girl had been flirting with him. He loved working at City Grill and would be starting at the Cooking and Hospitality Institute of Chicago in the fall. At 20, he felt like everything in his life was about to take off. He fell asleep as content as he could ever remember being.

He awoke two hours later at 4:00 A.M. to the sound of his mother's voice yelling for him and his sister, Carolyn. He ran to his mother's room and saw his father in what looked like a convulsion. He ran to the phone and called 9-1-1 and when he went back to the room, Carolyn was giving CPR. But it was no use. His dad was gone. A massive heart attack at the age of 56.

Within hours, the house was filled with Dante's aunts, uncles and cousins. Some having the same lugubrious fits he'd seen when his nonna died. Three days later, they put his father in the ground and a wound opened on Dante's soul that would never fully heal. Nonna had become very sick before she died, and Dante had a chance to make peace with her leaving him. But his dad was gone so suddenly. Dante never had a chance to imagine the world without his father in it. His dad would never see him married, never meet his kids. Even now, whenever anything good happened to Dante, he wished his father was there to witness it.

His mother, too, was devastated, but tried to hide how bad she felt. In spite of her brave face, she wasted away to nothing. Dante decided to forgo culinary school in Chicago to stay at home, and enrolled in the culinary program at Des Moines Area Community College. When he graduated, his mother told him it was time to chase his dreams. She had called her cousin, Marcello, and arranged for Dante to go and work in his restaurant in Rome. She would also pay his rent for the first year.

"You are meant for big things, Dante. This is my way to thank you for being here for me."

§ § §

Now, at Gloria's, when he looked up from his chair, he realized he was crying. Lauren came over and put her hand on his shoulder.

Dante looked into the faces of those around. Her children, he knew, didn't live near. Her son was in New York and her daughter was somewhere in Africa. Would they come home? Certainly for the funeral. But what about after? Judging by how Gloria was doing so far, she was going to need someone. Ativan might do the job in the short term, but he knew from his own experience that sooner or later she would have to face the reality of losing John.

"The worst part about all of this," Lauren said, "is that I've had to deal with business stuff all day today. It's not fair that the world keeps moving when a tragedy happens. I mean, we were right in the middle of a huge deal in San Jose and now everybody is calling trying to figure out what happens next. Were we far enough along to call it done? Who's going to own John's share? Hell, I don't know."

Jesus, Dante hadn't even thought of the business implications. Who would take over John's share of the restaurant? Gloria or some business entity? And what if this new owner decided to get out of the restaurant? Could they just shut it down? He hated putting the loss of a friend into that cold context, but this could directly affect his life on more than just the emotional level.

As Dante left Gloria's house, his stomach twisted and churned, and his head throbbed. This was a very bad day all the way around.

Chapter 19

The reception after John's funeral was at Gloria's house. Dante had offered to have it at Pane Rubato, but Gloria either didn't hear or pretended not to. At the reception, Gloria spoke to other guests, but turned her back or left the room if she saw Dante coming.

"Did I do something to offend Gloria?" he asked Lauren.

"Not as far as I know."

"Maybe she feels like I'm intruding on a private matter."

"Gloria's not always the easiest person to read."

"Don't I know it."

When Dante saw that Gloria was alone on the couch, he went over and sat in the chair to her right.

"I just want to say again that if there's anything I can do, please don't hesitate to ask." She looked at him and for the first time since John died, her eyes softened.

"John was a great man. He told me how you two met, how he couldn't keep his eyes off you when you walked in the room. It's a beautiful thing when two people find each other like that." A tear ran down Gloria's cheek and Dante thought he detected a tiny hint of a smile. "I know he loved you very much."

Gloria dabbed her eye with her handkerchief and took a deep breath. Then without a word, she stood and walked away.

He walked back over to Lauren. "I think I should get going," he said.

Behind him, a woman said, "Well, I heard she doesn't want to keep that restaurant anymore. I think she's going to sell it."

"I can see why," another woman said, "in that neighborhood."

Lauren, who obviously heard, shrugged her shoulders. Dante motioned for her to follow him.

"Has Gloria mentioned anything to you about Pane Rubato?"

"No, but she hasn't said a lot to me at all since this happened. Still, I wouldn't put too much stock in rumors at a funeral."

For the next few shifts at Pane Rubato, the staff was subdued by the news of John's death. They still laughed and joked around some, and told a lot of John stories. Lexi had one about a night when John was in with a table full of what looked like former frat boys who'd cashed in on their family names. One of the guys ran Lexi all over the restaurant: "Honey, can you get me this? Sweetie, can you get me that?" But when the guy said, "Hey doll, how about another beer?" John looked at him and said, "Her name is Lexi. Not honey, not sweetheart, not doll. Show respect."

"A guy like John," Lexi said, "could afford to be a big jerk if he wanted. But he never acted like he was better than anyone else."

"That's what made him such a great guy," Bird said. "He never treated any of us like we were his servants. He always made you feel like a friend."

After Lexi's food came up and she left the kitchen, Bird watched her the whole way out.

"What's up?" Dante said

Bird stared at the kitchen door. "Nothing."

"Something the matter?"

He pulled Dante aside and said quietly, "Not everything is always like it seems."

"You mean Lexi? She seems like a beautiful person with a big heart to me."

"Maybe. But she's got a big something else, too."

"What're you talking about?"

Bird crooked an eyebrow. "It was just the two of us here after work last night. And we both had too many glasses of wine. Things started to get a little heated up between us."

"And?"

"I asked if she wanted to come to my place. She said she really, really did, but she had to tell me something."

"That happened to me once. The woman told me she had herpes. Definitely a mood breaker."

"This might be worse."

"Worse?"

"She tells me she's saving for an operation. To have something—" Bird glanced toward his crotch—"removed."

Dante narrowed his eyes. "You don't mean . . ." He carefully gestured toward his crotch.

"Yes."

"No way."

Bird nodded.

"I would never have guessed. Did you freak out?"

"I was in too much shock."

"What are you going to do?"

"Nothing. I like my women to be women."

"I don't know. She's more woman than some women I know."

"Be that as it may, I don't drive stick." He half sighed. "Even if it *is* an incredibly hot Ferrari."

The next morning, Dante got a call from a friend of Charly's, Paige, who was the manager at the new La Cuisine cookware store in the Ferry building. Charly had texted Dante the night before that she had given someone his contact info, but he'd forgotten about it.

"I was talking with Charly yesterday," Paige said, "and I told her we want to have more cooking demos at the store. She said you'd be great and gave me your number. I love the food at Pane Rubato. So I thought I'd see if you're interested."

"I've always wanted to do something like that. I've been to the store and you have a great setup for classes."

"Fantastic. Why don't you come over some time and we can talk details. Any time is good for me. I'm usually here 'til 6:00."

"Is this morning okay? I could be there in about a half hour."

"Perfect."

Paige met Dante as soon as he came into the store. Dante shook her bony hand.

"It's so nice to meet you, Dante. I've heard a lot of good things about you."

They went to her office and talked about what Dante might do for a class. He wanted to do some recipes inspired by stories his nonna had told when he was a kid, like his Steak Diavolo, which was inspired by a tale about a heartbroken farmhand. They figured out what he would need and set a date for the class.

Afterwards, Paige stood. "I am so excited about this. We'll get to work on the promotion. And please let me know what we can do to help make the class a success."

A few days later, a woman came into the restaurant around three in the afternoon when there were only a few other tables in the restaurant. She had blonde hair and dark bags under her reddened eyes. It seemed you could shave ice with her cheekbones. She sat at a table alone and asked to see Dante.

"You have to help me," she said.

"What can I do for you?"

"I heard you cure heartbreak."

Dante took the seat opposite her. Out of fear that she might be trying to get him to say something about curing heartache, he said, "I'm not sure what truth there is about that."

"Really? I need something. Anything. I can't eat. I feel like I can barely breathe anymore. I—" She put her hand to her mouth, and a tear ran down her cheek.

Dante gave her a good long look. A voice whispered in his head, *It's safe*. "Let me see what I can do. Are you vegetarian or is there anything you won't eat?"

"I'll eat whatever you give me. And thank you. Thank you so much."

Dante went back to the kitchen and quickly whipped up fettuccini with pancetta, peas, red onion, tomato, and basil in a parmesan cream sauce.

He brought it out to the woman's table and set the plate in front of her. "I was going to run this as the pasta special tonight, so you can tell me if it's any good." He smiled.

The woman forced a smile, then slowly picked up her fork and twirled a single strand of fettuccini onto it. She closed her eyes, Dante thought almost prayer-like, and put the pasta in her mouth. As she chewed, her face seemed to change. She started to smile and Dante could have sworn her dark bags disappeared before his eyes.

She swallowed and took a deep, long breath. Then tears streamed down her face. "Oh my God, it's true," she said. "It really is true." She opened her eyes. "It's like you just poured light into my black heart. I can literally feel the toxins draining out of me."

Dante smiled. "So you think that'll be an okay pasta special for dinner tonight?"

The woman laughed. She wiped her tears away and said, "You're some kind of angel, aren't you? I mean literally. I wasn't sure what was going to happen when I came in today, but I didn't expect this." She shook her head, as in disbelief. "I just pray I'm not about to wake up."

"Me too. Because then I'll have to go back to my real life as a mail carrier."

"My name is Jill, by the way." She stood. "May I give you a hug?"

Dante opened his arms and she stepped into the hug.

"Thank you. And thank God for you."

When Dante went back to the kitchen, Bird said, "What was that about? Did you know that woman?"

"Nope. She just needed a good plate of pasta."

Bird raised his eyebrows dismissively. "Hey, can you believe that shit about the mayor?"

That morning, a scandal hit City Hall. The mayor's chief of staff very publicly quit his job over allegations that the mayor had an affair with the chief of staff's wife.

"I wonder if Charly's heard?" Bird said.

"No idea. I want to call or text her, but I don't want to butt in, you know? I guess if she wants to talk about it, she'll call."

More than a week went by and Dante still hadn't heard anything from Charly. A couple of days after the mayor scandal, he called but got voicemail.

She didn't return the call and he wasn't sure she was even in town. But she had to know. The scandal was all over the news, and her name was brought up several times.

Finally, he decided he'd better try to call one more time. At least let her know she could talk to him if she needed to. Not that she would ever admit to that, but he had to offer.

He dialed her number and waited to get her voicemail, but she answered. "Hey."

"Hi. I was just calling to check in on you."

"I'm fine." Her voice was raspy and worn. "Just busy as usual. Gina's going to be in town next week, so lots of stuff to get ready."

"You have dinner, yet?"

"I don't really feel like going out to find food."

"I could deliver a pizza to you. Personally."

"Who could pass up an offer like that?"

When Dante arrived, Charly looked like a nightmare wrapped in gloom inside a phantom. He set the pizza on the dining room table, a Margherita pizza, his specialty. Fresh buffalo mozzarella, tomato sauce and basil.

"I'm really not hungry," she said. "Maybe I'll have some later."

"Eat the damn pizza while it's hot." He put a cheesy slice on her plate. "It's *yummy*."

Charly rolled her eyes. "Well, when you put it like that."

She took a bite and closed her eyes, and Dante knew what was happening. A half smile formed as she chewed. Her eyes stayed closed for several seconds and she took a deep breath. When she opened her eyes again, she smiled and the light in her eyes returned.

"You know, I'm actually glad to be out of that relationship. I'd have preferred different circumstances to end it, the jerk, but the results are the same. I'm out of what obviously was a bad thing." She sipped her wine, then took another bite of pizza and closed her eyes again.

"So the pizza's okay? I mean you wouldn't rather that I had just brought over a protein shake so you could get your nourishment and be done with it?"

Charly shook her head. "That would've been fine," she said through a full mouth.

Charly had three pieces of the pizza and over the next hour, she and Dante finished the bottle of wine.

"So," Dante said, "Gloria Sierra is now my official business partner. I talked to Susan the other day, and apparently John left everything to Gloria. All of his shares in his businesses."

"Wow. Well, I guess the good news is she probably won't have time to bother with the restaurant."

"Or she might try to sell her share of it."

"There's got to be something in your agreement that keeps her from pulling it out from under you, right?"

"I have the right to buy out her shares. But I can't afford to do that, so she could sell to someone else or shut us down and sell the assets." He took a deep breath. "But, hey, I'm not going to worry about that right now. I'll just have to wait to see what happens."

"All you can do, really."

"Hey," Dante said, "remember I told you about my cousin, Marcello in Rome?"

"Yeah. The one whose restaurant you worked in?"

"I got an e-mail from him this morning that his twin sons, Renzo and Andrea, are coming to San Francisco. I haven't seen them since they were seven years old. They're graduating from film school in Rome and Marcello's graduation present is this trip. So I offered to let them stay at my place. Oh, and they're bringing their girlfriends."

"Wow. It's going to be a little crowded at Chez Dante."

Dante smiled. "Yeah, but it's going to be great to see them. They were so much fun when I lived with them."

For the rest of the night, Charly didn't say a word about the mayor. Instead, she talked a lot about her work. "I really feel like we're helping Gina do something good for the world. Somebody had to have the guts to do what's right, even when it looks like a bad idea politically. I loved it when she said, 'The day I put my own political ambition ahead of the people is the day I should be thrown out of office.' The opposition hates that about her. Every election they pour money into trying to defeat her, but it's never even close. People know she's the real deal."

Dante got ready to leave, and at the door Charly thanked him for spending the evening with her.

"I was worried about you," Dante said. "I just wanted to make sure you were okay."

"That's really sweet." She smiled and bit her lower lip.

"And?"

She kissed him, right on the mouth. Her soft and swollen lips pressed against his with so much desire that Dante couldn't help slipping his tongue into her mouth. He placed his hand on her face as they kissed more urgently. He wrapped his arms around her and pulled her closer. Her warm contours pressed against him. Dante's entire body throbbed. His fingers dug gently into her back.

Dante pulled back. He looked into her eyes, which seemed to ask for more. But did she really want him, or was this more about her breakup?

Her lips were rimmed with redness. She breathed heavily as they stared at each other for a few seconds.

God, she's so beautiful. Look at those eyes and that mouth. That mouth. I want to taste her again.

"I shouldn't have done that," she said.

"No?" Dante could feel his heart start to ache.

"Oh my god, that face." She placed her hand on his cheek. "Stay."

"Are you sure?"

"Yes. Just . . . be here with me."

They went back to the living room, and talked on the couch for another hour before Dante's eyes started to grow heavy.

"You're exhausted," Charly said. "Should we get some sleep?"

Dante yawned. "Yeah, I think that's a good idea."

Charly stood, then held out her hand.

Dante crooked an eyebrow.

"The guest bed has a bunch of junk on it, and I don't want you to have to sleep on the couch. You can sleep in my bed."

"Where are you going to sleep?"

Charly rolled her eyes. "In my bed."

"The same bed?" Dante smiled.

Charly blushed. "Yes. I just thought it'd be nice to have you there. But if you'd rather sleep out here."

Dante stood and took her hand. "No, the bed sounds better."

As they walked to the bedroom, Dante said, "Just to let you know, I sleep naked."

Charly laughed and jerked her hand away. "Not tonight."

"Well, I forgot my ducky jammies at home."

Charly laughed again, then said, "I guess those jeans won't be very comfortable. You're wearing underwear, I hope."

Dante grinned. "And if I'm not?"

Charly gave him a stern look.

"Oh, alright," Dante said. "Yes, I have boxers on."

"Good, then you can sleep in those." She grabbed a few things from her dresser, then disappeared into the bathroom.

Dante took off everything but his boxers, then climbed into the bed. Charly emerged from the bathroom a minute later in a pink tank top and boyshorts.

Dante caught his breath. *My god, she is beautiful.*

She crawled into bed and turned out the light. "You comfortable?"

"Yes, perfectly."

She sighed, shifted slightly, then sighed again.

"Everything okay?" Dante said.

"Yeah. It's just . . ."

"Just what?"

She took a deep breath. "Do you mind cuddling me?"

Dante said nothing, just slid over next to her. Charly rolled onto her side with her back to him. Dante pressed against her, and draped his arm around her.

She snuggled back into him more closely. "Thank you."

Dante took in a long slow breath, and slowly exhaled. His body hummed from the current coming off Charly's body next to him. The newness of this connection. The scent of her skin. As many times as they had hugged over the years, Dante never got to experience her in the way he did now—no perfume, the real Charly. Holding her, feeling her breathe, the faint beating of her heart.

Dante stayed awake and held her like that for at least an hour. He was pretty sure Charly was awake, too, though he said nothing to her.

Finally he fell asleep, and into several dreams. In one, he was on the roof at his mom's house, balancing close to the edge, having breakfast and trying not to fall off. In another, he was swimming at a beach in Palermo, Sicily, and kept getting water in his eyes so he couldn't see where he was going.

The last one was the strangest. He was walking through San Francisco, and he saw Abby ahead of him, about a block. Someone was right behind her, a guy, who kept reaching out for her purse. Dante tried to catch up, but no matter how fast he walked, Abby and the stalker stayed a block ahead of him. He tried to call her name, but his voice wouldn't make a sound. He ran after them, but still couldn't catch up. Then the guy grabbed Abby from behind, and Dante shouted, "Abby!"

The sound of his own voice woke him from the dream. Shaking, he opened his eyes to see Charly looking right at him.

"You were talking in your sleep," she said.

He knew, and he could guess what she heard him say. "Sorry. I was having a crazy dream."

Charly nodded, then rolled over to the other side of the bed.

The next morning, Dante woke up at 6:30 and Charly was already up and dressed for work. "I have a really busy day today," she said. "Just lock up when you leave."

"Do you want me to make a quick breakfast?"

"No, I have a Cliff Bar, and I'll grab a coffee on my way into work."

"Okay. I'll just get dressed and get going. Do you want to grab a drink later."

"Pretty sure I'll be working late, but I'll let you know."

"Everything okay? You seem—I don't know."

"Yeah." She forced a smile. "Still waking up."

As Dante started to get out of the bed, Charly said. "I really need to get going. I'll talk to you later, okay?"

Dante sat on the edge of the bed and nodded. "Okay."

Nice job of totally screwing that up.

Chapter 20

Dante didn't hear from Charly for over a week, so he finally called her.

"Hey stranger," he said.

"Sorry, I've just been crazy busy at work."

"But you're okay?"

"I actually feel really good. I went for an eight mile run this morning, and have had tons of energy all day. I got so much done."

"That's great."

There were a few seconds of silence. Then Dante said, "Okay, I'll let you get back to your business."

"Okay."

"Is everything alright?"

"Oh yeah. I'm just . . . .something on TV caught my attention."

"There's not a tsunami warning or anything is there?"

"No, nothing like that."

Dante took a deep breath. "I wanted to explain about the other night."

"You don't have to—"

"I know I said Abby's name in my sleep."

"You really don't—"

"I was dreaming that I saw some guy attack her and I called out."

Charly didn't answer for several seconds, and Dante fidgeted while he waited to hear her voice again.

"Look," Charly finally said, "I know you still have stuff to work out. I totally get that. And I'm sure I have to process what happened with Jack—I mean, it's only been a week. So it's not a big deal. Really."

Maybe you should tell her how nice it was to hold her, kiss her.

Charly said, "I think it's a good chance for both of us to start moving forward, you know what I mean?"

"Yeah, you're right."

She said she'd be in Washington D.C. for the next couple of weeks, but would call him when she got back and they could get together for a drink.

For the next few weeks, Gloria remained distant and uncommunicative. While her silence was nice from the standpoint of running the restaurant interference-free, it came with a certain amount of anxiety. Was she up to something?

"I honestly don't know," Lauren said when he called John's office. "Something's going on. I heard her son wanted to take over Sierra Properties, but John left his share to her."

"And she wants to run it herself."

"Or doesn't want him to run it."

"Why would she not want her own son to run his father's business?"

"Ah, that is just one of the mysteries of Gloria. I know there was some kind of family drama about ten years ago, but I never asked John, and he never volunteered any information."

John had mentioned that he didn't see his son much, but Dante just assumed it was because he was in New York. John didn't say anything about a falling out.

Dante did his best not to worry about Gloria, and instead focus on taking care of what he could control. And one of those things was his first cooking class. He arrived at the store a half hour before starting time and learned the class was sold out. He was impressed with La Cuisine's organization. They had all his stuff prepped. His vegetables were chopped and ingredients were measured. Pots and pans and equipment properly placed in his work area. And they had quite a set up. Lighting, sound. Chet Baker played over the PA as people gathered. People mingled about. A few recognized him and smiled.

Finally it was time to go on. The crowd took their seats and many people stood around the edges. Paige stepped in front of the crowd. "We're pleased to have with us here today, Dante Palermo, Chef and co-owner of San Francisco's Pane Rubato restaurant."

A few people clapped.

"Thanks, Paige. And thanks to La Cuisine for hosting this event. So we're going to do a few things today, but I want to start with this spicy steak dish, Steak Diavolo, that always makes me think of a story my nonna used to tell me when I was a kid helping her in the kitchen. She always said to use certain types of food to counter your mood. So if you're feeling cold and lonely, eat something spicy. I'm not sure there's any science to that idea, but it made for some good stories. This story is called *Ghiacciato, the Mule.*"

Once there was a farmhand named Ghiacciato, who lived in the barn with the animals, and loved his employer's daughter more than anything else in the world. But the farmer would not let poor Ghiacciato anywhere near his only daughter, Mimi.

"Ghiacciato is like a mule," said the farmer. "Just as strong, and just as dumb. My Mimi deserves better."

But Ghiacciato was determined to prove his worth. He worked from dusk until dawn through the scorching heat of summer and the coldest, rainiest winter days. He would pull the farmer's cart with the heaviest load on the longest journeys and always be happy to do so.

"When the farmer sees how hard I work," Ghiacciato told the pig, the sheep, and the horse one day, "he will allow me to marry Mimi."

But each of the animals had heard the farmer call the farmhand, "Ghiacciato, the mule," on numerous occasions.

"Mimi is not so pretty," said the horse.

"You can find someone better," said the pig.

The sheep added, "One who loves you as you love her."

But Ghiacciato ignored their counsel. "You will see."

One winter day, Ghiacciato spent the entire day in the rain, cutting wood for the farmer's house. When Mimi saw this, she asked the farmhand why he worked so tirelessly.

Ghiacciato simply replied, "For you."

And with that, Mimi fell in love with him.

Upon seeing what transpired, the farmer sent his daughter to live with her aunt in Messina. Poor Ghiacciato was heartbroken, but insisted his love would return any day. He waited day and night by the gate, refusing to eat or drink. In the cold and rain, Ghiacciato still refused to come inside. "I must be here upon my love's arrival," said he.

One night, a storm came, blowing freezing wind and rain straight into Ghiacciato's heart. The farmhand lasted but an hour before he collapsed, nearing death.

Seeing this, the animals rushed out and dragged Ghiacciato back to the barn. They put him by the fire, but he did not respond. They wrapped him in blankets, but Ghiacciato remained unconscious. The animals had given up hope when the owl spoke.

"He is cold not from the outside, but the inside. Not from the rain and wind, but from his heart. Feed him those hot red peppers to warm and restore him."

The other animals did as the owl instructed and soon Ghiacciato opened his eyes and within the hour was back on his feet.

The owl told him, "You cannot bring your love home by waiting. You must go on. Always remember the old saying, 'The sun will rise with or without the rooster.'"

From that moment on, Ghiacciato went back to work for the farmer and worked a hundred times harder in honor of his love, Mimi. Finally, the farmer saw the error of his ways and summoned his daughter home. He told Ghiacciato, "I will be proud to call you 'son.'" Three days later,

Ghiacciato and Mimi were married and lived out the rest of their days in happiness and without worries.

The audience applauded loudly at the end of the story.

"So, Dante said, "if, like Ghiacciato, the Mule, your heart has gone cold, this spicy steak will warm and restore you and allow you to get back to your life. First we need to get the ingredients together, We'll use four twelve ounce strip steaks . . ."

Afterwards, Paige approached Dante. "That was fantastic. How would you like to do these monthly?"

"I would love it." And so, *Cooking from the Heart with Dante Palermo* was born.

The following week, a new interview appeared in *San Francisco Magazine* with the title, "Lovelorn Chef Has Cure for Heartache." In the write-up, Dante said that there was no secret ingredient in his food. He had a passion for what he did and used a lot of recipes handed down by his family. "Maybe it's tradition and the love of my family that comes through in my cooking. And when people come into my restaurant, I try to do everything I can to make them happy and let them know I appreciate having them there. You combine good food, good music, good wine, and a pleasant atmosphere and it's easy to put a magical shine on the whole experience." The article mentioned his cooking classes and the next one was sold out well in advance.

One night at the restaurant, Charly said, "It's a great article, but I hope people don't really think you can cure a broken heart."

"I don't know. People come in and feel better when they leave. Maybe there's more to it than you know."

"Dante, you know I think you're a great chef, but come on. Really?"

"Why not?"

"Because that stuff doesn't exist outside of fairy tales."

"A lot of people believe in fairy tales."

"Yeah, five-year-olds."

"Maybe that's what's wrong with the world. We're not five-year-old enough. Maybe we need to stop being so serious and believe in a little more magic."

"Yeah, because magic puts people to work, and takes care of sick people, and keeps people in their homes."

"For a progressive, how can your heart be so closed?"

"My heart has nothing to do with it. And just because I live in the real world doesn't mean I don't have an open heart."

"Well, the 'real world' has a lot more magic than you know."

"Dante, you scare me."

As Spring progressed, everyone's love life bloomed. Bird was seeing a singer who sat in with Martin's band one night. And the rest of the staff all seemed to be sleeping with each other. Pane Rubato was quickly becoming known among the inner circle as Love Central.

One night Paige and Charly came to the bar at Pane Rubato.

As Dante went to say hello, Sal said, "Who's that woman with Charly?"

"Her name's Paige. Why?"

"She single?"

"She's never mentioned a boyfriend, or girlfriend for that matter, to me. Why don't you come over with me and I'll introduce you."

"Hello ladies," Dante said. "Paige, I'd like you to meet my friend, Sal."

They shook hands and Sal actually turned a little red-faced. The blushing Brooklyn Bull. But he and Paige locked eyes and their respective test tubes seemed to bubble over. Dante had to stifle a laugh when Sal nearly tripped on the leg of a bar stool as he left.

A minute later a guy walked up. Dazzling smile, dark wavy hair over his ears, steel blue eyes, a clean-shaven, flawless jaw line, not bony sharp.

"There you are," Paige said. "Dante, Charly, I'd like to meet my good friend, Hugh Lancaster."

He was the founder and president of the sustainability consulting firm, To Green Incorporated, and his new book, *Going Green and the Global Economy*, was just out.

"I just finished your book," Charly said. "What a coincidence that you're a friend of Paige's and here tonight." She gave Paige a look as if to say, *You planned this all along without telling me.*

Hugh smiled. "You might be interested to know I've started working on my next book about the national security issues of environmentalism. Definitely something people in government should read."

Okay, Dante thought, so this guy was smart, and attractive. But he seemed arrogant as hell.

Bird dragged Dante back into the kitchen. "D, you were glaring at the man."

"I was not. But I feel bad for Charly. Did you see the look on her face? She was totally annoyed."

"That wasn't annoyed. That was eating him alive with her eyes."

"It was not!"

Bird laughed. "D, are you jealous?"

Dante's face burned. "No." He shrugged. "Maybe I misread her."

That was three weeks ago and Charly had gone out with Hugh on a few dates since then. One night at Vesuvio, Charly met Dante and Bird for a drink.

"He's prettier than a lot of women I've slept with," Bird said.

"He's super smart," Charly replied, "and he cares enough about the world to do something about it." She seemed to be trying not to look at Dante.

Oh, well, good for him, Dante thought. He nodded. "Cool."

"It doesn't hurt that he's hotter than that Korean Suicide Burrito at John's Snack and Deli, does it?" Bird said.

Charly smiled, "No it does not."

Dante got up. "Be right back." *I have to go throw up.*

On a Thursday in May just after the lunch rush, Gloria walked into Pane Rubato for the first time since John died. A man who could have been the offspring of Ollie Hardy and Mama Cass escorted her. As Gloria showed her companion around the restaurant, he chortled and giggled. At one point, she whispered something in his ear and he snorted himself to coughing. He even had to remove his glasses to wipe the tears from his eyes.

Dante approached, smiling, and said, "Gloria, so good to see you."

Gloria turned and said, "Here we are." No smile and all the geniality of a pissed-on rattle snake. "Dante Palermo, meet my friend, Richard Godenot."

Dante shook his squishy, humid hand. "Nice to meet you, Richard."

"Ah, yes. You're the manager." Except in appearance, this guy was the mirror of Gloria; from her accent to the way she looked down her nose.

"Managing partner and chef," Dante said.

Gloria smiled at Richard. "Richard will be working here as my special consultant."

"Your special consultant?"

"Yes, I have a number of responsibilities now that require my attention, so Richard will be my proxy at Pane Rubato."

"Your proxy?"

"Richard will be producing a report detailing his recommendations on how we can become the kind of restaurant I believe we can be."

"We've actually gotten pretty popular recently, so I'm not sure—"

"I realize you're managing partner, but I think we could do so much more here. Richard is doing this for my own edification. And I hope you'll keep an open mind."

"I see." Dante's throat tightened so much he almost gagged. Gloria hadn't been around for who-knew-how-long and now she comes in one out of the blue with some obsequious hyena who was going to tell him how to make the restaurant better?

"I suppose," Richard said, "it's only fair to enumerate my credentials." He then launched into a desultory autobiography that started with his first trip to Paris, at ten years old, having fois gras and escargot, and ended with Gloria being like an older sister to him and how devastated he was over John's death.

As far as Dante could tell, Richard's qualifications for this new gig were that he took a week-long intensive course in restaurant management with Maxime Batard, executive chef at New York's popular restaurant Deux Cents Vingt Sept. (Batard also wrote a column for The *New York Times* where he typically bashed everything from celebrity chefs to vegetarians.) Richard also managed a restaurant in Atlanta for several years, an upscale French bistro. When it closed he became a restaurant consultant.

"Richard can bring a fresh perspective to Pane Rubato," Gloria said, "and I'll expect you to give him full access."

"I'll spend the first few weeks observing," Richard said, "then I'll write my report. By the way, how are the reservations looking for the weekend?"

"We're actually booked for the next two weeks," Dante said.

Word was spreading that Dante was a heart healer. At least once or twice a week, people would come to Pane Rubato, or approach him before and after his cooking classes at La Cuisine to request his help. To each request, Dante would simply say, "I'll see what I can do." Every time he fed the broken-hearted, they left satisfied.

"We've really become popular this spring," Dante said to Gloria and Richard.

Gloria seemed taken aback.

"Well," Richard said, "my goal is to see the reservations full months in advance. And I already have some ideas that will help get us there."

Us? Ugh.

Fortunately, Dante's cousins' visit from Rome kept him from

dwelling on Richard and Gloria and whatever it was they were up to. Renzo and Andrea arrived a few days later with their girlfriends. Fabiana, with long wavy black-tipped blond hair that reached down to the middle of her back, was Renzo's sweetheart. Velia, whose mother was Ethiopian and father was Italian, was with Andrea. When the twins were young, they were nearly indistinguishable, a fact they often used to play tricks on Dante. But now, Andrea's hair was a shabby-chic mass of black with blue streaks through it and Renzo's was shaved down to the nubs.

Dante had been speaking Italian to them since he picked them up at the airport. But once they got to his house, Andrea said, "We will like to practice our English—"

"So we can give a good Oscar speech one day," Renzo said.

"Is this okay?" Andrea said.

"Of course!"

"Thank you again," Fabiana said.

"I'm glad to have you here."

"Because you let us stay," Velia said, "we get to make a trip for Hollywood. Since I was a girl I always want to be in the movies and I always want to come to California, to visit Los Angeles."

Andrea smiled. "She is an excellent actress. She star in our final project for film school."

"And Fabiana," Renzo said, "is the best makeup artist in Rome. She make Andrea into a 150 kilo man for the film and he look so real."

"We bring a DVD if you want to watch it," Andrea said.

"I'd love to," Dante said.

At Pane Rubato that night, Dante talked about his first week in Rome.

"You guys probably don't remember," he said. "I was so scared and homesick. Your dad gave me the first week off in Rome to get used to being there and I think I spent the whole time trying not to cry."

Velia patted his shoulder. "Aww."

"You remember Savio?" Dante said.

The twins nodded.

"He was like your brother," Renzo said.

Dante nodded. "The night before I was supposed to start work, your dad asked him to take me out to meet some of his friends. So we went to his favorite bar and I got plastered. Savio and I stumbled home at three in the morning, singing American pop songs while people yelled out their windows for us to shut up."

"Sounds like these two," Velia said, pointing at the twins.

"That next night at the restaurant," Dante continued, "your dad put me on the pasta station. He said no one in America would care if I spent a year making salads in Rome, so he was going to toss me into the river and I would either sink or swim. I was so hung over and Savio, the little bastard, was on the sauté station next to me. He kept calling me girly man and telling me my food looked like crap. Finally, I got into a good rhythm and by the end of the night, I was fine. Not just with the restaurant, but being away from home, everything. That was when I realized how cooking grounded me, made me feel better. Like some kind of therapy."

The group took about a day to adjust to the time difference enough to function, and once they did, they were unstoppable. They walked all over North Beach, Chinatown, and Fisherman's Wharf. They went to the Golden Gate Bridge and Alcatraz and took a ferry around the Bay. They went to Sonoma and Napa. On their last night in town before leaving for L.A., Dante showed their movie at the restaurant after closing. The short film, *Uomo Grasso* [*Fat Man*], was about a young woman—played by Velia—who falls in love with a shy three-hundred-pound man—played by Andrea—and what she must do to convince him her heart is true and that he is worth loving.

Afterwards, teary-eyed, Kerry said, "That was so sweet and sad and funny."

To Andrea, Lexi said, "I can't believe it was you under all that.'

"Fabiana is truly a master," Andrea said.

On their way to the airport the next morning, Renzo said, "I feel bad. We did not spend enough time with you."

"You're on vacation," Dante said. "You didn't come all this way to sit around my restaurant and talk. When I come to Rome, that's what we'll do."

He said goodbye at the airport curb with many hugs and kisses and promises to see each other again, soon.

Chapter 21

Two months later, the Great Southern Sloth, Richard, still had yet to write his report. His "observation" consisted of coming into Pane Rubato two or three times a week to poke around or have lunch or dinner. He told Dante he wanted to understand every aspect of the restaurant: the menu, the location, and the entire restaurant scene in San Francisco. Gloria either bought his story or didn't care that she was paying him a hefty salary to eat free food at Pane Rubato and dine at other restaurants (which, in all probability, he expensed).

Richard also kept telling Gloria that if they could get Pane Rubato in shape, he could have Maxime Batard mention the restaurant in his column.

"Do you really think so?" Gloria said. "That would be wonderful. You know, I always eat at Deux Cents Vingt Sept whenever I'm in New York. It's an example of exactly what I wish we could do here." She evil-eyed Dante. Had his nonna seen that, she would have given Gloria the *mano cornuto*, the horned hand used to ward off evil. Gloria continued, "And to be mentioned in *The New York Times* would be exceptional."

When Dante suggested coverage like that might be hard to come by, Richard said, "You'll be surprised what a case of Bollinger Blanc de Noir champagne can get you."

Clearly he knew how to keep his paychecks from Gloria coming.

That night, Charly came into Pane Rubato. She sat on the barstool next to Dante.

"Where's Greenjeans?" Dante said.

"Would you stop calling him that?"

"I met the guy for like two seconds three months ago. How do you expect me to know his name?"

She slapped his arm. "You know his name is Hugh, now quit it."

"You'll probably dump him and then I'll have wasted brain space on his real name."

"What makes you think I'm going to dump him?"

"I don't know. Seems to be going pretty tepidly. Or have I misread your lack of enthusiasm?"

She said she liked Hugh but he kept pressing her about where the relationship was going. "So I said to him, 'Let's let this relationship go where it will and not try to *make* it go somewhere.'"

When Greenjeans walked into the restaurant, several people turned and looked at him. Kelly passed Dante and whispered, "I'd like to get into his green jeans sometime."

Charly gave Hugh a kiss. On the lips, though Dante would have sworn she didn't enjoy it. "Hugh, you remember my good friend, Dante."

Hugh gripped Dante's hand as though he were going to try a judo throw. "It's nice to see you again. Charly talks about you all the time."

Dante raised an eyebrow.

"Sorry, I'm late, by the way. Last minute meeting. The gentleman is from London and has to leave town in the morning."

"Don't worry about it," Dante said.

"I'm sure you know how it is running a business. You hate to miss opportunities. I've really been trying to establish more international ties and didn't want to have to do everything through e-mail. So I gave him a half hour tonight and we went a little long."

Dante forced a smile. "Really, it's okay."

Charly and Greenjeans stayed and had drinks for a couple of hours and Greenjeans droned on about sustainability and eco-assessments and organic farming and carbon footprints and abiotic resources and greenwashing and post consumer waste and biological magnifications and low-emission vehicles and vermicomposting.

"Oh, he did not," Charly said the next day.

"It sure seemed like it."

"He's passionate about his work."

"The guy's an inconvenient ecosexual. There's something fake about him. You can see it in his eyes and his smile."

"So you liked him?"

"Apart from a lack of sincerity, slight haughtiness and a bit of know-it-all-ity, yeah, the guy was great."

Charly narrowed her eyes and Dante asked what was on her mind. "Nothing."

"Come on. What?"

"No, it's nothing. I just didn't think you'd have this kind of reaction."

"What? I'm not crazy about the guy. Did you want me to lie?"

"Not at all." She sipped her drink.

The following Thursday after work, Dante and Bird stopped at Vesuvio. When they walked in, two women smiled from their table up front.

"Those beautiful women look lonely tonight," Bird said. "Shall we join them?"

One of them had long dark hair, like Abby's. Same jaw. Though the woman at the bar had brown eyes.

Dante shook himself out of his thoughts. "Let's just go sit at the bar," he said.

Bird nodded. "I get you. She reminds me of Abby, too."

They ordered a couple of beers and shots of Maker's Mark. Then

Bird said, "I know everything still reminds you of Abby. But the point is not to let this turn into a decade-long dry spell."

"I've never gone ten years."

Bird held up his of shot of Maker's Mark. "I don't know why you and Charly don't just stop fucking around and get together."

Dante took his shot, and threw back the whiskey. "I'm sorry, did you say something?"

Saturday arrived and Charly and Dante met at Justin Herman Plaza, across from the Ferry Building. Somehow, she had talked him into going for a run with her.

"Did you get my text to remind you to bring water?"

"No." Dante looked at his dead phone.

"Jesus, Dante. Learn to charge your damn phone once in a while." She shook her head. "Anyway, I brought extra water just in case."

"Thanks." He watched as Charly bent and touched her forehead to her knees. "You know," he said. "It's not natural to run unless you're being chased."

Charly straightened and rolled her eyes. "You *are* being chased. Your dad died of a heart attack at fifty-six, so you're running from heart disease. You want to be in good shape so all those women who come to your cooking classes will think you're a hottie, so you're running from ugliness."

She stood on one foot while pulling her other foot behind her to stretch her quad muscle. Her hair flapped in the breeze.

Dante bent over. His feet seemed much further from his fingertips than he remembered.

When he straightened up, Charly smiled. "You're supposed to be trying to touch your toes, not your knees."

"No, that's funny. Really. You are totally cracking me up."

"Okay, all set?"

"No."

"Too bad, Dorothy, let's see what you got." She had run three marathons; the most he'd run was three minutes. And she didn't appear to be in the mood to go easy on him.

She put on her black baseball cap and took off. She pulled away and her leg muscles flexed under the gray material of her running tights. A couple of guys running toward her turned to watch as she went by. Her butt barely rippled with each step.

Charly slowed after about a minute. When Dante pulled even, sucking wind, she was smiling and breathing as though they were walking. "I thought you wanted to run."

"Just getting my legs." For the next quarter mile, they ran silently at a pace that let him keep up with her.

"Hey," Charly said, "Hugh told me a good joke yesterday."

"Greenjeans tells jokes? Wait, let me guess. What did one locavore say to the other?"

"Do you want to hear it or not?"

Dante panted. "Hit me."

"A guy walks into a doctor's office with a parrot on his head. The doctor says, 'How can I help you?' and the parrot says, 'Get this guy off my ass!'"

Dante would have smiled if he could breathe. "That's pretty good." He huffed and puffed. "He's a regular Schecky Greenjeans."

After three slow miles filled with Charly calling out, "Can we go a little faster than geriatric-ward pace?" and "How do those toothpick legs carry you to work every day?" she finally let him stop.

As Dante walked to cool down, Charly said, "That wasn't so bad, was it?"

"Yes."

"You know I was just giving you a hard time to try to motivate you."

"Toothpick legs?"

"Sorry." She looked at his legs. "Actually, you have kind of nice legs."

Dante was glad his face was already red from running.

"And you did really well for your first time out. I was just happy you showed up." She rubbed his back. "What do you want to do for breakfast?"

"You have anything at your place for omelets?"

"Oh yeah. I have eggs and all kinds of cheese. Whatever meat you want to use. Veggies. Cream."

"Really?"

"No, dope." She punched his arm. "But there's a little produce store a block away. We can probably get something there."

"Do you even have anything to cook with?"

"I think someone gave me a Teflon pan one year for Christmas. What else do you need?"

"A bowl. A spatula would be nice."

"I think I have those."

"Then let's go."

Charly didn't leave a crumb on her plate of the spinach, mushroom, and feta omelet, and two slices of toast.

"So that was okay?" Dante said.

"Nah, I hated it." She smiled.

Dante finished the last of his coffee and said, "Okay, you've given me enough of your day. I'm going to get going now. Besides, I really need a shower."

Charly held her nose. "Yes, you do." She winked. "So same time and place next week?"

"Yeah. This was great. I'm already looking forward to doing it again."

At the front door, Charly hugged Dante and kissed his cheek. She looked into his eyes. "I'm glad we did this."

Now he kissed her cheek. And this time they held their embrace for several seconds. Until Dante realized he wasn't letting her go. He finally broke away and said, "Okay, I'm off."

As Dante drove home, he realized he was smiling. For no reason in particular. And that was something he couldn't recall doing for some time now.

The next Wednesday, Dante fired Darryl. It was bound to happen sooner or later. Nobody liked Darryl and he wasn't a good worker. Below average. Not your first choice, but the kind of guy you can get by with in a pinch, like regular parmesan instead of Parmigiano-Reggiano.

It was the middle of the lunch rush and Darryl was coming back from the walk-in with a pack of porterhouses. He came through the door and turned to look at Lexi's ass as she walked by. He then smacked right into Sammy, whose arms were loaded with a large stack of plates. In spite of his effort to hold on, Sammy lost the plates which partially landed on Darryl's foot. Darryl bent over and howled in pain. And even though it wasn't Sammy's fault, he immediately said, "I'm sorry, Darryl."

"Watch where you're going, you stupid fucking retard," Darryl said. He then pushed Sammy.

Dante grabbed Darryl by his shirt and pushed him all the way to the back alley. He gave him one last shove out the door and said, "Don't ever show your fucking face in my restaurant again." Dante got back to the kitchen to a round of applause from the entire lunch staff. Then he put on an apron and got on the grill.

That night, Darryl returned with Gloria and Richard.

"Now what's this all about?" Gloria said. "Darryl lost his temper, but it's hardly a *terminable* offense."

"I'm not sure you have all the facts," Dante said. "Darryl insulted then assaulted another employee. Very much a terminable offense."

Blotchy patches of red appeared on Gloria's face and neck. "I understand the retarded man ran into Darryl and dropped plates on him."

"It was Darryl who ran into Sammy."

"And you saw this?"

"Of course I did. The whole kitchen did."

Gloria rolled her eyes. "I'm sure it's what you would have me believe."

"What the hell does that mean? Of course I would have you believe it because that's the way it happened."

Richard cleared his throat. "You know, if I might interject—"

"No you might not interject. Darryl is fired and that's the end of it."

"Dante," Richard said, "I must say your management style leaves much to be desired. If your so-called kitchen manager did any work—"

Bird shot forward. "If I did any work? You see this?" He pulled up his sleeve to reveal the garnet burn mark on his forearm. "You don't get that by showing up a few days a week to eat for free. I got my job by working hard, not by having my lips on the ass of the owner."

Richard and Gloria gasped. Then Gloria said, "I'll not be spoken to in that manner in my own restaurant. Get that man out of here. He's fired."

"Unfortunately," Dante said, "You don't have the authority to fire anyone."

"I'll not truckle to you or the staff at this restaurant. You *will* fire him."

"Bird's not going anywhere."

Gloria glared. "Clearly, John's death was a blessing to you and you think you can just run roughshod over me now. I'll write you a check today and you can take your whole vulgar crew elsewhere."

"You are not going to buy my restaurant out from under me. This is my dream, my life, not just something to try to cure my boredom. If anything, I'll buy *you* out."

Gloria laughed. "With what? Your wit and charm?"

"Get the hell out of my kitchen." They all just stared. "Now!"

Gloria and Richard stomped away, towing Darryl.

As if the week wasn't bad enough, Dante had several dreams about Abby. In one, they were getting married. A big outdoor wedding in the hills, the Golden Gate Bridge in the background. Zoe was the flower girl. During the vows, Abby said, "You are my life, my love, my heart and I will be forever blessed by having you by my side."

Dante woke up and sat up in his bed. He shook his head then banged the heel of his hand against his forehead. "Knock this shit off!" he said aloud.

At their weekly run, Charly berated him. "Maybe if you actually tried to move on, things would get easier. All you do is think about Abby. It's no wonder you have dreams about her. Don't you think it's time to let her go?"

"I'm trying."

Charly rolled her eyes.

"I know things are over with Abby. I know it. And it pisses me off to have these dreams. Like my own stupid head won't listen to itself."

"Are you sure you really *want* to let her go?"

"Yes, Charly."

Charly narrowed her eyes. Then she pulled on her cap and said, "Alright, let's move it, chicken legs."

That night, when Dante got home from work, Nonna was in the kitchen sautéing rapini while a pot of pasta boiled away on another burner. Dante walked over and stood next to her.

Nonna smiled and said, "*Una volta ho conosciuto una ragazza di nome Antonella, la ragazza più bella della città di Bagheria, in Sicilia . . .*"

I once knew a girl named Antonella, the most beautiful girl in the town of Bagheria, Sicily. She was set to marry a young man named Lazzaro whom she had fallen in love with the first time she saw him. Antonella was so happy and exuded such joy and calm that the people of the town called her Quercia Bella, Beautiful Oak, because of her majestic stature.

But the week before the wedding, it was discovered that Lazzaro had gotten another girl pregnant. The expectant girl's family insisted Lazzaro marry their daughter (or face disembowelment), and Antonella was left behind, heartbroken.

She was devastated, and for two years was so wretched that she became skinny as a bird's leg and her face became permanently tear-stained. The once-beautiful young woman was now called Ramoscello Brutto, Ugly Twig, by everyone in the town.

Antonella tried everything to cut out the sadness in her heart. She prayed for healing and when she got no satisfaction from God, she tried amulets, charms, spells, and conjurations of every kind. Still she remained crushed under the weight of her broken heart.

Until one day I was visiting my cousin in Bagheria. I saw Antonella and asked, "Quercia Bella, what has happened to turn you?"

The young woman, who had heard of my healing powers, explained the situation. "If you can help me, I will become your disciple and attend to you the rest of my life."

"I cannot help you," I said.

Antonella cast her gaze to the ground. "Then I will be forever hopeless." She began to walk away.

"I cannot help you because you do not believe you can be helped. You do not believe your heart can heal."

"But I have tried—"

"No amount of effort or desire can heal you if you do not believe you can be healed. For the next three days, go to a quiet place and bring yourself to believe you will recover from your broken heart. After that, come to me and I will help you."

Antonella did as she was told. On the fourth day, she found me. When I looked deep into her eyes, I smiled. "Now I can help you."

I made for Antonella this butterfly pasta, farfalle, with rapini, capers, and olives. "The butterflies to remind you of life's beauty and the possibility of transformation," I said. "The bitter rapini and strong flavors of the capers and olives to remind you that though not everything we experience is sweet, life is to be savored, even in its bitterness."

Antonella took one bite and was cured. The next morning, she arose, Quercia Bella, once again.

Chapter 22

A few weeks later, the recently-dumped celebrity Layla Corey, in town to shoot a new movie, came into the restaurant for dinner. She was the lead singer in the band, Dollhouse Incident, about ten years ago. Before she became a movie star, she was singing songs like "Princess Lolita," wearing a tube top as a skirt and thigh high boots. She was covered in tattoos and piercings. She was on the cover of *Rolling Stone*. She was in those saucy videos. Dante never thought she was all that, but Bird had a thing for her. Every time she had a new movie out, he said how he preferred the finger-flipping, ass-flashing Layla Corey. She'd calmed considerably since then, though no one would have called her America's Sweetheart. But nothing about her had ever caught Dante's eye before he met her.

In person, though, she was stunning. Short blond hair and unbelievable green eyes. She looked elegant in her low cut gray sweater and blue skirt. Her smile seemed shy for a woman who had made a living out of outrageous behavior.

After eating at Pane Rubato, she swore to anyone who would listen that her heartache disappeared. "It's the most amazing thing," she said in an interview for *People*. "I took one bite, and it felt like all the healing power of the universe came into my heart."

Reservations at the restaurant had increased steadily ever since the article came out. Richard, always eager to keep his lips as close as possible to Gloria's ass, mentioned the article one day when he and Gloria were in. "I don't think this kind of publicity is at all good for our reputation. Curing broken hearts? It makes us look gimmicky."

"I can't see how national attention could ever be a bad thing," Dante said.

Richard and Gloria both rolled their eyes. Then Richard said, "The real reason we're here today is to let you know you have a new landlord."

Gloria tossed her arms in the air. "*Moi.*"

Dante narrowed his eyes. "Okay. I didn't think you were a fan of this location. But I guess you've come to see the value of being here."

Gloria said nothing, just perused a menu. Then she said, "Why is it you always have a vegetarian special? And bother with calling out all the vegetarian entrees? Those annoying people. They think they're all so much better than the rest of us because they don't eat meat. Let them go to Greens."

Richard chimed in. "Our friend, Maxime Batard, would advise that the restaurant have a single vegetarian option of a few grilled vegetables because it suits the food costs much better."

"Look," Dante said, "I don't care why people choose to eat or not eat anything. That's their business. But I'm not going to offer a single entrée of a few grilled vegetables and charge seventeen bucks a pop for it. I want vegetarians to be as blown away as anyone else who comes in here. We'll never serve anything at this restaurant I wouldn't pay for myself."

"So Gloria owns the building now?" Bird said later.

Dante nodded.

"She's up to something. And it's no good. I can smell it."

"It does stink," Dante said. "But I'm not sure what we can do." He recognized Gloria had given herself more leverage by buying the building, but he decided he couldn't worry himself about all of Gloria's moves. "I'll take care of myself, my staff, and my restaurant. What I can't control will take care of itself."

On the love front, Sal and Paige had started dating. Bird, however, rarely saw any one woman more than a few times before moving on. He and Lexi continued their little dance. But it never seemed to go beyond flirting. Bird, for his part, was all smiley-faced whenever she was around. Got her whatever she wanted. Gave her a wink here and there when he thought no one saw. If he hadn't known she was anatomically male in the one place it counted, he might have acted on his crush.

Dante's running therapy was also going well, though the sessions with Charly were getting to be fewer and fewer. Between work and Greenjeans, he hadn't seen much of her over the last month-and-a-half. But she called last week.

"Hey, stranger, you avoiding me?" she said.

"I'm not the one painting the town green with Mr. Hugh Greenjeans."

"Remind me to kick your ass next time I see you."

"Well, since I never see you, I don't really have anything to fear."

"What about next Saturday night? I could do it then."

"That's kind of you to offer, but—"

"We need to catch up. You're becoming quite a celebrity now that you cured Layla Corey's broken heart. Dante Palermo, heart healer to the stars."

"Such a smartass."

"I'm sorry. But I really do want to see you."

"Okay, why don't you and Greenjeans come to Pane Rubato for dinner?"

"Eh," she said. "You won't be yourself if he's there."

"What makes you think—"

"You never are. And maybe since I've been such a terrible friend lately, we should have some one-on-one time."

Dante smiled. "Okay, what about dinner at my place?"

"That sounds great."

§ § §

That Saturday, Dante stood in his kitchen putting the final touches on the dinner he prepared for Charly. The menu for the night was a Tuscan style tomato and bread soup, spare ribs roasted with vinegar and red pepper, and roasted pears with brown sugar and homemade vanilla ice cream for dessert.

He took in the savory aroma of the soup, the spicy and pungent smell of the ribs, and the sweetness of the pears. The sound of Bill Evans' piano drifted in from the stereo in the living room.

The doorbell rang. Dante opened the door and his heart stuttered when he saw Charly. She wore a taupe sweater and denim hip-huggers. Her straight hair fell over her forehead and was tucked behind her ear.

"Can I come in or shall I take my dinner out here?" She handed him a bottle of Etude Cabernet as she pushed past him. "Wow, it smells incredible in here."

"Yeah, the SpaghettiOs are in the microwave and the Sara Lee apple pie is in the oven."

"Well open up that Mad Dog 20/20 and let's get this celebration started."

Charly followed him into the kitchen. "What can I do?"

"You can pour some wine if you like. Dinner'll be ready in a few minutes." Dante ran a wooden spoon around the edges of the soup, watching as it left a mini wake in the creamy pink mixture.

"You look nice tonight, by the way," he said. He didn't look up from the stovetop for fear he was blushing.

"Thanks." He jumped when she put her hand on his shoulder and she laughed. "I didn't mean to startle you, sunshine. I just wanted to hand you this glass of wine." She rested her hand on the middle of his back. Dante's flesh got goosey and he had to use all his strength to suppress the chill that wanted to run screaming up his spine.

"Maroon is a good color on you," she said.

Dante's face burned. "Hey, I got a call from my friend, Savio, in

Rome this morning. He's finally opening his own restaurant. I really should get back to see him and my cousins some time."

"You should," Charly said. She put her hand on top of his fuzz-topped head. "You ever planning to grow your hair all the way back?"

"Does it look bad this way?"

"I was just curious. Actually, it looks pretty good like this." She rubbed his head.

He cleared his throat. "I think we're ready. Have a seat."

She removed her hand, but he could feel it there long after she was sitting at the dining room table.

He ladled the soup into a bowl in front of her. "Careful, it might be a little hot."

"This smells wonderful." She leaned forward and her nose hovered above the steaming bowl. She raised her glass. "Cheers."

They clinked glasses.

"I don't know if Paige mentioned anything to you, but La Cuisine wants me to do demos at their stores in L.A., Portland, and Seattle."

"That's great! Won't be long before you have your own cooking show."

After they finished eating, they sat on the couch in the living room where they worked on a second bottle of wine. Charly had her shoes off and her feet pulled up next to her. Her toes touched Dante's thigh, which sent a wave of warmth from his leg up to his chest.

He looked into her eyes. "Thanks for helping me get myself together. I'm not sure I could have done it without you."

"You couldn't have, you loser."

Dante smiled. "You're my guardian angel."

A happy little pop tune came on, and Charly stood. "I love this song. Dance with me," she said and held out her hand.

Dante took her hand and she pulled him to his feet. He stumbled a bit, then they danced as the song told the story of a love that began in September. When the song finished, a slow one started up. "If You Don't Know Me By Now." Charly put her arms around him and they swayed to the music. Dante's palm pressed against the muscles of her back. He moved his hand up, then back down, noticing how she was soft and solid at the same time.

Charly threw her head back with a big smile on her face. "I love to dance," she said. "I should do it more often."

"You should."

She looked into his eyes.

Her lips were much too close to Dante's and he couldn't resist pulling her closer. Their bodies were pressed tightly together.

Kiss her, kiss her, kiss her.

"Charly?"

"Yes?"

Greenjeans, Greenjeans, Greenjeans.

He stopped dancing. He couldn't move, couldn't speak.

Finally, he said. "Nothing."

They still stared at each other.

"Dante?" Charly bit her lower lip.

"Yeah?"

She took a deep breath. "Do you— Is there—"

She let go of Dante and sat down. She picked up her wine glass. "I think I've had a little too much of this stuff."

"Well . . . You can stay here if you don't think you should drive."

"Hugh dropped me off. He's coming by soon to pick me up."

"Well, I guess you're all set."

She smiled weakly. "Yeah, all set."

Dante watched Charly drive off with Greenjeans. His top teeth dug into his lower lip. Then a hand touched his shoulder. He jumped and stumbled over the ottoman. His heart pounded in his head.

"*Scusami,*" Nonna said. She apologized for startling him. "*Non volevo spaventarti.*"

Dante caught his breath. "*Non fa niente*"—It's okay. "But could you maybe give me a warning when you're going to show up?"

Nonna shrugged. "*Vedrò cosa posso fare.*"—I'll see what I can do. She sat on the couch and motioned for Dante to join her.

Dante grabbed his glass of wine. "Would you like a glass?"

"Nice of you to offer, but I'm dead."

"I understand." He sat next to Nonna.

"Why don't you tell that beautiful girl you love her?"

"Is she my one true love?"

"How should I know?"

"You said my reward for being a heart healer would be the heart of my one true love. If she's not it, why do you want me to tell her I love her?"

"Because it's the truth in your heart. There's an old Sicilian saying. *Testa che non parla si chiama cuccuzza*—the head that doesn't speak is called a pumpkin. And when you reveal the truth of your heart, the truth of life is revealed to you."

Chapter 23

The next month, Dante barely had time to close his eyes. He'd spent three of his Saturdays in Los Angeles, Seattle, and Portland doing cooking demos at La Cuisine stores. And he was spending practically every waking hour at the restaurant. More and more people came in asking for Dante to cure their broken hearts. And even more came in just to see what all the buzz was about.

He'd also been talking to Charly more than at any other time as long as he'd known her. Charly would give him the ins and outs of political wheeling and dealing. Or talk about the triathlon she had started training for. Or the gig as a lobbyist for the Sierra Club she'd been contacted about. But she never talked about Greenjeans. Dante always asked about him, and Charly would always say that he was fine, and that was about it.

"Hey," Charly said one night on the phone. "We still on for your birthday dinner this Friday?"

"Yep. We're meeting at Vesuvio first, right?"

"As long as that works for you."

"It does."

"Then I'll see you Friday."

During the lunch service on his birthday, Dante made his way around the dining room to thank people for coming in. A smiling woman sitting with a couple of friends said, "I just read a story about you in *7x7* magazine, and all the broken-hearted people who come to your restaurant. None of us are broken-hearted, but the food is still amazing."

Dante smiled. "Thank you. I really appreciate it."

"Can you please sign a menu for me?" The others nodded that they wanted theirs signed, too.

"Thanks again for coming in," Dante said.

He then turned to see a mid-twenties Asian woman sitting at a table with a mid-forties, half-moon-faced, angry white woman, who appeared to be the boss in the relationship. She was giving her subordinate—and it was clear that's how she saw it—a good talking to. Dante circled back around the boss and went over to their table to see if he could break it up. As he approached, he heard the boss say, "I expect more from you. I need you to proactively drive and manage our strategy in a continuous improvement framework."

Continuous improvement framework? Dante wanted to ask her not to use that kind of language in his restaurant.

He stepped up to the table behind the boss. The young woman looked up and the boss said, "At least look at me when I'm talking to you."

"How are your lunches?" Dante said.

The boss turned, red-faced. The subordinate smiled, clearly relieved the woman across from her had shut up for the moment. "Wonderful, thank you."

The boss said nothing and the young woman's eyes apologized for her ill-behaved boss.

Dante smiled graciously. "Sorry for the interruption. Enjoy your meals."

As he walked away, he heard the boss say, without even trying to lower her voice, "I expect the work to be done. And if you can't do it, there's no shortage of people happy to take your position."

That poor woman, having a manager like that. Maybe Cruella De Vil needed to be taken down a notch. Dante checked in on a few other tables before he went to one of the busboys, Tommy. He told Tommy to give it about five minutes, then go spill the water on the boss. He was the best spiller they had. In fact, the best Dante had ever seen. Dante told Sal to comp their lunches and Sal knew immediately what was going to happen.

It was so natural. Tommy grabbed the boss's water glass and poured. And there it went, slipped out of his hand, landed right in her lap. Tommy looked like he'd seen a kitten turned inside out. His cleanup routine was even better. He started speaking Vietnamese quickly to himself and grabbed whatever he could find to throw into the spillee's lap: napkins from the empty table behind him, he even chucked in his own apron. Then he acted like he was going to dive right into her crotch, but pulled back at the last instant. He did all this without ever touching her, the whole time looking as though he'd cry at any moment. When it was over, Dante wanted to applaud, but instead he had to go hide his joy in the kitchen.

"Having a little birthday fun, are we?" Bird said as Dante walked in. "Mr. Broken Heart celebrity."

"He's our great big shiny star," Lexi said.

Peanut nodded. "I want your life, boss."

"Okay," Dante said. "We need to change vendors for the laundry. There's a party for fifty next week and they still haven't set the menu. Gloria's been bugging me to meet with her about God-knows-what. And I have to teach cooking classes in Corte Madera, Berkeley, Palo Alto, and San Jose over the next month. Call me if you need anything."

Bird laughed and put his hand on Dante's shoulder. "Remember just a few months ago? Little Mary Sunshine here would've told you that nobody should have his miserable life. Poor skinny Dante with the sunken cheeks and dark circles around his eyes. He would've told us all about how since his love was gone, his life was gone." He rubbed Dante's stubbly head. "It is *good* to have you back."

§ § §

Later, Dante and Charly sat at the bar at Vesuvio.

"Happy birthday," Charly said, holding up her martini.

Before Dante could raise his glass, his phone rang. Bird.

"D, a water pipe busted in the dining room and water is spraying everywhere. Get up here, fast!"

"Find the shutdown valve. Call a plumber. I'll be right there." He looked at Charly and told her what happened. "I have to get up there."

"I'll come with you."

Fortunately it was only a two minute walk. And when Dante burst into the front doors, everyone in the restaurant yelled, "Surprise!"

His entire family was there. His mom. His brother, Frank and his brother's wife and kids. His sister, Carolyn, and her husband and kids. His mom was the first to give him a big hug. "Happy birthday, honey." Then he was surrounded by his brother and sister and all the little rugrats, who hugged all around him.

The place was decorated with hearts of every kind. Balloons, cutouts, posters. Strings of heart-shaped lights lined the dining room. After a rousing rendition of "Happy Birthday" by Martin and the band, Dante made his way around the room where he was greeted with pats on the back, hugs and lots of happy birthday wishes. Lots of people he'd worked with over the years. Lots of friends who had started out as customers. The night was a steady stream of talking with people, some of whom he hadn't seen in years.

After a couple of hours, and as the crowd began to thin, Charly brought Dante a Scotch. "Here you go. You've been talking so much I don't think you've had a chance to have a drink."

He took a sip. "Oh that's good stuff." He looked around. "Where's Greenjeans?"

Charly shook her head. "*Hugh* is at the bar. It was his idea for me to bring you this."

"Oh."

When Martin started "My One and Only Love," Dante put his hand out. "May I have this dance?"

Charly took his hand. "With pleasure."

They slowly danced to the guitar, bass, and drums which wove the hypnotic melody. "By the way," Charly said, "you look pretty sharp tonight."

"I've been working out. Can you tell?"

She squeezed his biceps and frowned. "You have?"

"Funny." Her body felt nice against his. They stared into each other's eyes. "You look beautiful yourself."

Charly's face turned a little pink and she lowered her eyes.

Dante sighed. Charly looked into his eyes again. He could stay like this for, oh, maybe four or five hundred years. Every part of her felt so good next to him and the longer she looked into his eyes, the stronger the desire to kiss her became.

When the song ended, Dante held Charly's hand. Another song started up, and Dante wanted to keep the dance going, but then he saw Greenjeans at the bar talking with Bird. He let go of Charly's hand.

"I guess I shouldn't keep you away from Greenjeans."

Charly smiled. "Okay." She started to walk away, then turned back. "At least come over and have a drink with us."

"In a minute. I see some people over there I should go talk to."

At the end of the evening, people drained from the restaurant. More birthday wishes as folks went out the door. The family headed off without too much drama from the kids. Little Frankie was cranky, but the others were quiet and sleepy.

Most of the Pane Rubato staff, both those who worked the party and those who were there as guests, were at the bar having a drink. Sal sat with Paige and Bird stood close to Lexi. Dante told the staff how much he appreciated those who worked that night and in general what a great team they were. "You make things here run so well that I have the time to run off and do all these cooking demos." He motioned Bird and Sal toward him. "And these two guys could run any place in the city. I'm glad they put up with me and stick around here." He held up a glass. "*Saluto.*"

Before leaving, Greenjeans shook Dante's hand and said, "Listening to the people in here tonight, I have a feeling things are really going to take off for you in the next year. Good luck with everything. You deserve it."

Okay, maybe Greenjeans was a decent guy. Charly cared for him, so that should be good enough for Dante. Maybe it was just how things were meant to be: Charly with Greenjeans.

Dante got home and went straight to bed. It had been an interesting night. A good night.

Dante woke to the clang of a pan. When he heard "*Ciuri, ciuri,*" he knew what was going on. He walked into the kitchen as his Nonna pulled braised pork shanks from the oven. Dante looked into the pan. Beautifully browned pork, with porcini mushrooms, prosciutto, a mirepoix of carrots, celery and onion. The zesty aroma of the meat and vegetables, plus garlic, sage, rosemary steamed up.

Nonna looked at him and said, "*Siediti.*" She did not smile.

Dante sat at the table and she placed a plate of food in front of him.

"*Cosa stai facendo*?"

"What do you mean, 'what am I doing?' I'm sitting, like you said."

This time, the cranium-cracking glare accompanied the real thing.

"Ow!" Dante rubbed the side of his head.

"What are you doing to your heart, *saputo*?"

"Doing the best I can to heal it."

Nonna clenched her jaw, then said, "Like what?"

"Like running. I'm in the best shape of my life."

"Still, you're not doing right by your heart. That's why you haven't won your true love."

"I don't even know if true love exists for everyone."

Nonna's eyes softened. "Every heart has true love. We're born with it. But sometimes we let bad experiences get the better of us and let true love get obscured, buried by hurt and grief. By ideas of how life and love are 'supposed to be.' True love is there. You must simply uncover it."

"But what have I been missing?"

"Sometimes, the mind will mislead you. It will tell you things that keep you from seeing the truth in your heart."

Charly came into his mind, how she felt in his arms while they danced earlier in the night.

"But remember, you must learn to overcome your grief. Make peace with your heart and allow it to heal. For only a mended heart can truly love again."

The next night, Dante and the family got together for dinner. Charly, who was left on her own for the night because Greenjeans had a business dinner, joined the family. The kids couldn't get enough of her. Frank's daughter, Chloe, and Carolyn's daughters, Mia and Nicole, hung on her. Little Frankie wanted to do everything with her and Frank's eldest, Chelsea, grilled Charly.

"Why do you have a boy's name?" Chelsea said.

"My real name is Charlene. But ever since I was a little girl in Texas, everyone has called me Charly. Like everyone calls you Chels."

"Do you work in a restaurant, too?"

"No, I can't cook like your Uncle D."

"Do you like to dance?"

"I *love* to dance. Do you like to dance?"

"I do, to mom's crazy music. Do you have a horse?"

"I don't have anywhere to keep one. But I love horses. They're my favorite animal."

"Mine too! And tigers. Have you been to Iowa?"

"I haven't been, yet. But it sounds beautiful."

"Yeah. Do you like Uncle D?"

To that one Charly reddened. Then she whispered something in Chelsea's ear that made Dante's niece giggle.

After Charly left, Dante's mom said, "She's going to be a wonderful mother."

Dante's sister-in-law, Holly, said it was time he and Charly hooked up.

"You guys are great together," she said. "I don't know what's wrong with you two, except that you're both too stubborn." Even Carolyn, who almost never talked to Dante about his love life, chimed in saying she thought Charly would make a wonderful addition to the family.

Dante rolled his eyes at all of them.

"She already has a boyfriend."

Dante saw the family off the next morning, then went into work. Gloria arrived shortly after he did and came into his office.

"I think it's time for Pane Rubato to leave this location," she said. "With the restaurant enjoying so much attention now would be the perfect time to make a move."

"I don't—"

"There's a new condo building opening in South Beach. You know, get away from some of our neighbors here."

"South Beach?"

"Yes, it's perfect. Richard says it is *the* place to be. Very trendy and there are lots of people with money who would want to go to a truly special restaurant."

"We already have a special place here."

"Please, Dante. We're surrounded by riffraff. I personally know several people who won't come in here because they don't like all the filth we're surrounded by."

"Then they're not the kind of people I care to have here."

"It's a good thing you're not the sole owner or God knows what kind of people we would have in here."

"Gloria, maybe it's escaped your exceptional attention, but Pane Rubato is packed every night. We get national media coverage. Wake up!"

"Don't you dare talk to me like that. We will move, or I'll see this place closed."

She turned and walked away.

Yeah, Dante thought, just try to shut me down.

Chapter 24

The next two months flew by and Pane Rubato continued to get more popular. Dante himself was also getting more and more attention, and his e-mail inbox was always overflowing. One night toward the end of September, he glanced through his e-mail and the subject line, "you saved my life," caught his eye. He clicked to open the message.

From: Sydney Ingram
Subject: you saved my life
Date: September 29, 2013 7:59:57 AM PDT
To: dante@panerubato.com

Dear Dante,

I just had to write to tell you how much you've done for me. My husband left me last year and our divorce was final a couple months ago. I won't bore you with too many details but this man was the father of my children and a man I loved with all my soul. When he told me he had an affair with another woman and that he was leaving, I was devastated. I really thought I might die. Though I didn't (obviously) I had a hard time pulling myself out of depression. I'd heard so much about you, so I knew I had to go to one of your classes at the Ferry Building. I finally got into one about a month ago. When you told the story about the woman who didn't believe she could be healed, I knew you were talking to me. Well I knew you weren't really talking to me, but you were talking to people like me. Anyway, as soon as I tasted the food you made at the class, it was like someone started draining the unhappiness out of me. I went to my car and started crying. When I got home,

> I was still crying, and my son, who is old enough to notice my sadness on a daily basis, asked me what was wrong, and I said nothing, just the opposite, I was going to be alright. I was as happy as I could ever remember. For the last month, everything in my life has changed. I look and feel completely different. I even met a new man and have been seeing him regularly. Life isn't perfect, but I know one thing, my broken heart is cured and I owe it to you. You may really have saved my life. Maybe not from ending, but from being miserable and depressed. Thank you!
>
> Sincerely,
> Sydney Ingram

E-mails like that one were by far the most common: people writing to tell him he had cured their heartache. And media coverage had started to build. Dante made his first TV appearance on *San Francisco Morning* with Michael Martinez and Kitty O'Shea.

Kitty was all smiles and perk. "Dante, as you know, I went to one of your cooking demos here in San Francisco, and I loved it!" She practically bounced on her stool. "But you've become almost a cult figure. So many people talk about how your food cures heartache. Why do you think that is?"

"I think it's the healing power of cooking and the connection we all share through food. Plus, I think the stories I tell are easy to relate to. They remind people that they're not alone in their feelings and they realize they're not the first to believe they could actually die of a broken heart. That makes them feel better. And I get to pass along a lot of my nonna's wonderful folk wisdom."

Then they got to cooking: a chanterelle mushroom and fontina cheese frittata. Quick and easy, like the show's producer had asked.

"Fontina Val d'Aosta" Dante explained, "has been made in the Aosta Valley up in the Alps since the twelfth century. It has a subtle, nutty flavor and its velvety melted texture makes it ideal for a frittata or quiche. It's great with mushrooms or for stuffing a zucchini flower. The chanterelles have a mild and delicate fruity flavor that works well with the fontina and the eggs."

Kitty and Michael ooh-ed and ahh-ed over the food. Dante gave a final plug for the restaurant and his cooking classes, and he was out of there.

That afternoon he got an e-mail from Charly. She wrote, "Saw you on TV this morning. You did great. And you looked good, too. Aren't you glad I made you start running? Camera got a good shot of your bum. Very cute. ;^) " Between his schedule and hers, Dante had only seen her once since his birthday party.

Two days later, Dante was doing another class at the La Cuisine store in the Ferry Building. A blonde woman in a clingy red T-shirt and black mini-skirt sat in the front row, about ten feet from his work area. She could have been a Playboy Bunny. With her legs crossed, she showed a fair amount of thigh. She kept looking at him and smiling. After Paige introduced Dante, he was met with applause as he stepped up to the table.

"I always like to have a theme that deals with matters of the heart when I do one of my classes. So today we're doing the spinach and portobello lasagna, a favorite of my ex-girlfriend, the woman who broke my heart and really got me started on all this."

Quiet groans and boos rippled through the audience.

"I know, some of you might wonder how or why I would ever make food connected to someone who broke my heart. But I'm sure many of you understand that just because she broke my heart, it doesn't mean I want to erase the good memories. Sometimes it's food she loved, sometimes it's a night we spent together. But they were wonderful experiences, and making food tied to them is another way of healing. I didn't want to be bitter or angry. True, I didn't want to hurt, but when I think of how happy it made her to eat something I'd prepared, and how good that made me feel, why would I want to throw that away?"

The crowd gave a warm ovation.

"And just so you don't think I'm too well-adjusted, I have a few recipes borne out of bitterness, sadness, and utter despair. But I like to confine those to my private kitchen so you don't have to experience my crying in public."

The audience laughed and *awww*-ed.

"Let's start with the sauce. The white sauce in this lasagna really complements spinach and portobellos. And with the mozzarella and cream, this will fill even the most devoted carnivore."

Red T-shirt licked her lips. She hiked up that skirt, but it couldn't go much higher. Dante named the ingredients and got lots of smiles and nods from the audience.

He started making a roux by cooking flour and butter for a couple of minutes. "Then we'll add the garlic, salt, nutmeg, and pepper. For the nutmeg, I like to take the ball and give it about three strokes over the grater. That should be perfect." He tossed in the spices and stirred the mixture.

He stuck his head above the pan and took a good whiff. "Oh this is starting to smell good, don't you think?" More nods from the audience. "The smell of garlic cooking is unmatched. It always reminds me of when I was a kid smelling my nonna's cooking on Sunday mornings. That sweetness is intoxicating." Dante closed his eyes and took another deep nose full.

He looked out at the audience again and made eye contact with Red T-shirt. She licked her lips and opened her mouth. Then she quickly looked down toward her lap. Dante followed her glance to see her legs were slightly apart.

And she wasn't wearing underwear.

Dante dropped the wooden spoon and his face burned. Red T-shirt had a wicked smile.

What the hell was he doing? Oh yeah, cream sauce for lasagna. "Of course, you'll want to maintain control of your utensils at all times." A few people laughed. "Now we'll gradually add the cream, two tablespoons at a time until the flour and butter are absorbed."

He would not look directly at Red T-shirt again.

"Once the butter and flour are absorbed, add the rest of the cream and turn up the heat to a simmer until the sauce thickens." He stirred the sauce until it was the desired creamy consistency. He pulled the spoon up and let the sauce drizzle off of it. "See that? That's what we're looking for. Now toss in the parmesan and test for salt." Dante put a spoon into the cream and tasted it. "Oh that's perfect. Remove from heat and that part is done. Not too bad, right?"

The audience applauded lightly.

"Let's move onto the filling. We'll need two pounds of fresh spinach, sautéed in a little olive oil." He tossed the spinach into a skillet. "It won't take long to cook, but make sure to cook off all the moisture or you'll have one soggy lasagna." He put the sautéed spinach aside.

"Then we'll take four large portobello mushroom caps and thinly slice them." Dante showed his slicing technique on a mushroom cap. "When you're slicing, keep those fingers curled in. Remember, this is a vegetarian recipe so no finger pieces."

He put the mushrooms in a large skillet.

"Then we'll sauté them in a bit of olive oil as well. Like the spinach, the mushrooms hold a lot of moisture, so make sure you cook off all the water." As the mushrooms cooked, Dante took a couple questions.

The woman in the black vest: "Can you use frozen spinach?"

"Yes, frozen is fine. Just thaw it in the microwave, then wrap it in a tea towel and wring the water from it."

The gentleman in the blue polo: "Do you have to grate your own parmesan or can you use the stuff that's already done?"

"I like to have mine freshly grated because it always tastes better than the other stuff. Plus, when you buy it already grated, you'll often get anti-caking additives that aren't necessarily sauce-friendly. Yes, it takes a little more time to do the grating, but in the end it's worth the effort. And if you've ever had your sauce separate, you'll know what I mean."

Then he built the lasagna: layers of sauce, mushrooms, spinach and lasagna sheets.

"Finally, top it off with the sauce and cheese." He gave some final baking instructions before he slid the lasagna into the oven. "Of course, through the magic of La Cuisine, we have one already done." He pulled out the finished version and cut a slice. He placed it on a plate and ladled a small amount of the cream sauce over the top. A couple quick turns of the pepper mill. A sprig of parsley and a few diced fresh tomatoes as a garnish. "And there it is." He tipped the plate, allowing everyone to see. The crowd applauded. "Easy recipe. You can do that, right?"

Store staffers then came out to a table and dished up small paper plates with little squares of lasagna for everyone to taste.

Red T-shirt came up to Dante. "Thank you for such a wonderful demonstration."

Dante smiled. "Glad you enjoyed it. Thank you for coming."

She handed him a card, but held it as he went to take it. He looked up to see that wicked smile again. She said, "Let me know if you'd like to see more." A quick glance at the card showed it was her name and number. She turned and stuck her butt out as an exclamation point.

Then a producer from Cook Network, Sonali Rai, approached Dante and congratulated him on the demo. She said, "La Cuisine is interested in sponsoring a new show on the network, and they asked us to take a look at you."

"Wow, I don't quite know what to say."

"I'm very impressed with what I've seen. If you're interested, we'd like to bring you in to talk more about coming on board with us. Maybe next Thursday?"

"Of course I'm interested. And next Thursday should be good."

"Perfect. Someone will call you with the details."

"Great. I'll see you then."

He immediately called Charly.

"Hey, sunshine," she said. "I only have a few minutes before my next meeting. What's up?

"I've got big news."

"I *love* big news. What is it?"

"Well, you know how I've been doing these cooking classes all over for La Cuisine?"

"Yeah."

"They want to sponsor a TV cooking show on Cook Network and want me to be the host."

"Wow, that's huge!"

"Yeah, so they want to fly me to New York for a meeting with the network."

"Amazing!" Charly paused. "And what about Abby?"

"The producer I talked to didn't mention her, so I don't know if she knows."

"Dante, really? I highly doubt she doesn't know about it. Isn't she the VP of Marketing? Wouldn't it be her job to know something like that?"

"All I can tell you is what I know. And what I know is that Abby's name didn't come up."

"Probably wants to keep her affiliation with you on the down-low."

"You're such a conspiracy theorist. And remember, she rejected *me*. If anything, when she finds out, she'll kill it."

"I got a hundred bucks says she won't."

Chapter 25

Since Gloria brought up moving the restaurant, Dante did everything he could to evade the issue, but Gloria and Richard continued to press him about it. The spot in South Beach was still available and after Dante had gotten about twenty e-mails from them about meeting to talk about moving, he finally sent this reply: "Restaurant booked for weeks. On pace for very profitable year. See no need to discuss move. Cheers, D."

After that, Gloria had sent Richard after Dante every day. Dante would simply tell him he wasn't moving the restaurant, so there was no point in meeting about it. Gloria called and left messages on his cell phone, demanding a meeting. She tried showing up one day when he wasn't there and waited for four hours, even though Sal told her Dante was in Napa for the day. She left a note saying she wanted to meet immediately upon his return or she would start selling the restaurant's assets. Having avoided Gloria as long as he could, he told her he'd meet with her when he was back from New York and his meeting with Cook Network.

Two days later, Dante fidgeted as he waited for the meeting at Cook Network to get underway. How cool would it be to have a show on national television? He had thought it would have been fun to be on San Francisco public television. But a national audience? It was odd to even be in a position to talk about it. He thought his career had reached its pinnacle when he opened Pane Rubato. He couldn't imagine doing much more and certainly no better. He was happy running his little place and getting good reviews and working with wonderful people. Yeah, maybe he'd open another restaurant in the Bay Area, but that was about it. And he expected Pane Rubato to carry him for a long time, even to retirement.

Dante wondered what his dad would have thought of it all. His father never had much in terms of material things, but he had a tremendous amount of love. He had such a gentle way about him. Rarely lost his temper. And when his dad put his hand on Dante's shoulder to congratulate him on his grades or getting a big hit in Little League, he made him feel important. At times like this, Dante could feel his father's hand on his shoulder again, telling him how he knew Dante would be cooking on national television the day he started culinary school. He'd say this was about accomplishment, not ego. He'd say Dante should be proud of his success, but not use it as a tool to try and get things he didn't deserve.

It was lessons like that that Dante wanted to pass on to his own children. He wanted to be the father his father was. He wanted his children to know that they'd always have his love and support.

"Dante." Sonali came through a door behind him.

Dante stood.

Sonali said, "Good to see you again. Thanks for making the time to come in."

She led him down a long hallway and explained that they'd be joined by one of the programming VPs and a few other producers. "I have to tell you, we're all very excited about the prospect of bringing you into the Cook Network family. We like what you bring to the table." She smiled and winked. "So to speak."

In the conference room, everyone was all handshakes and smiles. Once they settled, Sonali explained that the purpose of the meeting was to decide if they were all a good fit for the project, understand the basics of the show, and maybe brainstorm some ideas. And finally to determine the next steps. She handed Dante a dossier outlining Cook Network and its programming. She gave a quick overview of the network and its history, how they were growing into quite a force in the cable space and had among the most loyal audiences on television.

About a half hour in, Abby peeked into the room and asked if she could join them. When she walked in, Dante stood and she shook his hand. The scent of her perfume brought him right back to Las Vegas. She said, "Good to see you."

Sonali gave Abby a quick overview, and they continued the meeting.

The show would be called *Cooking from the Heart*, after Dante's popular La Cuisine classes. The format would be basic cooking show stuff: a couple of recipes in each show. Sounded easy enough. They also talked about things like field trips, maybe even to Europe. Special shows. Just throwing out ideas. They asked Dante how he felt about taping in New York.

"We want to have a live studio audience," Sonali said, "and we have a studio perfect for it. It means you'd be spending a couple weeks a year here."

"I think I can handle that."

"You'll be a big hit in New York," Abby said.

"What do you think so far?" Sonali said. "We're not looking for a contractual commitment. We just want to know if you're interested in taking the next steps. Then we'll let the lawyers hammer it out."

"I'm definitely interested in moving forward."

"Great," Abby said. "The show sounds fresh and fun and I know Dante has the charisma to carry it off."

After the meeting, Abby offered to walk Dante to the lobby. On the way down the elevator, she said. "Victor has Zoe this week and I'd love to catch up. How about dinner tonight? You're at the Millenium, right? There's a new restaurant near there I want to try."

Okay, well, this was awkward. But there was no reason it had to be. They were adults and could be working for the same network very soon. They could still be friends, right?

"Sure. That sounds good."

At dinner, Dante filled their wine glasses for the third time, emptying the bottle of its few last clinging drops. "I was pretty shocked."

"Well, you got flashed. Who wouldn't be?" Abby smiled. "You're such a rock star. And you look really good. Not that you didn't look good before, but now. . . Have you been working out?"

Dante smiled. "I've become a runner."

"It shows." She wiped her mouth with her napkin, then said, "You ready to trade plates?"

"Hit me."

She handed him her cider-braised monkfish with salsify and sugar cane-marinated prawns. She took his *cinghiale agrodolce*, wild boar in a sweet and sour sauce.

Dante took a bite. The sweetness of the prawns was perfectly paired with the monkfish. He and Abby both said, "Wow," at the same time.

"So," Abby said, "Zoe asked me the other day if I could have a super power, what would it be?"

"And?"

"I went with flying."

"I suppose that's okay. A little uninspired."

"Oh? What would yours be, Mr. Inspiration?"

"You're not going to like this."

"Come on. How bad can it possibly be?"

"The ability to make people lose control of their bowels."

A look of disgust wrenched her face. "I didn't expect you to go scatological on me."

"I know it's foul, but can't you see the good you could do?"

"No, actually, I can't."

"It's the ultimate way to knock someone down a few notches when they need it."

Abby grimaced again. "I guess."

"Well, here's how I came up with this idea. When I was in culinary school in Des Moines, I was on my way to a bar one night downtown. There were these two big guys in front of me. Muscle shirts showing off arms the size of tree trunks, dark tans, macho types. One of the guys says to the other that he really feels like fucking somebody up tonight, been a long time since he really kicked someone's ass."

"Guys suck sometimes."

"So I'm thinking, okay, someone's probably going to get hurt tonight because these two idiots are bored. And it's bugging me all night long. I tell my friends and we start talking about ways to deal with guys like them."

"And you hit them with Diarrhea Man?"

Dante rolled his eyes. "Well, I tell them that I can see how the scenario is going to play out with these guys. They'll wait until the right guy bumps into them, then pull the 'Dude, what's your problem?' And off they go. But, I say, what if right after they pull their 'what's your problem?' these two guys shit themselves? The only problem now is how fast can these guys get the hell out of there. Crisis averted."

"Diarrhea Man, protector of the meek."

"Something like that." Dante smiled. "And I'd go a step further. I'd keep crooked politicians in line." Abby arched an eyebrow. "No really. Every time they made public appearances, I'd go to work. No one votes for someone who starts every speech, 'My fellow Ameri—pthhhht!'" She shook her head, but couldn't keep from laughing. "You see," Dante continued, "it's perfect. You don't hurt anyone, except maybe a little rash. And I'd only use my power to fight for truth, justice, and the American way."

"I don't even want to know what Diarrhea Man's costume looks like."

"No costume. And no name. I'd quietly do my thing with no one ever knowing the cause."

"How very noble. The mark of a true hero."

As they left the restaurant, Abby stumbled over a crack in the sidewalk. "Tonight reminds me of our first night together in Las Vegas." Her eyes danced with that familiar carnality.

She was a beautiful woman, no doubt. And maybe Dante had a trace of lingering affection for her, memories of all they'd shared together. But all he could think was how much he wished he could be celebrating this Cook Network thing with Charly right now.

"That was a long time ago," he said and hailed her a cab.

Before getting in the taxi, she whispered in his ear, "It wasn't so long ago." She kissed his cheek and slid into the cab without looking at him again.

As Abby rode away, Dante stood dumbfounded. What was she playing at? He shook his head.

Chapter 26

The day Dante got back to San Francisco, Gloria and Richard were at the restaurant waiting to meet with him about moving. The creases in Gloria's face were deeper than the last time he saw her. And she'd lost weight.

"Gloria," Dante said, "I really think this conversation should be between the two of us. So Richard, if you'll please excuse us."

Richard made to protest, but Gloria held up her hand. "It's alright, Richard."

The self-styled special consultant pulled his heft from the chair and said, "I'll be outside if you need me."

Gloria's eyes were hard. Dante went behind the desk, but before his ass hit the seat, she nearly barked, "I've grown very tired of the lack of respect I get around here. You allow employees to insult me without consequence and you ignore me as if I'm nobody. I do own half this restaurant."

"I don't ignore you, Gloria."

"Oh yes you do." She scowled at him. "I want this move."

"You know, Gloria, North Beach is one of the most popular neighborhoods in the entire country."

"Among people who know no better."

"*And* it's been my neighborhood the entire time I've lived in San Francisco, I can't imagine us being anywhere else. It doesn't make sense."

"It makes perfect sense."

"Look, Gloria, we're doing—"

"Please stop with the 'we're doing great' and 'if it ain't broke, don't fix it' talk. I know you're content with the way things are. I know you fear change."

"Why would I *want* to change what is clearly working so well? I could see if we were having trouble filling tables, but we're packed every night of the week. You don't move from a location that people are already coming to."

"Let me make this more clear," she said. "I know John had no problem bringing his friends and business associates in here. And I'm sure they would occasionally visit some of the neighbors. They were men and that's the way men are. But do you know what an embarrassment it is to bring my friends here? I'd love to have events at the restaurant, but I can't imagine my friends and associates having brunch on the patio while some whore passes on her way to sell her ass on the stage next door."

"We're in San Francisco. That's part of the charm of—"

"Don't give me that 'San Francisco charm' flummery. It's time we moved out of this 'charming' space and over to something a little more dignified."

"I don't agree."

"Obviously." She cleared her throat. "But perhaps the strength of my feelings on this matter haven't been made apparent. So let me spell it out for you. Pane Rubato is moving to South Beach." She stopped and glared. "I've already spoken with my lawyers, and I'm prepared to buy you out."

"Ha! If there's going to be a buyout, it's going to be me buying you out."

"I won't allow Pane Rubato to stay in this place."

Vitriol seethed just below Dante's surface and he wasn't sure he could contain it from spewing right into Gloria's face. He paused a moment to let his temper settle. When he spoke, it was barely above a whisper. "With all due respect, Gloria, the only reason Pane Rubato exists is because your husband was a friend and put up the money as a favor to me. And because I have worked my ass off to make this place a success. Without those two factors, there would *be* no Pane Rubato."

"Yes, without John, there would be no Pane Rubato."

"He was half of this. I'm the other half."

"I won't let my husband's legacy be tarnished by a restaurant that decent people won't patronize because it's surrounded by filth."

"John loved this place exactly where it is. You really think trying to move it away from here is what he would want?"

"I'm his wife. Do *you* really think he wouldn't want me to do what I think is best?"

"I don't think he'd agree that moving is what's best."

Gloria pulled a compact from her purse and checked her face. Without looking at Dante, she snapped her compact closed and put it back in her purse. "I guess we're at an impasse."

"I guess so."

"You'll be hearing from my lawyers," she said, then walked out.

For the rest of the day and night, Dante's head jack hammered. He wondered if this was the universe telling him it was time to move to New York. If all went well he would have a TV show. Maybe he could use that cachet to open a little place in the West Village.

He woke up the next morning with a hunger for bread that reached up from inside him. He went to the kitchen and grabbed his ceramic bowl, then went to Pane Rubato.

When he got to the restaurant, he gathered everything he needed to make a batch of bread.

"What're you doing, boss?" Peanut said. "I already got pizza dough going."

"That's okay. This is just something I'm trying out."

"You need me to do anything?'

"Nope, I got it under control, thanks."

Dante took a deep breath and looked at all the ingredients in front of him. He imagined the beautiful loaves he wanted to pull from the oven. He imagined the smiling faces of people who tasted his bread. He considered the ingredients, the effort it took to make the flour, the olive oil. The work of the bees to make the honey, of the people to harvest the honey. He thought about the work the yeast had yet to do. He wanted to pay proper tribute to all that labor by creating something of beauty. A simple loaf of bread made from earth, air, water, and fire.

The rest of the world and his concerns started to fade away.

He concentrated on every aspect of mixing the ingredients. The way it felt in his hands, the way it looked in the bowl. The smell of the yeast and flour and water and oil and honey. The sound of the dough as it formed in the bowl.

When he turned the dough out onto his board, he thought only about his hands pushing and folding and turning and rolling. Over and over. Feeling the elasticity develop with his touch. Pushing and folding and turning and rolling. When it felt ready, he placed the dough back in his bowl with all his intention and covered it with a damp towel. He placed it on top of one of the ovens to rise.

He went to find Bird, who was by the back walk-in refrigerator.

"You were in a groove back there," Bird said.

"I was. It felt good. So I think I'm going to do the soups today. And I'll take a shift on the line. Keep the groove going."

"Really feeling like cooking, huh?"

"Sometimes I just forget that's what I do."

"I hear you, brother, I hear you."

While waiting for his dough to rise, Dante set about making his soups the same way he did the bread, focusing all his attention on the food at hand. The vegetarian soup of the day was tomato and bread soup made with a garlic broth. When he peeled the garlic, he tried to think of nothing but peeling the garlic. When he crushed the tomatoes, he tried only to think of crushing the tomatoes.

When he finished the first soup, he took his bread bowl and punched down the risen dough. He placed the towel back over the top to let it rise a second time, then went to work on the second soup, andouille black bean. Again, chopping the vegetables, slicing the sausage, dicing the jalapenos took all his attention and intention.

When the spicy soup was on the stove, he again retrieved his dough and turned it out onto his board. He cut it into two equal pieces. He folded and shaped the loaves and placed them on a greased sheet pan. He cut small slices on the tops and put them in the oven. An hour later, they were done. After letting them cool, he sliced one open.

Lexi looked over his shoulder. "It's beautiful."

"Yeah? I don't know." Dante sliced a piece for her. "Here, how's it taste?"

She took a bite. "It's really good."

Peanut and Amaya appeared and Amaya said, "Looks alright." She motioned for Dante to hand over a slice. Dante gave her and Peanut each a piece.

Amaya sniffed at the bread and pulled it apart before putting some in her mouth. "Pretty good."

"Pretty *damn* good if you ask me," Peanut said.

Dante chewed on his own bit and smiled. The rest of the morning, he felt calm and relaxed, his mind clear. Lunch service got into full swing and he stayed in the groove. He took the pasta station where the special was salmon and kale fettuccine with crème fraîche and dill. First he broiled the salmon and then wilted chopped kale in butter and garlic. Then he mixed fettuccine with the crème fraîche, butter and dill. He added the kale to the pasta, some salt and pepper, and finally broke the salmon into pieces and tossed it with the pasta and kale until it was all lightly coated.

"Okay," Kerry said. "This is wild. I have a table of three regulars. One had the pasta special and the two others had the soups. They are raving over the food."

Kelly said, "The pasta is crazy popular."

"Boss," Peanut said, "We're gonna have to eighty-six the soups pretty soon. I'm almost out."

Bird laughed. "Dante, everything you've touched today has been like gold. You still got the magic."

Dante worked the line for the dinner service, too, which went as well as lunch. At the end of the night, he was exhausted. He left Pane Rubato late that night, smiling.

The next morning, when Dante got to Justin Herman Plaza to go running with Charly, she was already there, pointing at her watch. She wore her black running tights, a royal blue hoodie and a black stocking cap. She sure could be devastatingly cute when she wanted to be.

"Sorry I'm late."

She smiled. "Only a couple of minutes. I'm just giving you a hard time." She hugged him. "Feels like I haven't seen you forever."

"I know. And I've got big news."

"You got the Cook Network gig?"

"Looks like it."

"That's great!" She hugged him, and Dante felt electricity run through him.

Charly pulled back and narrowed her eyes. "And what about Abby?"

"What about Abby?"

"Don't be coy. Did you see her?"

Dante looked at the clock tower, then across to the fountain, then back to the Ferry Building. "Yes."

"You owe me a hundred bucks."

He bent to tie his shoe. "I didn't bet you."

"So you saw her? At a meeting?" Her eyes had the spikes out and the hammer ready to nail him to the closest tree.

"Yes, she joined the meeting."

"And?"

"And we had dinner."

"Jesus, you slept with her, didn't you?"

"No! Good lord, Charly. We just had dinner."

She just shook her head with a disgusted look on her face. "You're such an idiot."

Dante's jaw tightened. Then he said, "Thanks. I appreciate your support."

"Do you not remember what Abby did to you?"

"This has nothing to do with Abby, other than that she works for Cook Network. It's not like I went and sought her out."

"It's not like you've told her you want nothing to do with her, either."

"What was I supposed to do? Just say, 'Oh, hey, just in case you're wondering, I'm not interested in getting back together with you.'"

Charly said nothing. She just stood there with that *whatever* look of hers. The one that said *I don't care if you've got a point, I'm still going to crucify you.*

"I'm an adult," Dante said. "I can have a professional relationship with Abby."

"Right."

Every muscle seemed to get tight in Dante's body. His head throbbed. *This is so fucking futile*!

"How's Greenjeans, by the way?" he said.

"There is no similarity whatsoever between my relationship with Hugh and your inability to move on from Abby. What does he have to do with this, anyway?"

"Oh, well, I thought you wanted to talk about being an idiot?"

Charly didn't respond. Just turned and started running. Dante watched for a few seconds, then turned and ran in the opposite direction.

That afternoon he baked bread again. He mixed and kneaded

the dough, but found it difficult to focus. Why did he even care what Charly thought? She was in her lame-ass relationship with the beautiful but boring Greenjeans. Oh, and he did something "good for the world." Well, whooptie-fucking-doo for him.

After he finished his bread, he went into the restaurant and made a four-cheese red and white lasagna for the dinner service. He made the pasta sheets himself. Each layer had ricotta, provolone, mozzarella, and parmigianno reggiano. He alternated the sauce on the layers between red marinara and white garlic cream sauce.

Throughout making the lasagna, he tried to concentrate, but he couldn't stop thinking about that morning with Charly. Couldn't stop seeing her turn and run away from him.

Chapter 27

The week passed with Dante's mind continuously on Charly. Why did she always have to be so damn difficult? But even when she was being a total pain in the ass (which seemed to be most of the time), he loved being around her. She had this way of getting his blood going, making him express all his passions. He hadn't ever been quite able to describe it, but sitting in his kitchen one morning, having espresso, he said to himself, "It's beautiful tension." The question was, what could he do about her? Should he even try?

At the moment, though, he needed to make a decision on the latest offer from Cook Network. They had just offered him a hell of a deal: more money than Dante thought he was worth and even a couple of trips to Italy. So at this point, it was more of a formality that he accept the offer officially.

Then there was the question of the Pane Rubato buyout. Dante met with his lawyer, Susan, after she received Gloria's offer.

"$500,000," Susan said. "She basically just wants the name. You get the rest."

Dante's face puckered with displeasure.

"It's not a bad deal."

"She still wins, though. Pane Rubato moves."

"Yes, but you stay."

"In her building. How long do you think she'll let me stay there?"

"So maybe we ask for a fifty year lease."

"You know, it's not about the money, or the location. I just hate the idea of her using my restaurant's name. I worked hard to get to this place in my career, and the name, Pane Rubato, represents everything I've done, and all the people who've helped me get here. It's part of me, who I am. Gloria's done nothing to help the restaurant, and has only ever tried to change it into something it's not. And if I let her walk with the name, she gets to make my restaurant into god knows what."

"I think you have your answer on what to do."

"So what are my options?"

"It's pretty simple. You dissolve the partnership, divide up the assets, and go your separate ways. No one gets to use the name. Is that what you want me to communicate to Gloria's lawyers?"

Dante took a deep breath. "Yes. And I'd like to have three months so my staff has plenty of time before having to find new jobs. And so I have some time to see what I can get going."

The next morning, he held an all-hands meeting to tell everyone what was going on. He got in and when he walked into the prep room, Bird was talking to Lexi. She yanked her hand away from his arm. They both smiled nervously and Bird went over to Dante. "Yo, D."

"Hi Dante," Lexi said, red-faced.

Bird looked all doe-eyed as she walked away.

"What's up with you two?" Dante grinned at Bird.

Bird frowned. "Nothing's up. She was just asking me about the specials."

"Sure." Then Dante leaned in and in a low voice, said, "She's sweet. A guy wouldn't be doing so bad with her."

"I'll keep that in mind," he said, then he stomped off.

At the meeting, Dante said, "I just wanted to let you all know that Gloria is trying to buy me out and move Pane Rubato. I want to keep Pane Rubato going right where it is. So the only option she has left me is to dissolve the business."

Several people groaned.

Dante continued. "I'm sorry, I know this situation sucks. I'm trying to keep us open at least three months so we have some time. I do plan to open something else, and I would sincerely love all of you to stay with me. Gloria may be able to get us out of this building and make us change our name, but she can't shut us down."

The room erupted with hoots and applause.

After the meeting, Dante and Bird went into the office.

"What's the plan?" Bird said.

"To get the word out that I'm looking to open someplace new. In North Beach if possible. Something's got to open up, right?"

"I hope so, D. I hope so."

"I'll call a real estate agent and get someone looking. I have to go to New York at the end of the week to work on the show, but maybe you can keep your eyes and ears open. I'll tell Sal, too. I'll have the agent call you guys while I'm out. You know what kind of place we have here, so if you hear about something, I'll trust you if you tell me if it's worth pursuing."

A few days later, Dante was in New York for a day of meetings with the network's PR department. The welcome party would be later that night. He'd leave the next morning for home.

When he got to Cook Network, he was shuffled off to a conference room where a very thin blonde woman introduced herself, "Shawna McClure. I'll be handling most of your PR." She told him he was booked on a few television shows: *The Today Show*, *Rachael Ray*, *The View*, *The Ellen DeGeneres Show*.

"Wow," Dante said. "So soon?"

"Yes," Shawna said. "We want to get your face out there so when your show premieres, a lot of people will have seen you on TV before."

At the network's welcome party, Dante met several Cook Network stars, including Sonny Rigetto and Lara Diaz, whose shows he would be making appearances on.

"You're going love it here," Sonny boomed. "We like to have a lot of fun. And when you're on my show—a couple of Italian boys? Forgetaboutit. It'll be a blast."

A hand brushed Dante's shoulder. Abby came from behind him, looking as stunning as ever. But now her looks had a different quality. Not so much of the pure beauty he used to see in her.

"Hey there." She hugged him. "It's great to have you on board."

"I'm really looking forward to working with these two." He nodded toward Sonny and Lara.

"They're two of our best." She took Dante's elbow. "Can I steal him away for a minute?"

She pulled Dante to an unoccupied corner. "I've been thinking about the last time you were here."

"Oh?"

"I really enjoyed having dinner with you." She discretely ran her fingers over the back of his hand. "And I was hoping we'd get to spend some time together while you're in town. But I know you're leaving in the morning."

"Abby, I don't—"

"I have a little present for you." She turned her back to the rest of the room, then opened her purse. She handed him something silky and red, barely enough material for an eye patch.

The instant the panties touched his hand, he heard Sonny holler from the other side of the room, "Dante, get over here. I want you to meet someone." Sonny stood next to the legendary Jacques Pepin. Dante quickly shoved the underwear into his blazer pocket and escaped.

At the end of the night, Dante was exhausted. He'd met dozens of people, and felt how truly blessed he was to have this opportunity. In his hotel room, the one person he wanted to talk to most about all of it was Charly.

Chapter 28

When he got home the next day, Dante walked in the house and tossed his blazer onto the chair by the door. Then he called Charly. He needed to tell her he'd moved on from Abby.

"Can I come over?" he said when she answered.

"I'm at work."

"What about tonight?"

"I'm having dinner with Hugh tonight."

"Tomorrow?"

"I'm working all day tomorrow."

"On Sunday?"

"Yes, is that okay with you?" She huffed. "What do you want, anyway?"

"I need to talk to you. What about tomorrow night?"

After a long pause, she finally said, "I suppose."

Sunday night, Dante headed out the door from his house on his way to see Charly. The fog had rolled in and the breeze put a chill into him. He quickly grabbed his blazer from the chair just inside the door and slipped it on.

At Charly's, when she opened the door, he said, "You're still mad at me, aren't you?"

"Yes."

"Well, stop it."

"Give me one good reason."

"Can I come in first?"

She stood aside and let him in. She pointed to the couch and he sat.

"You know, there's nothing there for me with Abby."

"That's nice."

"But you don't believe me."

"She's got you exactly where she wants you now."

"Where she wants me? What, you think she can do anything she wants and I'll just go along?"

She cocked her head in that *damn right I'm telling you your business* way. "Pretty much."

"Oh, that's rich, coming from you."

"What's that supposed to mean?"

"You've been with that plain white rice Greenjeans for how long now?"

"Hugh is *not* white rice. He's—"

"A waste of time."

Charly laughed and stood. "At least I know he loves me."

Dante stood. "Big fucking deal. He loves you. You can live a very long and dull life together."

They stood face to face, nearly out of breath, staring into each other's eyes. A second later, they were in a passionate embrace, kissing, tongues in each other's mouths, knocking teeth, mashing noses into each other's face. Charly practically tore Dante's blazer off and threw it to the floor. He pulled her sweatshirt off as they kiss-stumbled their way to the bedroom.

Then Charly stopped. "Okay, we have to wait."

"We do?"

Charly nodded. "I have to talk to Hugh first."

"You do?"

She laughed and put her hand on his face. "Yes. Because when we get back to this, I don't want to have anything else on my mind."

"I hate that you have scruples. Okay, call him. I can wait."

"I'm not calling him. I have to see him in person."

"Is it too late to go see him tonight?"

"He's out of town until Wednesday."

"Ahhh! You're kidding me!"

Again, Charly laughed. "Sadly, no." She moved down the hall to pick up her sweatshirt. Dante followed. He got to the living room and picked up his jacket from the floor. A tiny red thong fell out of his pocket.

Dante's heart stopped. He quickly shoved the panties back into the pocket.

Oh, God, please don't let Charly have seen that.

He remained bent over. He needed to get rid of those panties, or get out of there. Or both. He slowly straightened himself and looked at Charly. She stood smiling. Then her smile disappeared and she quickly walked over.

"You okay? You look like you're about to pass out."

"Head rush. I just need to sit."

They moved to the couch. "So," Dante said, his mind divided between the panties in his pocket and wanting Charly in every way possible, "Do you have to talk to Greenjeans before we can have dinner together?"

"I guess dinner would be okay."

"How about tomorrow night?"

"I have a work dinner tomorrow. But Tuesday is good for me."

"Great. My place?"

"I think we'd better be somewhere public. Not sure I trust us to be alone with wine."

Dante laughed. "Good point." He paused a moment. "How about Slanted Door? I can pick you up around 8:00?"

"Perfect."

The next day, Dante floated. Even Richard coming in to ask for a copy of the accounting records didn't bring him down.

"We don't do the books here," he said. "We have an accountant who handles all that. Have Gloria contact Donna at Morales Accounting Group. She'll have everything you need."

Richard took off his glasses and set them on the office desk. He rubbed his eyes. "Here," he handed Dante a card. "Have the records sent to Gloria's attorney at this address ASAP."

Dante only smiled. "Gloria's a co-owner. She can make her request to Donna directly."

Richard simply turned and walked out.

When Dante walked out to the dining room, he was all smiles. It was 5:30, so the restaurant only had a few tables.

Bird was just coming into work through the front door when Dante saw him.

"Yo, D," Bird said. "Was that Richard just leaving?"

"Yeah."

"And you're smiling? Ain't never seen that before. What happened?"

"Oh." He waved his hand dismissively. "Has nothing to do with him."

"Then you must've had a good meeting in New York. I haven't seen you look so happy in a long time."

"New York was a bit surreal, to tell you the truth. And the welcome party was even weirder."

"How so?"

Dante lowered his voice. "I'm in the middle of meeting all these Cook Network stars, and Abby comes over and pulls me away and tells me she wishes we could spend some time together."

"I assume not for a meeting about your show."

"No."

"That woman confuses me. I thought she was done with you."

"Just wait. Gets better."

Birds raised his eyebrows. "Do tell, D."

"She hands me her panties right there in the room, with all those people around."

"For everyone to see?"

"No. We were in a corner and she had her back to everyone."

"Good lord. Is she just playing with you, or what?"

"I don't know what the hell she's doing. She rejected my marriage proposal, but now that I have a show on her network she seems interested again. Or at least interested in sex."

"Seems you're pretty happy about it, though. I thought you were off her?"

"I am."

"You just getting some strange pleasure out of her wanting you now?"

"No."

"Then what's with all the smiles?"

Dante couldn't help grinning. "Charly and I kind of hooked up last night."

"You mean you two finally did the deed?"

"Not quite."

Bird crooked an eyebrow. "How do you 'not quite' have sex with someone?"

"We stopped short because Charly wants to breakup with Greenjeans before we do anything."

Bird laughed and shook his head. "Damn, she's always doing the right thing. I hate that about her." He smiled. "But it's about time you two hooked up. It's been a long time coming."

Dante laughed. "It has." He shook his head. "I'm telling you, it has got to be about the strangest twenty-four hours I've ever lived. And I've lived some strange twenty-four hours lately."

Birds eyes grew wide. "Brother, it's about to get even stranger." He nodded toward the front of the restaurant.

Dante turned and Abby was standing at the maître d' stand. She had with her a small piece of wheeled luggage. When she looked over and saw Dante, she smiled. She walked over. Something about her seemed different than when Dante saw her the night before. Her eyes showed a vulnerability he'd never seen before.

"Hi Bird," Abby said.

"Hello Abby. Been a long time."

"It's nice to see you." She turned to Dante. "You look a little shocked. Didn't you get my text?"

"No." Dante pulled his phone from his pocket. He pressed a few buttons but nothing happened. "Because my phone seems to have died."

"Oh, good. That explains why you didn't text back. I thought maybe you didn't want to see me."

"I'm going to leave you two," Bird said. "Nice to see you, Abby."

Dante pointed toward a table. "Do you want to have a seat?"

"Is there some place private we can talk?"

"Sure."

He showed her to the office and they both sat.

Abby took a deep breath. "So, you want to know why I'm here."

Dante nodded.

Abby shook her head and looked down. "I acted so inappropriately the other night, and it has been eating me up from the moment you walked away from me."

"I was a little taken aback."

"I had been thinking about the first time I did that, and I've always remembered that joke you made about preferring to wear a thong. I guess I was hoping I could create a little of that old magic. But as soon as I saw your eyes, I knew I made a mistake."

She looked up into Dante's eyes.

"I couldn't let that little stunt sit with you, so I booked myself on a flight to get me here as soon as I could. I had to come see you face to face and talk to you."

She shifted in her seat.

"It's just, seeing you in New York these last few times has made me realize how much I miss you. And after all we've been through, after all I've done to you, I'm not even sure I have a right to be here now."

Abby's words seemed to slowly penetrate his numb head.

She continued. "I've been stupid and stubborn not to realize what we have. And after what I did the other night, I knew I had to come here tonight to show you how serious I am." She paused a few seconds. "I had to tell you I want you in my life."

Dante could only raise his eyebrows.

"I still don't want to get married. At least not yet. And I'm not planning to move back. I don't expect you to move to New York, either. But I think there's a way to make this work, especially now that you have your show on the network and you'll be in New York fairly often. And I would fly out here at least once a month."

Dante's mouth seemed completely unable to function.

There was a light knock at the door.

"Yeah," Dante said.

Bird peeked his head in. "Sorry, D. Can I see you for a second? We've got a bit of an emergency situation out here."

Dante looked at Abby who said, "Go ahead. I'm fine here."

"Be right back," Dante said.

"Hope everything's okay," Abby said.

As Dante closed the office door, he said, "What's up?"

Bird looked at Dante. "Jesus, D, what's happening in there?"

Dante could only shake his head and blow out a long breath.

"Well, you've got bigger problems, my friend." He directed Dante's eyes to Charly having a seat at the bar.

"Son of a bitch," Dante said. "What's she doing here? She's supposed to have a work dinner tonight."

"Not sure. And Kerry already told her you were here, so I couldn't cover for you."

"Alright, I'll go talk to her."

"I'll be in the kitchen if you need me," Bird said.

Charly looked stunning. Her hair was pulled back, and her dress had sinuous block panels of black in back, mocha in front, and white on top. The cutaway shoulders revealed just enough of her beautiful skin. When she saw him, her eyes lit up and she smiled. "Hey, sunshine." She stood and hugged him.

"Hi," he said, a little shakily. "I thought you had a work dinner tonight?"

"I do. Didn't you get my text saying I was going to come in for a drink beforehand?"

"No, my stupid phone's dead."

She rolled her eyes. "Doesn't matter. You're here and so am I." She bit her lower lip. "Though I'm starting to question my decision to come in. I'm having a very hard time not kissing you."

Dante forced a smile.

Charly put her hand on his shoulder. "You sure you're okay? You look like you're ready to keel over."

"I think it's just a little jet lag." Okay, he had to get her out of here and he needed an excuse, fast. Then it came to him.

"And Richard's in the office now pestering me about the books."

"Oh, I'm sorry. Why didn't Bird just tell me?"

"Guess he forgot."

"Is he going to be long? Should I just wait?"

"He's being a real pain. It'll probably be a while."

Just then, Richard walked back into Pane Rubato. Dante's stomach dropped out of his body, and his heart tried to follow.

Charly knitted her brow. "I thought you said he was in the office."

"Uhm, he was. Guess he finished and left without me noticing."

Richard came over. "I believe I left my glasses on the desk in the office."

"I'll go check," Dante said.

Dante went back to the office. The glasses were on the desk, but Abby was not there.

Oh, Jesus. She's out there somewhere. Where would she have gone? Must be the bathroom.

Dante grabbed the glasses and hurried to the kitchen to get Bird. "I think Abby's gone into the bathroom."

"Shit!"

"I need you to help me get Charly out of here."

They both went back out to the dining room. Dante gave the glasses to Richard who took them with a terse, "Thank you," and left.

"Okay," Dante said, "I just need to finish one more thing, then I'll meet you and Bird at Vesuvio, okay?"

"I'd rather just stay here. Is that okay?"

Now his stomach was trying to re-enter his body through one ear, and his heart through the other. "Uhm, I need a break from this place. Why don't you go over to Vesuvio, and I'll be there as soon as I can."

"Yeah," Bird said, "let's just go."

Charly stared at them both for a second with a frown on her face. "Well, can I finish my drink here, first?"

"Of course." Dante laughed and his voice cracked pubertesquely. "Here. I'll get it for you." He reached for her martini and intentionally knocked it over. "Oh crap," he said.

Bird gently took Charly's arm. "Okay, why don't we head over, and Dante will be there in a minute."

Charly pulled her arm away from Bird. "What is *with* you two?"

Dante's throat froze. He could feel Abby about to come out of the bathroom.

Bird said, "Nothing, why?"

Charly shook her head. "I don't know what's going on. But I'll humor you. Let me just go to the bathroom—"

"No!" Dante and Bird shouted together.

"I mean," Bird said, "Can you hold it until we get to Vesuvio?"

"No, I have to pee. Is that okay with you two?"

They could only look at each other.

"Freaks," Charly muttered and stomped away. With every step she took toward the bathroom, Dante felt like he was being seared.

Oh, please let them miss each other.

Just as Charly got to the door to the bathroom, it opened.

Charly stood motionless.

"Oh, hi Charly," Abby said.

Charly turned, and two laser beams shot from her eyes and instantly incinerated Dante. As she headed out of the restaurant, she went by Dante without giving his smoldering ashes a second look.

Dante took a step to follow her. "Charly, wait."

Without breaking her stride or looking back, she held up her hand to halt him.

Abby came over, and said, "I just caused something very bad to happen, didn't I?"

Dante could only weakly raise his eyebrows.

"I'm so sorry, Dante. I never ever considered that possibility." She sighed. "I guess that explains a lot. Do you want me to talk to her?"

"I think that would only make things worse."

Abby nodded, and smiled sympathetically.

She got her bag and apologized again before she left, saying she'd see him in New York as they geared up for his show.

Chapter 29

The next morning, Dante went straight over to Charly's. He texted her when he got there. "Can I come over and talk to you?"

She replied. "No, I don't want to see you."

He knocked on her door. When she opened it and saw him, she slammed the door in his face.

He knocked again.

"Go away," she said.

"Please just let me come in and explain."

After a long pause, he knocked again. Still she wouldn't answer. He knocked one more time, and the door flew open.

Charly stood with rage in her eyes. "Go away. I do not want to talk to you."

"Please, just—"

"No. I don't care what you have to say. The fact that Abby was there and you were trying to hide that from me is all I need to know about where I stand with you."

"It's not like that."

"I. Don't. Care." And she slammed the door.

Dante got home and looked at his bottle of Scotch. No, he thought, not this time. Charly was right. Had he just been honest, everything probably would have been fine.

He sat in the living room and closed his eyes. He could only see the fury on Charly's face when she said she didn't care.

"I think this time the damage is permanent," he said aloud.

He should have known better than to expect things with her to work out, anyway. Maybe it was just another of life's unpleasant realities: some people will never experience true love. His life could be a hell of a lot worse. He had plenty of other things to be happy about, things other people would never experience. Maybe this was just how things balanced out for him.

Then Susan called.

"Gloria's agreed to three months before closing, But she's also upped the offer. $750K, and a lease that lasts as long as you own a restaurant in that building."

"I don't want her to be my landlord, and I still don't want her to have my restaurant."

"Are you sure your ego's not getting in the way here?"

Dante was silent for a moment. "Maybe. But if she wants to be in the restaurant business, why doesn't she just open something else?"

"I think it's the John connection."

"But John was a silent partner, and that's the way he wanted it. He always told me the reason he was so successful was because he let good people do what they do best and didn't interfere. He never made a single suggestion for Pane Rubato. And even when I asked him if there was a favorite dish he wanted on the menu, he just told me that he trusted me, and that he knew he'd love whatever was on the menu. And now, Gloria wants to take the name away from the guy her husband gave free rein. It doesn't make sense."

"Maybe you and Gloria should meet in person to hash this all out."

"The only thing we ever seem to hash out when we're in the same room is who can piss off the other more."

§ § §

A week later, Dante hit the road for two weeks to do the talk show circuit and some public appearances. His first spot was on *The View*. He showed Jenny McCarthy how to make marinara. Each stood with a bowl of whole Italian tomatoes in front of them. "If you're going to make the best marinara," Dante said, "you have to crush the tomatoes by hand."

Jenny lowered her hands into her bowl. "Really? You can't just get them already crushed?'

"Of course you can. But there's a higher level of commitment to the sauce if you crush them yourself. Plus you can get the exact consistency you want." He crushed his tomatoes and grinned. "But really, it's just an acceptable way to play with your food."

He got his plug in for the TV show and off he went.

With Rachael Ray, it was all about meatballs. "My nonna's meatballs were like nirvana for your taste buds."

"And it isn't that difficult," Rachael said.

"Exactly. You learn a few tricks and you're on your way to making great tasting food at home. Not only do you feel better physically because you control the ingredients that go in, but there's a sense of satisfaction you get in seeing your efforts produce such a wonderful meal."

A couple of days later, Dante got a call from Shawna at Cook Network. Her voice was nearly three octaves above normal. "Have you seen *The New York Times* this morning?"

"No, why?"

"Maxime Batard wrote about you in his column."

"That's not good?"

"Not when you read what he wrote."

"Let me read it first," Dante said. "Then we can discuss how to handle it."

He went down to the hotel lobby and bought a copy of the newspaper. Batard, wrote, "When you see Dante Palermo—and you will, the media blitz is already starting—you'll get charming and good-looking. He talks a good game, too. But to be on TV, you have to have a hook and Palermo's is this curing broken hearts thing. Without the gimmick, there's nothing special about his recipes. No pizzazz, no razzle-dazzle. It's quotidian Italian fare. But the gimmick is world-class and should be good for maybe ten or fifteen minutes of fame."

When Dante finished, he could only shake his head. Gloria's influence wasn't something to take lightly. But he wasn't bothered by such an obvious attempt to slander him. In a few more days, he'd have a national TV appearance on which he could respond to Batard.

On *Today*, during his segment with Kathie Lee and Hoda (making fried zucchini patties with a yogurt-dill dipping sauce), he said he wanted to make something clear. "I have never said my food can cure a broken heart. But I have always said that cooking is great therapy for whatever might be bothering you. Probably because we so often connect our food to celebration. If anything, cooking is a way to recall festive occasions and in that way it may make a hurting heart feel a little better. There are those who call the idea of cooking as therapy gimmicky, but I think they're dead wrong."

"You're referring to Maxime Batard's column in *The New York Times*," Hoda said.

Dante smiled, "Oh, did Batard write something like that?"

At his hotel that night, he wondered if Charly had read Batard's article or watched him on any of the morning shows. And if she had, what she thought of his response. The whole situation seemed a lot like politics and she'd probably have great advice.

On the cab ride from LAX to his hotel, Dante caught a glimpse of himself in the rearview mirror. His eyes glowed pink and were rimmed with black. His head ached.

Once he got to his hotel, he spent the afternoon on his laptop, looking at commercial real estate listings and reading articles about the tough real estate market in San Francisco. None of it gave him a lot of confidence that he'd find a decent spot to open a new place.

At one point, while saving one of the articles, he came across a picture of Charly and him at Bird's birthday party before he had met

Abby. They posed cheek-to-cheek with big grins on their faces. Sitting in his hotel room and looking at Charly's smiling face on his computer screen, he felt like he was floating in the middle of the ocean. Nothing around. He closed his laptop and put his face in his hands.

The next day, he was on the set of *The Ellen DeGeneres Show*. During his demo (chicken parmesan), Dante said, "Now we'll season the chicken with—"

"Now wait," Ellen said, "I read recently that your food cures broken hearts."

"Well, I—"

"So you've got some kind of *love* potion?"

"No, I—."

"Or some kind of magic spell?"

Dante smiled. "That would do it, I guess," he said. "Seriously, though, Elsa Schiaparelli said, 'A good cook is like a sorceress who dispenses happiness.' I can't account for how people feel before or after they've had a meal I've prepared, but when they're with me and I'm feeding them, their happiness is my main concern. At my restaurant, my house, wherever, I want to see happy smiling faces when people eat my food. So I talk to people, I pour wine. It can be communal. It can be intimate and personal. I tell stories about heartache so people know they're not alone in what they're going through and I give them something good to eat. It's bound to make a few people feel better."

On his short flight back to San Francisco, as the plane started its descent, Dante looked out the window and watched the lights below get closer and closer. He knew things were changing and he had a sense that he wasn't prepared for what was coming. When the plane arrived at the gate and the flight attendant welcomed San Franciscans home, Dante didn't feel like she was talking to him.

Chapter 30

When Dante got to his house, the feeling that started on the plane remained. The familiar suddenly looked different. He felt like a stranger in his own life. And the mood persisted for weeks. There was a numbness, a cloudiness, a vagueness.

He felt out of place no matter where he was. Walking around North Beach. In whatever city he was doing a demo. Especially at Pane Rubato, knowing it'd close soon. It was a funk like he'd never experienced before. The pain wasn't as sharp and intense as it had been after Abby. It was more like a migraine.

In the midst of this, Dante continued trying to find a new place to open a restaurant. North Beach was his home and where he started his career in San Francisco. He loved having Pane Rubato there and the thought of leaving the neighborhood was heartbreaking.

He called Gloria. She didn't answer, so he left a message. "It's Dante. I'd like to meet with you to see what we can work out. No Lawyers, no advisors. Just you and me."

That afternoon, Susan called. "Gloria wants to know if the name, Pane Rubato, is on the table."

"I was hoping I could talk her into opening something named after John. I have a perfect concept for her. The kind of place John would absolutely love, and that's much more her style. An upscale steakhouse with French flare."

"Sounds great. But she won't meet with you if the name isn't on the table."

"It's not on the table. But can you tell her people I have a restaurant concept she might like."

"I can try."

It didn't take long for Susan to call back. "No Pane Rubato, no meeting."

"Well, then I guess Pane Rubato will be closing."

Dante continued his search for a place to open a new restaurant, and a few days later, he found a property in the Marina district that looked promising. On Chestnut street. It had been an Indian restaurant before. Good sized, would hold maybe a hundred seats. The location would get plenty of foot traffic, though definitely not the tourists that North Beach got. Still, Dante could imagine his new place there.

He told the property management company he was interested and it seemed he had a good shot at getting it. The next day, however, his agent called and said the place had already been rented.

"How could it already be rented? I just saw it yesterday and nobody mentioned that someone else had already put a claim on it."

"That's what the property manager told me."

A couple of weeks later, Dante found a place in the Mission he liked, only to find out that it was no longer available.

"How is this possible?" Dante said to his agent. "As soon as I want a spot, it goes off the market?"

The fruitless search for a new place certainly hadn't helped Dante's depression, but his bread, which he'd been baking religiously, was helping. He'd gotten better at concentrating on all aspects of making the bread. It was like meditation for him and he was coming away from bread-baking sessions with a sense of calm. It rarely lasted for more than an hour or two, but he had started looking forward to the times when he could bake the bread.

§ § §

And Dante's life continued to get crazier. He went to New York every few weeks to work on *Cooking from the Heart*. He and the producers decided on the recipes for each show and Dante gave his input on the new set. He wanted a few personal touches, like pictures of his nonna, his father, and his mother. Just small pictures to remind him how he got to this place. They also assembled a top-notch back kitchen staff. People who had been in the TV cooking business for years and knew how to best support the person on camera.

Shawna also wanted him to promote the show and worked a deal with La Cuisine to have him do demos at more of their stores. So on top of travel to New York, he went to places like Kansas City and Memphis. Indianapolis, Philadelphia, and Charlotte.

Finally, Dante was back in New York for the first taping of his show. On the first day of taping, he got to the studio early to check out the set. It looked great, especially considering they finished it late the night before. Maple cabinets with a hand-rubbed stain finish, blue slate countertops, Viking cooktop and ovens.

When he checked in with the back kitchen, they had already started work on the dishes for the day's two shows. For the first show, they would do gato di patate and a Sicilian fennel and blood orange salad. The entire second show would be devoted to tomato sauce with meatballs, brasciole and pork ribs. The back kitchen staff of four did the bulk of the prep work: chopping, measuring ingredients and making the finished versions for each dish. Dante checked in to talk about preparation and answer any questions, but they had it all well under control.

The technical crew arrived just after Dante and set up the cameras, lighting and audio. Since they were taping live, the Culinary Producer wanted to go with a performance feel. The floor director, Iris, told Dante, "You go where you have to go, do what you have to do, and we'll make sure to get the shot." So along with the typical floor cameras, they had a boom camera and a hand-held for "rock star" shots like when he sautéed something that would flame up.

After makeup, he was shuffled onto the set. Iris was his connection to the control room and the director in the booth, and she assured Dante she'd take good care of him.

Right before they let the audience in, Dante ran through the show segments for the director and the cameramen.

Sonali arrived and wished him luck. "You're going to be great," she said.

The first show was going well. The potatoes for the gotto di patate were mashed and the ground beef and peas for the filling were simmering. Then came the breadcrumbs. Dante broke a few pieces of stale bread into chunks and dropped them into the food processor. But when he hit the power button, nothing happened.

He tried again. Still nothing.

As he leaned over the processor to see if it was securely plugged in, a hissing power surge buzzed it to life, blasting the lid off and spraying breadcrumbs everywhere. The lid caught Dante's forehead and knocked him back. He stumbled and put a hand on the edge of the bowl of mashed potatoes which flipped into the air. He ended up flat on his ass and the bowl landed, potato side down, on the floor next to him.

Sonali ran over. "Are you alright?"

"I am, but my potatoes aren't." He rubbed the spot where the lid hit his head.

Iris moved his hand. "There's a welt forming." Then she picked up the potato bowl. "We need more potatoes right away."

"That'll take some time," Dante said. "I've already used all the potatoes the back kitchen made. Why don't we just use the ones on the floor? No one has to eat it, and this way we don't have the delay." Then he turned to the audience. "This isn't acceptable if you're serving the dish to guests. But if you're making it for yourself, what you do in the privacy of your home is nobody's business but your own."

He got a little makeup to cover the red spot on his forehead and they finished taping the rest of the show without incident. They had a slight break then started taping show number two.

He showed the audience all the ingredients they would need and said, "My nonna taught me how to make this meat sauce when I was five. I was always standing around, watching and one day she decided if I was going to be 'between her feet' then I was going to work. I rolled meatballs, I deglazed the pan with wine, I crushed the tomatoes with my hands. In fact, that may have been the day most responsible for my becoming a chef."

Through the second taping, all the equipment worked and he managed to stay on his feet. As the audience filed out, Dante exhaled and thought he'd get to do it all again tomorrow. Sonali turned to him as she left the set. "Postmortem in fifteen minutes?"

"Great, I'll be right there."

Charly would love to hear about the potatoes.

Dante's heart sank at the thought of her laughing about him landing on his ass in the first show. "Only you, Dante," she'd say. She'd tell him she wasn't even surprised, that she would have been much more shocked if something dumb *hadn't* happened.

Over the next two weeks, they taped an entire season. They prepared spicy shrimp and scallop linguine and pancetta-wrapped shrimp for show number six. Duck saltimbocca (sautéed boneless, skinless duck breast with sage and prosciutto in a marsala wine sauce) and mozzarella en corroza (fried Italian toast with mozzarella, prosciutto, and basil in a pomodoro sauce) for show fourteen.

In show nineteen, the hand-held camera operator nearly caught on fire. Dante was making a vodka cream sauce. The camera guy got too close to the pan when Dante added the vodka and the flames singed the hair on his forearm. It elicited nice oohs and ahhs from the audience and gave Dante a chance to talk about the dangers of using alcohol in a hot pan. For the other shows, they made parmesan-encrusted halibut, stuffed chicken breasts, chicken marsala, handmade gnocchi, rosemary penne (with sausage and sweet peas in a tomato rosemary cream sauce), ricotta pudding, and zabaglione. They worked with asparagus and broccoli, eggplant and zucchini, beef and lamb. They grilled, roasted, baked, and fried. When it was all over, Dante couldn't believe that they pulled off an entire season in such a short period of time.

After finishing the last show, Dante went into the restroom. He looked at himself in the mirror. "Damn," he said. "A pimply-faced kid from Des Moines. Who'd have ever guessed?"

Chapter 31

Dante went home the next day and arrived in San Francisco after midnight. He dragged himself through the door when he got home and went right to bed. But he laid there feeling like someone was poking at him from every angle. It was only a few days until Pane Rubato would close, and still no prospects for a new space. At least for now, it didn't look like he'd be opening a new place in San Francisco in the very near future. All because Gloria insisted on uprooting Pane Rubato from North Beach.

He'd never again get himself into a partnership and be at somebody's mercy. From now on, he'd have control. No one would be able to force his hand.

Oh hell, he wasn't going to think about that now. He was too damn tired. He rolled over and punched his pillow into shape. Not long after, exhaustion won.

On the day before Pane Rubato closed, a forbidding presence clung to Dante. It didn't help that the morning was enveloped in fog. He went for a run, but the darkness remained. Tomorrow, people he cared about would be out of work. And he hadn't spoken to Charly in weeks.

That night, Dante threw a small closing party. He called everyone together and said, "I want to thank you all for everything you've done, and for sticking with me to the end." Tears rolled down his cheeks. "And the minute I find a new place, I want you all there. You're my family and I'm so sorry I haven't been able to—" He bit his lip and strained to keep his composure. Finally, he said, "But let's not make this a night of sadness. Pane Rubato closing is a chance for all of us to start something new. And if we can start something together, so much the better."

All night, Dante noticed Bird was no longer hiding his affection for Lexi. They stood close to each other and held hands. And when they looked at each other, their eyes spilled with care and affection.

Dante felt a hand on his shoulder. He turned to see Paige who was there with Sal.

She gave him a hug. "Hi there, sweetie."

"Glad you could make it," Dante said.

"Wouldn't have missed it for anything. And I know you'll have a new San Francisco restaurant soon. Maybe not soon enough."

"Thanks."

Paige smiled. "I wondered if Charly and Hugh would be here. Things are getting pretty serious between those two. I'm sure Charly's told you they're going to Rome at the end of next week for some big international environmental conference." She lowered her voice. "And I probably shouldn't say anything, but Hugh's going to propose. At the Trevi fountain. He showed me the ring. Isn't that wonderful?"

Dante's heart sank. That would just be the perfect ending to all of this: Charly married to Greenjeans.

Neither Sal nor Bird smiled.

Paige looked around. "What? What'd I say?" Dante looked away and Sal tightened his lips. "Oh my God, Dante. I can't believe how stupid I am. I never realized you—Charly—I'm so sorry."

At home, around two in the morning, Dante wanted to call Charly and tell her about everything. He wanted to tell her that it all felt uneventful without her there to share it with him. He sat watching the shadows from the light of the TV and missed her so bad it ached.

Early the next morning, Dante met Susan at Pane Rubato. Gloria's lawyers would be coming by at 8:00 to finalize the dissolution of the partnership. There were a few minor items left to settle, but there shouldn't be any surprises.

Dante poured Susan a cup of coffee as she yawned.

"I don't know why they insisted on meeting so early," Susan said.

"Because it's a pain." Dante smiled.

It dawned on him that it was John Sierra's birthday. He decided to whip up John's favorite parmesan-herb frittata while they waited and prepared for the meeting. Dante had just pulled the frittata from the oven and brought it out to the dining room when Gloria came in with two lawyers and Richard. Her eyes were full of annoyance.

Dante leaned in to Susan and said, "Didn't expect to see her here. I haven't actually seen her in months."

Susan shrugged.

As everyone took seats around the table, Dante said, "It's John's birthday today. When I remembered, I decided to make one of his favorite breakfast dishes."

Gloria's eyes softened a bit.

"Would any of you like a piece?" Dante said. "In honor of John."

"I suppose there's no reason we can't be civil about this," Gloria said.

Dante cut six pieces which he gave to each person. He also poured coffee for Gloria and her people.

Susan handed Gloria's lawyers a packet of documents. Dante perused the one Susan had given him earlier.

Susan said, "I'm sorry, Gloria. I didn't realize you'd be here, so I don't have a packet for you."

When Dante looked up, Gloria had just taken a small bite of the frittata.

Dante smiled. "You know Gloria, I think that's the first thing I've seen you eat in this restaurant in a very long time."

Gloria closed her eyes. "I can see why John liked this so much." Tears started running down her face. She stood and said, "Go ahead without me." She turned and walked out of the restaurant.

The others looked at each other. Richard shrugged, then followed Gloria out.

The rest met for about a half hour. At the end, Dante signed the documents to dissolve the partnership and business.

One of Gloria's lawyers said, "We'll get you a copy of the documents with Gloria's signatures."

After everyone had gone, Dante sat for a few minutes in the dining room until the quiet was too much to take.

When Dante got home, his stomach churned. The fog outside was draining the life out of him. He needed to get out of the city.

Right then.

Maybe Tahoe. He could be there in about four hours. The mountains, the air might help him clear his head.

He threw a few shirts and pairs of pants into a bag. He had travel-sized toiletries already in a case. Anything else he might need, he'd buy. Quick shower and within twenty minutes, he was out the door. On the road, heading east on I-80.

A few hours into the drive, he started the ascent into the Sierras. There'd been a fire on that stretch of road. The grass was black and burnt tree trunks stood, stark, feebly reaching toward a mocking blue sky. When he reached Truckee, he knew he wasn't far enough away, yet, so he kept going.

Beyond Reno. He drove through the Nevada desert, trying to empty his mind. Stopped for a sandwich at a little deli on the railroad tracks in Lovelock. Carried on through Battle Mountain.

Into Utah. Through the Great Salt Lake Desert. Past Salt Lake

City. Up and down, twisting and turning through the Rockies. At around 1:00 A.M., he came to the town of Rock Springs, Wyoming. Somewhere along the way, Dante decided to drive to Des Moines. He hadn't been there in a while and now might be a good time for a bit of home. If he remembered right from when he moved to San Francisco, Rock Springs was about half way. This was a good place to stop.

He checked into the Motel 6 and on the way to the car, he heard something behind him. A dog. German shepherd mix. No tags. No collar. No one near taking responsibility for it. The thing looked lonely. Judging by the smell, this dog hadn't had a bath in a long time.

When Dante put his hand out to greet the pup, it gave him that pure face of gratitude only dogs have.

"Hi there."

Quick look showed it was a she. Her tail sliced the air and she smiled a big yellow, toothy grin. She lowered her ears and licked his knuckle.

She looked hungry, so Dante reached into the car and grabbed the other half of the ham and turkey sandwich he got for lunch. He unwrapped the sandwich and handed it to her.

"Here you go."

Though she appeared ravenous, she gently took the food and held it in her jaws as if she wasn't sure she was allowed to eat it. "Go ahead, it's yours."

She wouldn't eat her sandwich. Just kept it in her teeth. Maybe she didn't want to let it get away. Food without decay. Not a single fly had buzzed it yet. No maggots to pick through.

Dante bent down and pet her head.

"I don't suppose you bother to pick through the worms, do you? But go on, it's good."

Her ears perked up and her head tilted.

"Eat... Mmm... Yummy," Dante said rubbing his belly. Finally, she put the sandwich on the ground, placed her paw on it, and pulled off a chunk. Within seconds she devoured the rest, wagging her tail the whole time. When she finished, Dante scratched behind her ears. She closed her eyes and leaned into it. Dante could feel her appreciation coming through his finger tips.

"My name's Dante." He offered his hand to shake. She licked his thumb. "What's yours?"

No response. Maybe she was waiting to tell him.

Dante stayed for several minutes, stroking her and making chit-chat. How did she like the mountains? Would she like a change of scenery? Her coat was matted and rough, but she had beautiful colors: silver and gold, browns and blacks. She had amazing light eyes, too. Maybe she was a Husky mix.

"Come on, honey," Dante said, doing his best Mae West. "You can stay with me." They got in his car and Dante immediately put the windows down. She was much more potent in a confined space. They drove around back to where his room was. As soon as they were in, he took the dog to the tub and gave her a bath. He scrubbed her down with his shampoo. His fingers ran over her too-exposed ribcage. It took time, but he managed to wash most of the smell out of her. Then it was his turn to shower the road off.

He crawled into bed and motioned for the dog to follow. She hopped up and circled a couple times before curling up next to him. They watched SportsCenter. The Yankees beat the Rangers 7-4. Dante channel-surfed for another hour before turning off the TV. In the blackness of the hotel room, he finally let the tears go.

He finally drifted off to sleep, but after a few hours, he woke up when he felt the bed move. He drew back when he opened his eyes to see a figure at the foot of the bed petting the dog.

"*Sono io*,"—it's just me, Nonna said.

Dante rubbed his eyes and sat up in bed. "*Ciao. Come stai*?"

"The question, Dantelino, is how are you?"

"I'm not sure I know anymore."

"That's no good."

"Any advice?"

Nonna petted the dog again. "I'm glad you're taking this trip. I think you will find some truth at home. Just make sure to keep your eyes and heart open to it."

Dante sighed. "I seem to be terrible at seeing the truth in anything. Can't you just tell me what I need to know?"

"I just did. Keep your heart and eyes open to the truth. The rest is up to you."

"Why did I know you were going to say something like that?"

"See how good you're getting at seeing the truth?" She smiled. "I have to go now. *Ciao*."

"*Ciao*, Nonna."

Chapter 32

Dante awoke the next morning with a dog licking his face. She probably wanted to go home. When he let her out, she ran over to the grass, sniffed around briefly and did her business. At any moment, Dante expected her to wander off and keep going. But then she came back, smiling and wagging her tail. He stood aside in the doorway to his room and she ran in and jumped up on the bed.

"Well, I guess you're sticking with me."

Dante checked out of the hotel and got directions to a pet supply store where he picked up a bag of kibble and a couple of bowls for food and water. Stopped at the gas station to fill up and get a bottle of water for the dog. Fed her. Grabbed a fast food breakfast sandwich for himself and they were off.

"I should call you something other than 'sweetie,' shouldn't I?"

The pup sat in the passenger seat and tilted her head.

"Let's see. I found you in Rock Springs." He rubbed his chin. "Rocky might be a little masculine. What do you think?" The dog didn't give any discernable sign that she liked the name. "How about Roxie?" She smiled, panting, then gave him a big kiss on the side of his face.

Dante laughed and said, "Okay. Roxie it is."

He took a deep breath. "So Rox, let's make a deal. If you see me starting to mess up, bite me on the ass, okay?" She tilted her head. "And

I promise to do the same for you. Deal?" Dante put out his hand to shake, but she just licked him again. "Good enough for me."

The miles piled up as they headed through Wyoming, passing towns like Table Rock, Elk Mountain. Snow-topped mountains off in the distance. Stretches of road, straight for miles. They rolled through Laramie and Cheyenne as the sun crept higher into the bright blue sky. They stopped for gas and a pee break in Pine Bluffs, on the Nebraska border. Home of a thirty-foot high, gleaming white statue of The Virgin Mary, Our Lady of Peace. They saw her from the highway as they came around the bluff. She stood like a typical Madonna, arms open and welcoming them to Nebraska. Dante said, "You ever wonder if she slapped Jesus on the back of the head and told him to stop picking on his baby brother? 'Jesus, stop teasing little Joey. He's only four and you're the Messiah. Start acting like it!'"

They kept moving east. North Platte, Kearney. The plains gave way to more greenery. Trees and grass. The interstate followed the Platte river for miles. Another gas and pee stop in York. They were definitely into Midwest humidity now. The last road sign said Omaha was a hundred and six miles away, about an hour-and-a-half. And Des Moines was less than two hours from there. It wouldn't be long. Dante thought about calling his mom, but his phone had died and he forgot to pack a charger. They'd just have to show up at home. They wouldn't get in too late.

They crossed into Iowa with the sun lingering barely over the horizon in the rearview mirror. The familiarity of home settled on Dante. The rolling green hills could be right out of a Grant Wood painting. The names of towns on the road signs now had connections. One fall semester at Iowa State, Dante dated a girl from Atlantic. Lisa. She had great tan lines. He went to his pal Don's family reunion near Anita. Another friend, Beth, got married and moved to Panora. He streaked through one of the bridges of Madison County in Winterset. He jumped on a trampoline in Waukee.

On the freeway in Des Moines, he drove by all the familiar places:

downtown, the capitol building, his high school. He remembered how much he loved growing up in Des Moines, but somehow always knew he'd leave. Maybe someday he'd move back.

His mom's house was dark when they pulled into the driveway.

Could she be asleep already? She wouldn't be out, would she? Dante knew she liked to go to the movies or for dinner with her friends. Would she be out at ten o'clock?

Dante opened the car door and the humid air hit him in the face. He got out with Roxie and walked around to the back patio. Roxie sniffed around. A sticky film of sweat and humidity covered Dante's body. Oh, those Iowa summer nights.

A car pulled into the driveway, and his sister, Carolyn, got out. "Dante?"

Dante's mom followed and hurried up to him.

"What are you doing here?" She grabbed his face and kissed him. "You're so skinny." She looked at him, at the car. "Did you drive all the way here?"

Dante nodded as the dog ran up. "Oh, this is Roxie."

"It's skinny, too," she said. "Did you have dinner?"

She put her hand on his face again. "Those dark circles around your eyes. You look like you're starving. Come in and get something to eat."

In the house, Carolyn and Dante sat at the kitchen table while their mother put out a plate of sharp provolone and cured black olives along with a large loaf of bread. She poured three glasses of red wine.

The house hadn't changed much since Dante moved. The walnut cabinets and table in the kitchen were exactly as they'd been all his life. The shelves of pots and pans. A stainless steel double sink replaced the wide porcelain single one.

While they ate and drank, Dante told them about the restaurant. They asked a lot of questions. Will he open a restaurant in New York? Does he think he can find a new spot in San Francisco? Why had he driven all the way there? Was he okay? Why didn't he call?

"I had to get out of San Francisco," he said. "I didn't intend to drive all the way here when I started, but somewhere along the way, it sounded like a good idea." He put his hand on Roxie's head. "Plus I got a dog out of the deal." The pooch smiled. "Well, actually, she kind of got me."

His mom looked at the three olive pits on his plate. "What's the matter? You don't like the olives? You want me to make some pasta? I have some peaches and plums."

"No Ma, I'm not that hungry."

She shook her head. "You're tired. You'll eat tomorrow."

After an hour, Carolyn left and his mom set Dante up for the night. "You want to sleep in your old room? The bed has some boxes on it because I was packing up a bunch of old clothes for Saint Vincent de Paul."

"I'm fine on the couch in the TV room for tonight." She promised she'd clean up his room tomorrow, then went up to bed.

Dante sat in the room where Frank and Carolyn and he would fight over who got the rocking chair when their dad wasn't in it. Where they watched TV and played games. Where he interrupted Frank with his hand up some girl's shirt late one night.

He thought about all his friends. He couldn't resist the urge to go into his old bedroom and pull out his high school yearbook and take it back to the TV room. God, how young they all were. Flipping through the pages and seeing faces and names he hadn't thought about for years. Strange how he didn't even remember some of the people. He sat there on the couch, Roxie at his feet, and he knew why he came here. A part of him that used to seem so far away was much closer now.

Chapter 33

When Dante rolled off the couch the next morning, the smell of espresso and toast filled his nose. He stood and his legs ached with the stiffness of two days in a car. He hobbled into the kitchen where his mom sat with Roxie. They both turned and smiled. "I gave the dog a piece of cold chicken," Ma said. "You have dog food for her?"

Dante rubbed his eyes. "Yeah, in the car. I'll get it."

"No. Sit. You want coffee?" He nodded. "I'll make you some eggs."

"No, Ma. The toast is fine."

She poured a demitasse of espresso. "No wonder you're so skinny. I'll make frittata."

"No really. I can't eat it. Too early."

"*Testa dura.*"

Dante smiled. "I got my hard head from you."

She laughed, then sat and tried to have a conversation. "How are you?"

"Okay."

"How's Charly?"

"I don't know. She's mad at me."

"Why? What did you do?"

"It's a long story."

"I got time." Dante's face must have showed the pit forming in his stomach. "But I can see you don't want to talk about it." She got up and poured herself another espresso. "When do you think you'll go back home?"

Dante shrugged. "A few days. Maybe a week. You in a hurry to get rid of me?"

"Of course not!" She looked out the window. "It's supposed be ugly with this heat all week."

"Great." Dante finished his coffee and toast, then excused himself to go shower.

Once he finished cleaning up, his mom had gotten busy with other things, so he easily made his escape with Roxie. It was only nine o'clock, but when Dante stepped outside he understood how a steamed pork bun must feel in its final moments before being plated and served.

They walked up to the field at Dante's old junior high. Almost nothing had changed since he went to school there. Even the houses hadn't changed much. A few new paint jobs. Maybe an addition here or there, but the neighborhood looked about like it did twenty years ago.

After a short, sweaty time, they went back home and Dante told Roxie how he used to think it was such a long walk. Especially in winter.

Dante walked into his mom's house and wiped the sweat from his forehead. "Good lord, how do you people live in this place?"

His mom peeked in from the dining room. "I don't know. You used to do it. Maybe California has made you weak." She smiled.

That afternoon, Dante went to visit his dad's grave. While at the gravesite, Dante stood quietly for a long while. Out of nowhere, an image of himself standing at a big wood-fired oven popped into his head.

"You trying to tell me something, Pop?"

Nothing else came to him, but as he stood there, he thought maybe this was the truth Nonna had mentioned. Could it be time to come home?

Maybe he could open a bakery. Maybe like Papireto in Nonna's story, he needed to master the bread to master his life.

Come on, Pop, Nonna, anyone. Give me something I can understand. Am I supposed to move back to Iowa? What am I supposed to do?

Later that night, the entire family was at his mom's for a cookout. He sat on the bench swing in the shade and rocked back and forth. He started to sweat, but the juniper-scented breeze cooled him. Roxie sat next to the swing, panting.

"D," Frank said, "You ever think about coming back here?"

"You know," Holly said, "you could open something up here in Des Moines."

Carolyn jumped in. "Can you imagine how popular your place would be here? Plus we'd get you full time."

"Yeah, Uncle D," Chelsea said. "Move back to Iowa." Then she lead a chorus of all the kids, chanting, "We want Uncle D! We want Uncle D!"

"You've been in California long enough, D," Frank said. "Time for you to come home."

His mom stayed conspicuously silent on the issue, but Dante knew she was happy with the other family members doing her bidding.

Holly sat at the picnic table, digging in her purse. "Oh, hey, I have pictures from San Francisco," she said. "I was looking through these last night. There's one you really need to see."

"You still develop pictures?" Dante said.

She shrugged. "I'm old school."

She found an envelope of photographs, opened the flap and thumbed through to what she was looking for. She turned quickly and yelled, "Frankie, get your face away from the dog's butt right now!" She looked back at Dante, smiled and pulled out the picture. She held the photo out as she walked toward him. "You and Charly. I don't remember seeing it when I first had them developed. But when I saw it last night, I don't know how I could have missed it."

The picture was of Dante and Charly dancing at his birthday party.

Dante's hands held her waist. Her arms were around his neck. They looked into each others' eyes, and looked like they were exactly where they were supposed to be in the world. Right there, holding each other. As Dante took in the picture, his chest nearly collapsed, and the wave of regret that hit him nearly flipped him backward in the swing. Why hadn't he called Charly weeks ago?

"You okay, D?" Frank said.

His mother sat next to him and took the picture. After a moment, she said, "You need to get back to San Francisco, don't you?"

"Yeah," Dante said.

Chapter 34

Dante packed up his stuff the next day and he and the dog drove back to California. He had the picture of Charly and him, and when they'd stop, he'd look at it. Every time he did, he'd become more and more convinced that not only did he love Charly, but she loved him as well.

After two days of driving, Dante and Roxie arrived back in San Francisco. Dante stepped out of the car onto the sloping sidewalk outside his house. The dog jumped out right behind him.

He patted her head. "This is it, Roxie."

The cool night air smelled of North Beach and all its wonderful food a couple of blocks away. He stood for a moment on top of his stairs and looked over the neighborhood. He still didn't feel like he was home.

When he got in the house, he knew he needed to call Charly. But he'd have to work up to that one, so he knew he'd better call Bird, first.

"I'm back in San Francisco. Anything interesting going on here?"

"Well, I haven't seen anything come up for restaurant spaces. But I did talk to Charly."

"Oh?"

"She and Greenjeans are flying to Rome tomorrow morning. She thinks he's going to propose, D." Dante sat on the floor in his living room. Roxie came over and licked the side of his face. "I asked her what she was going to do."

"And?"

"She said she's probably going to say yes."

Dante pressed his palm to his eye. "Probably?"

"That's what I said. She said if he asks."

"What's that mean? If he asks, she's going to say yes?"

"I don't know. But if I was you, I'd want to find out."

He looked at his watch. It was almost 10:00. "It's already late. And I'm not sure what good it would do me, anyway."

"I'm not sure what bad it'd do you, either."

After hanging up with Bird, Dante sat on the floor for at least an hour. Roxie stayed right beside him.

Finally, he yawned and crawled over to his chair. He didn't even have the energy to get up, so he just leaned against it. He dozed off on the floor in front of his chair, and woke up after what felt like only a few minutes. But it was 4:30 A.M. The sleep was a black void. No dreams, no rest. Just a loss of consciousness. He blinked hard.

But the black sleep had done something, given him an unmistakable clarity about what he had to do. He knew he couldn't let Charly go to Italy without telling her he loved her.

He stood. If he took a quick shower, brushed his teeth (he couldn't tell Charly he loved her with body odor and halitosis), it'd be about 5:15, maybe 5:30, when he got to her place. If she was on an early flight, she may already be gone, but if it was a later flight, she may not be too happy with him if he woke her up so early. But what did that matter when he was there to proclaim his love?

"Rox, I may be nuts, and God knows where this'll take me, but I gotta do it."

He went to the shower and twenty-three minutes later, he was in his car, driving to Charly's. Doubt sat in the back seat of the car and smacked his head repeatedly, yelling, *This is a stupid idea!*

"A stupider idea would be letting her marry Greenjeans," he said aloud.

He arrived at Charly's, and the house was dark.

Please let her be here, please let her be here, please let her be here.

He took a deep breath and rang the doorbell. Nothing. He waited a few seconds then rang again. This time a light came on and Greenjeans opened the door. Okay, didn't anticipate that possibility. The plan thus far was not going so well. Greenjeans looked at Dante through squinty sleepy eyes.

Finally, Dante said, "Uhm, is Charly at home?" Greenjeans said nothing, just turned and walked away, leaving the door open.

A minute later, Charly, wrapped in her royal blue silk robe, her hair pointing in seventy-two different directions, came in. "Is everything okay?"

"Yes and no."

She motioned for him to sit and said, "Let's start with the yes part. No one is dead or sick? No other tragedy has befallen someone I know and love?"

"Yes, no one is in any kind of serious trouble. But me that is."

"Okay, what kind of trouble are you in?"

Greenjeans came into the room. "Everything okay?"

Charly nodded.

"If you need me," Greenjeans said, "I'll be in the bedroom."

Charly turned back to Dante. "So?"

"Charly, I've been an idiot." He paused, but she said nothing. "And I need to tell you something I probably should have told you a long time ago."

Finally she gave him a inquiring look.

"I'm in love with you."

Dante thought he saw a tiny spark in her eyes, but she quickly replaced it with the same indifference that had been there for most of the conversation so far.

Finally, she said. "So things didn't work out with Abby?"

"It's not like that. It was never like that."

"What is it like, then?"

"It's that I have no doubt about the truth in my heart, and that truth is you. It's no more complicated than the fact that I love you."

Charly pursed her lips. The silence rang in Dante's ears. Then Charly said, "And what am I supposed to do with this information now?"

"Whatever you like."

Again the agonizing silence. There was no reciprocation of his feelings in her face.

"At this point, I don't think there's anything I can do with it."

Dante felt like he'd been rammed in the gut by a jet ski. He couldn't speak.

"I don't think you know or understand your heart any better than you did before," Charly said. "I know you're upset about closing your restaurant and maybe you're grasping at some kind of control in your life. But whatever you think you feel now is too little, too late, and probably won't last, anyway."

"That's not true."

Charly shook her head. "When Abby came here, it was a personal visit, wasn't it?"

Dante took a deep breath. "Yes. She came to tell me she wanted me in her life. But I didn't want to be back in her life. Not like that."

"But the fact that you tried to hide her visit from me showed me that at some level, maybe one you don't even recognize yourself, you were considering whether you wanted to be back in her life. And with you two working together now, I decided I don't want any part of it."

He stared at her. He could see her mind was made up and to continue arguing his case would be futile. He got up to leave. "I think you're the one who's got it wrong. I do love you, and I just wanted you to know."

Chapter 35

Dante drove home. When he walked into the house, he was hit with a smell he remembered from hundreds of Sunday mornings: his nonna's meatballs. He went to the kitchen and Nonna pulled a pan of steaming meatballs from the oven.

In the sunlight, the earthliness of Nonna Isabella was undeniable. The age spots and bluish veins on her hands. The wrinkles around her laughing hazel eyes. Her crooked teeth. The smell of garlic coming off her. She had a smudge of flour on her cheek. He thought he might have been a ten-year-old in her kitchen on a Sunday morning again. He wrapped his arms around her and when he felt her warmth against him, he began to cry. In every one of her previous visits, there was a dreamy, ethereal quality about her, even when she touched him. But now he couldn't deny she was really standing right there in his kitchen with him and knew he had missed her more than he had ever realized before.

Roxie came over and wagged her tail. Nonna patted her on the head. "She's a sweetheart. And she loves meatballs."

Dante couldn't help but smile.

"*Siediti*," she said. "Why are you letting the love in your heart go?"

"Charly may be in my heart, but I'm not in hers."

"Did she say she does not love you?"

"Not those words exactly, no."

"Then there may still be a chance. You must go to her and cook a meal filled with all your love for her. If she is in love with you, the moment she tastes your food, she will be yours forever. If she has no love for you, the food will taste of goat urine." She stood. "You must be aware of one other thing. Your Charly is a stubborn woman. If she sees you before this meal, she will run away. If she runs away, you will lose her forever." She kissed his forehead, then stepped behind him.

"No pressure there."

Roxie barked.

When Dante turned, Nonna had disappeared.

He sat, trance-like, watching the sunlight on the table. Finally, he took a deep breath. When your dead nonna told you what to do, it was probably a good idea to heed her advice.

But the question was, how?

He popped the rest of the meatball in his mouth then got his laptop. At the kitchen table, he got on the Internet to find out what conference Charly and Greenjeans were going to. He had to get to Charly before Greenjeans proposed.

Dante found Greenjeans' company web site and found the International Alternative Energies Conference and Expo at the Nuova Fiera in Rome. And Greenjeans would be speaking: "Going Green and the Global Economy." Half an hour later, Dante had booked a flight to Rome and called his cousin, Marcello. "I'm coming to Rome tomorrow and I need your help. Tell Andrea and Renzo I'll need their help, too."

"Of course we will help. All of Rome will help, you will see."

Then he rang up his friend, Savio, and explained the situation and the favor he needed.

"*Assolutamente*!" Savio said. "I will do anything I can."

Then he called Bird. "Can you watch my dog for a few days?"

"Why? You making another trip on Dante's Excellent Adventure?"

He told Bird his plan to go to Rome and cook for Charly to prove his love.

"D," Bird said, "you might be the craziest man I know, but I hope it works."

An hour later, as Dante packed, his phone rang. He picked it up and saw that it was Gloria calling. His first thought was that she must have been deleting him from her contacts list and accidentally called.

"Hello, this is Dante," he said.

"Hello Dante. It's Gloria."

He sat on the bed next to his bag. "Hi Gloria. What can I do for you?"

"I'd like to meet with you, if I may. Are you available any time soon?"

"I'm kind of busy. I'm leaving for Europe tonight."

"Can I possibly come to your house? It's important. And if you're leaving the country, I'd like to take care of this before you go. It won't take long."

"Can we just do it over the phone?"

"Not really. I understand you're probably very busy, but I promise this will be fast."

"Uhm, okay. I'm here if you want to come by this morning."

"I'll be there in fifteen minutes."

True to her word, Gloria arrived fifteen minutes later. When Dante opened the door, he noticed that something was different. She was smiling. An actual genuine smile.

"Thank you for agreeing to meet with me, Dante. I appreciate it."

Dante offered her a chair. "Can I get you anything?"

"No thank you," she said. "As I said, I'll make this brief." She took a deep breath. "Dante, John thought the world of you. Not just as a chef and business partner. You were a friend. And I'm afraid I haven't honored his friendship with you by the way I've acted."

"Well, I certainly bear some responsibility for the tension in our relationship, too."

"In any case, I know John would not have wanted to see Pane Rubato close. And you've worked so hard and done great things to make it such a special place. John would be so proud. And I want to honor his memory by keeping it open. And what's more, I want to give you the other half of the restaurant so you'll have sole ownership. I've had all the papers drawn up."

She handed Dante a small stack of documents.

Dante stood silent. All the words Gloria had said just seemed to be colliding into each other, like some kind of smash-up derby, in his head.

Finally, he said, "You what?"

Gloria laughed. "I want to give you your restaurant."

"Really?"

"Yes, really. I just need a few signatures from you, and it'll all be settled."

"But what made you change your mind?"

"The day you signed the closing papers. When I had that frittata, I had an extraordinary feeling that John was there with us. And so much of the pain I'd been feeling just floated off of me. I didn't quite know what was happening, so I had to leave. Over the past few days, it all became very clear to me what needed to be done. This is what John would have wanted, and it's what I want."

Dante shook his head, still not sure this was all real. "What can I say? I am incredibly grateful. This is so kind. Thank you."

"I have to tell you, Dante, I feel thirty years younger. So thank *you*."

Five minutes later, Gloria was out the door with the promise to visit Pane Rubato often.

Dante called Bird. "You are not going to believe this."

He told Bird all about Gloria's visit.

"That is just some crazy ass shit, D."

"So call Sal, and between the two of you, hire back as much of the staff as you can. We can re-open tomorrow."

"I'm on it, D. Man, if this isn't a good omen for your trip to Rome,

I don't know what is."

"Let's hope so."

A day later, Dante was at Rome's Fiumincino airport, embracing Renzo and Andrea.

"You are a big shot TV star now, eh?" Renzo said.

"My show hasn't even been on the air yet."

Andrea took Dante's bag. "But you *will* be a big star." He smiled.

"We take you to our parent's house," Renzo said. "You are hungry?"

"Starving."

"I hope we can get out of here quickly," Andrea said. "The taxi drivers are striking to protest a new tax. The streets of Rome are *un caos completo*"—complete chaos.

They got to Andrea's car, a little light green Fiat, circa 1990. "She doesn't look like much," he said, "but she handles Rome's streets as well as anything." He crawled through the driver's side window. "I have to weld the doors shut because they come open when I drive."

Renzo maneuvered himself into the back seat and Dante slid into the passenger side front seat.

As they drove—more like crawled in the gridlock—through Rome, the evening light fading, Dante was surprised how much of the city came back to him. Such a beautiful place. Perfect, he thought, for winning the heart of his true love. Suddenly, he hit a wall of tiredness.

I can't believe you're doing this. It's never going to work.

But if he really believed this couldn't work, he wouldn't be here. The worst case was simply no change in the situation. But if it did work, he'd have his true love forever. If Charly rejected him, he'd just have to go home and figure out a way to put his life back together.

Once they got to their destination, Marcello, his wife, Anna, Nonna Cara, Velia, and Fabiana all greeted Dante with hugs and kisses. Nonna Cara could stand only for a moment and her hands trembled. She was so much thinner than when Dante last saw her.

Dante thanked Marcello and his family for letting him stay and for their willingness to help. "*Grazie per avermi lasciato rimanere qui e per la vostra disponibilitá ad aiutarmi.*" Aside to Marcello, Dante said, "Is your mother okay?"

"She will not eat," Marcello said. "She does not sleep. She cries all the time and prays for God to take her to my father."

"Maybe I can help."

"I don't know how."

"Let me cook dinner tonight."

"You are exhausted. I cannot let you cook."

"Please. As my way to thank you. And you'll see. Nonna Cara will change before your eyes."

Anna said she had bought dried cod that morning that he should use. Dante decided to make *bacala con peperoncino*, dried cod fish with red chili flakes, and *tonnarelli cacio e pepe*, pasta with sheep's cheese and black pepper.

While Dante cooked, Nonna Cara, who spoke no English, told many stories of her late husband. Dante had heard them all many times before when he lived in Rome, but that she still missed her husband was apparent in every word of her memories.

"When I was a young woman," she said, "the man I loved was going to leave for America. I was sure he would ask me to marry him, so when I heard he was leaving, it nearly killed me. How could this beautiful man who I had given all my heart leave me behind? The day before he was to leave, I learned an evil man who wanted me for himself told my Vincenzo that I had slept with him. I found the liar and slapped that troll's face so hard I think I broke his teeth. Then I ran to Vincenzo and nearly split his head open for believing the liar. After that day, he never again left my side. Until the day he died." She wiped a tear from her eye and Andrea hugged her.

When the food was ready, Marcello poured everyone a glass of Frascati, a local dry white wine. He held up his glass and toasted. "To love."

"Nonna, eat," Andrea said.

"I will keep it for later. I'm not hungry right now."

"That's what you always say but then you never eat. Please, have just a little. For me so I don't worry."

"For you." She took a bite and closed her eyes and said it was the most wonderful thing she had ever eaten. "*È la cosa più buona che abbia mai mangiato.*"

Marcello, Anna, Andrea and Renzo exchanged shocked looks.

After she had eaten half her plate of food, Marcello said, "I have not seen her eat like that in a year."

"It is true, isn't it?" Anna said. "You cure broken hearts."

Dante nodded. "I think so."

"When I was a little girl, my grandmother used to tell me stories about a man in Palermo who could do this. I thought it was just another folktale."

As Nonna Cara sopped up the peppery oil on her plate with her bread, Marcello said, "God bless you, Dante. Whatever you need from me and my family, you will have."

"Well, you know, I do need some help." He then told them all why he was in Rome, his nonna's counsel, and the meal he must make to get Charly. "I know it sounds crazy, but I have to try."

"*L'amore è pazzo*," Nonna Cara said—love is crazy.

Marcello nodded. "And beautiful. I have been with my wife for twenty-five years and we work together every single day. Still, her face is like my own sun, lighting up all of my life. If all the world could have this kind of love, there would be no war."

"I hope I can have that kind of love."

"You will! You have a heart as big as Rome. One thing I know is that if you give love, you get love. And we will help."

Dante smiled. "Okay, so here's my plan."

He said that they would go to the conference and Greenjeans' presentation, after which Andrea, posing as a business executive would invite Greenjeans to a dinner meeting. "At Savio's. He's going to keep

Greenjeans there and ply him with aperitifs while he waits for you to show up."

He asked Velia if she could pretend to be from an Italian government agency interested in establishing ties with Speaker Farello and set up a meeting with Charly at Marcello's restaurant. "At the same time Greenjeans is at Savio's."

"*Si*," Velia said. "It will be fun."

"Great. So Greenjeans will be waiting at Savio's out of the way while I cook for Charly. Assuming it's okay if I cook at Quattro Uccelli, Marcello."

"Of course!" Marcello said. "I will be honored if you will use my kitchen."

"What about me?" Renzo said. "Maybe I can be at Savio's and slip some laxative into his aperitif. That will make sure he stays out of the way."

Marcello and Anna rolled their eyes and Dante laughed.

"It's a nice thought, but I think we'll need you to direct all of this. You'll be the one behind the scenes making it all work together smoothly."

"Okay," Renzo said. "I will be the director."

Dante smiled. "Thank you. All of you. You have no idea how much this means to me. You may actually be saving my life."

Dante stroked his chin. "I'll need a disguise so I don't get spotted."

Renzo frowned. "Why will you go in at all?"

"You're going to need me to point out Greenjeans."

Renzo shook his head. "It's too risky. We will figure another way."

"Oh, no," Dante said. "There's no way I'm waiting outside while all this happens. I'll go out of my mind."

Renzo stood. "But—"

"I have to go in," Dante said. He stood. "I have to."

"Okay," Renzo said.

"And I can't just show up in a wig and fake mustache."

"What about the fat suit?" Andrea said.

Dante raised an eyebrow. "The fat suit?"

"The one I wore in our film, *Uomo Grasso*."

"Will that work on me?"

"It can be done," Fabiana said. "But it will take many hours."

Dante nodded. "As long as it's done in time to get to the conference at one o'clock. By the way, how do we get to the conference? It's at Nuova Fiera."

"We take my car," Renzo said.

"It won't start half the time," Andrea said. "We should take my car."

"*Donnicciola*," Renzo said. "Your car doors do not open. You expect him to squeeze through your window in the fat suit?"

"*Forse*"—maybe. "No?"

"Hmm," Dante said. "And the taxi drivers will still be on strike tomorrow?"

"*Si*," Marcello said. "There has been no settlement."

"Then Renzo's car will have to do."

Fabiana turned to Dante. "I think it will be best if we start first thing in the morning at my flat."

"7:00?" Renzo said.

"That will be enough time," Fabiana said.

"Okay, Dante I will pick you up here at 6:30 and bring you to Fabiana's," Andrea said. "From there we will go to Nuova Fiera."

After the twins and their girlfriends left, and Marcello and family went to bed for the night, Dante set the alarm on his phone for 6:00 A.M., then settled on the couch.

"Nonna," he said to himself. "I hope you're right and that this all works." He closed his eyes and within minutes he was out.

Chapter 36

The next morning, Dante dozed away with a little smile on his face. In his dreams, he was at his mom's house in Des Moines. The entire family was there around a big table filled with food: pasta, bread, vegetables, meat. Even Nonna was there. They all held up their glasses of wine and toasted, "To Dante and Charly. *Cent'anni*"—a hundred years.

Next to him, Charly sat smiling and they kissed. Nonna said to Charly, "Let me see the ring again." Charly held out her hand and Nonna said, "It looks better on you than it ever did on my fat fingers."

They all laughed and then his nephew, Frankie, made a beeping sound. No one but Dante seemed to notice. Dante tried to tell him to stop but no one heard him. The beeping got more and more intense until Dante opened his eyes.

The morning light peeked in through the windows. Dante sat up and took a deep breath. He whispered, "Let me find my Charly today and let my plans all work."

After he cleaned, up he went to the kitchen where Nonna Cara poured him an espresso and handed him a brioche roll with egg, prosciutto di Parma, and fresh mozzarella.

"You will need your energy today," she said.

"Thank you." While Dante had his breakfast, he and Nonna Cara talked about the meal Dante would make for Charly.

"It's an easy choice. The first food of mine she ever ate was gnocchi with gorgonzola cream sauce."

"*Farai gli gnocchi a mano*?"—You will make the gnocchi by hand?

"Yes, so I can put all of my love into each bite."

Nonna Cara smiled. "*Che bella*"—how beautiful.

He finished his sandwich a minute before Andrea arrived. As he left the house, Nonna Cara wished him luck. "*Buona fortuna, caro.*"

The ride to Fabiana's was not too bad, but slower than usual according to Andrea, who said, "It is already getting congested. We will want to leave plenty of time to get to the Nuova Fiera."

Shortly after dropping Dante off at Fabiana's, Andrea said, "I must go change my appearance, too, so I can look dignified. I will be back at noon."

In the next five hours at Fabiana's, Dante transformed into a balding three hundred-pound man with rosy cheeks, a mustache, and three chins. His olive suit strained to keep him all in. Dante barely recognized himself when he looked in the mirror.

Velia and Andrea arrived at 11:30. As soon as they got a look at Dante, they howled.

"Oh, it is *perfetto*," Velia said.

Andrea clapped his hands. "Fabiana, you are a master." To Dante, he said, "No one will know it is you in there."

Velia and Andrea were both dressed smartly in business suits, Velia's blue pinstriped and Andrea's grey herringbone. The blue streaks in Andrea's now-tame hair were gone.

"You two look great," Dante said. "But Andrea, you look too young to be a company president. Fabiana, can you make him look a little older?"

Fabiana nodded and quickly went to work adding a touch of gray to Andrea's hair and a hint of wrinkles around his eyes.

"Perfect!" Dante said.

"Now you look mid-thirties," Fabiana said.

Renzo handed Andrea a small stack of business cards he'd just pulled off the printer. "Don't forget these." The cards read Roberto Andolini, President of VerdeItalia; they even included an e-mail address, and phone number. "The phone number is mine," Renzo said. "The email address will just bounce if he tries to send to it."

"I'm so glad you thought of this."

Renzo handed Velia printouts of a picture of Charly he'd gotten from Dante's laptop. "Here, so you can make sure you have the right person when you see her." He looked at his watch. "You must go. It is already 12:15."

Two minutes later, Dante sat in the passenger seat of Renzo's blue 1970s BMW 316. Renzo turned the key but nothing happened. He tried again. Still nothing.

Renzo slapped the steering wheel. "*Merda*!"

Andrea came to the window. "We do not have time for this. Get him to my car."

They rushed over to Andrea's Fiat.

"I'm supposed to go through the window?" Dante said.

"It's the only way," Andrea said.

Andrea and Velia pulled from one side while Renzo and Fabiana pushed, stuffing Dante into the front seat of Andrea's car.

"Careful not to tear him," Fabiana said.

Finally, everyone was settled and Andrea put the car into gear and they tore off. Renzo and Fabiana followed on her scooter. Andrea grinned as he weaved around people, buses, and cars. He honked at a truck pulling out in front of him. He yelled out the window, "*Stronzo!*" He turned to Dante. "It is crazy out here today." Velia screamed and Andrea faced front again just in time to see an old man standing on the sidewalk. He jerked the wheel and flung Dante into the door. "But I can get anywhere in this city fast. My friends all call me Speed Racer. You know, after the cartoon."

The way they dodged in and out of streets and alleys, Dante was more convinced that his nickname should be Crash. All of a sudden, everyone was thrown forward when the car stopped. Nothing moved on the road in front of them.

Andrea pounded the dashboard. "The road is blocked." They were completely pinned in with nowhere to go.

Fabiana pulled up next to the car. "I will go up ahead and see what's going on," she said, then scooted ahead between cars, and around the curve in the road.

A minute later, Andrea's phone rang. It was Renzo and he said that the backup was caused by a bus that had collided with a truck. The accident, he said, had nearly been cleared enough for traffic to get through.

After what seemed like a year, they finally got clear of the gridlock and Andrea said, "We are so late!" He hit the accelerator and they rocketed down a narrow road, walled in by shuttered buildings. "Out of my way!" he shouted out the window again. "I carry a man in love!"

Dante gripped the dashboard. "I'd like to get there alive."

"You missed your turn!" Velia yelled.

Dante turned back to see Fabiana making the correct turn, Renzo on back waving for Andrea to follow.

"*Merda*! Hold on." He stomped on the breaks and they did a one-eighty degree turn.

Several twists and turns later, the car came to an abrupt halt in front of the Nuova Fiera conference center. It was already 1:15.

"I probably shouldn't be seen crawling out the window of your car out front," Dante said. "Can we go around the corner?"

Andrea sped around the corner and screeched to a halt. Again Renzo and Fabiana pulled while Velia and Andrea pushed. This time Dante felt something come loose near his backside. "I think my butt is coming off," he said.

"Your butt?" Renzo said.

"His *culo*," Fabiana said.

"I know what it means, but how does it come off?"

Once out of the car, Dante wiggled his butt which didn't feel as secure as it had before. But the others assured him it looked okay from the outside.

They all headed toward the front of the conference center; Dante's thighs zip-zip-zipped as he went.

When they got to the front doors, it was nearly one-thirty. When they tried to go in, a Roman god in a blue blazer stopped them and asked for their badges. "*Dove sono i vostri distintivi?*"

"*Non ci siamo ancora registrati,*" Velia said—We haven't registered, yet.

The staffer pointed to a large sign that said *Registro*. Forty people must have been lined up to register. After another half hour, Dante, Velia, and Andrea got to the front of the line and learned three day-passes would cost $450.00. Small price for the chance to show Charly how he felt.

Once inside, Dante said, "The session is almost over, but if we hurry we might be able to catch them afterwards." He picked up his pace, but then he felt it. His left butt cheek came loose and was traveling down his pant leg. Velia gasped. He grabbed a hold of the wayward buttock and held it in place long enough to get to a restroom where he and Andrea ducked inside and went to a stall. Through a series of ties and tucks they got his butt close to where it had been before. When he came out of the bathroom, Velia gave him a quick check.

"You're a little crooked," she said.

"Well, it's going to have to stay that way or we'll miss Charly." He pulled his belly up and walked as quickly as his cockeyed *culo* would allow.

By the time they found Greenjeans's session, it was over. People milled about and Dante spotted Greenjeans talking with a few other people. No Charly in sight. He leaned over to Velia and Andrea. "See the man in the blue jacket? That's Greenjeans, the boyfriend."

"He's very beautiful," Velia said.

"Oh, well that makes me feel a lot better about all of this."

"Sorry. But underneath all of that, you are beautiful, too."

"Thanks." Dante smiled a fat smile.

Renzo and Fabiana walked up, Renzo grinning.

"How did you get in?" Dante said.

"We snuck in through the loading dock."

Andrea pointed out Greenjeans to his brother and Fabiana. Still no sign of Charly.

Dante put his hand on Andrea's shoulder. "Time to go in." He straightened his belly. "I'll come with you."

They walked over to Greenjeans and his entourage. "Excuse me Signor Lancaster," Andrea said. "I am Roberto Andolini, President of VerdeItalia." He shook Greenjeans' hand then gave him his card. He motioned to Dante, "This is my associate, Luca Brasi. Do you have a moment?"

Greenjeans nodded and excused himself from the group he'd been talking with.

"I am hoping," Andrea said, "to meet with you for a dinner this week and propose for you a partnership."

"I'm sorry," Greenjeans said. "I'm leaving tomorrow for Tuscany, a little vacation."

Leaving? Tuscany? Tomorrow?

Dante took a deep breath and said to himself, *Calm*.

He'd just have to cook for Charly tonight. His life depended on it.

Andrea looked at Dante, and his eyes pleaded for help.

"Perhaps," Dante said, "we can meet tonight—"

"I'm afraid I have a previous appointment." He paused a moment, then said, "But you know, I have to be over at the Trevi Fountain tonight. I could give you maybe a half hour before my business there. At, say, 7:00. How does that sound?"

Son of a bitch! Dante thought. He's going to propose tonight.

"That will be perfect," Andrea said. "There is a café near there. Casa della Panna, about a block away at Via delle Muratte."

"That sounds fine." He pulled his phone from the front pocket of his man purse. "Let me just put this in my calendar." He thumbed the device. "Seven o'clock. That was Casa della Panna. And the street was

Via delle Morat?"

"M-u-r-a-t-t-e."

"Thanks. Then I will see you at seven."

Greenjeans' face lit up. Dante looked over to see Charly walking right toward them. The blue of her eyes seemed to light up the entire hallway. His heart rate jumped and the ache to hug her nearly overwhelmed him.

"Charly," Greenjeans said, "I'd like you to meet Mr. Andolini, and Mr. Brasi."

She shook Andrea's hand. "Nice to meet you." She then reached over and took Dante's squishy hand.

Dante cleared his throat. "*Piacere.*"

"Sorry to interrupt," Charly said, then turned to Greenjeans. "I'll let you get back to your conversation."

"No, no," Andrea said. "We are finished. *Signor*, I look forward to meeting you later." He nodded toward Charly. "*Signora*, very nice to meet you. *Ciao.*"

They hurried over to the group. Dante said, "He's proposing tonight." Everyone's eyes bulged. Fabiana put her hand over her mouth. To Velia, Dante said, "But I set a meeting for seven. We have to get Charly to Quattro Uccelli then."

"*Si*," Andrea said. "*Deve essere là alle sette*"—she must be there at seven.

"She leaves right now," Velia said.

As Charly walked away down the corridor, Greenjeans said to her, "Don't forget: Trevi Fountain at 8:00." Greenjeans held up his phone. "Text me if you need anything."

"I'll see you tonight," Charly said. She walked off and Velia followed.

Dante waddled in the same direction as the others, but within seconds he had fallen yards behind.

Renzo came up from behind. "Dante, your *culo*."

Just then, Dante felt his bad cheek slip down toward the back of his knee. Renzo grabbed it and put it back where it was supposed to be.

"People are staring," Dante said.

"Think of how they will look if your *culo* falls out of your pants. Fab, you have to fix him. We'll catch up to Vel in a minute."

The four of them ducked into the men's restroom and fixed Dante's butt up as quickly as they could. How bad it looked at this point, he didn't care. Out of the restroom and past a few raised eyebrows, they rushed in the direction they saw Velia and Charly go. They got all the way out front and saw Charly get into a car and pull away. Velia stood at the curb.

"Please tell me," Dante said, "she got the meeting."

When he finally got to Velia, she said, "I talked to her, but she says she cannot meet. She was surprised I knew who she was. She says she is not here in an official capacity so cannot meet on behalf of the Speaker."

Velia sighed deeply. "I'm sorry," she said.

Chapter 37

Dante pressed his palms to his temples. He wanted to stay positive and believe it would all work, but he couldn't help feeling everything was slipping away.

"We have to figure out how to get Charly to the restaurant at seven." He bit his thumb knuckle. "But we don't even know where she is, where she's going." His head throbbed and his stomach churned. "What time is it, anyway?"

"Almost 2:30," Velia said.

"So we would have to get her to Quattro Uccelli in four-and-a-half hours. I still have to cook, too. I just don't think this is going to work. I can't see how—"

"Wait," Fabiana said. "What if you appear at the *Fontana di Trevi* at eight o'clock along with the boyfriend. It will be awkward, but the choice will be there for her."

"I can't even imagine how mad she'd be at me. And when my nonna came to me, she said Charly can't see me before I cook for her."

"And you must cook for her?" Andrea said.

"That's what Nonna said."

"Maybe," Renzo said, "that is not meant to be. Maybe your nonna made a mistake. Or you misunderstood her."

"No," Dante said. "I have to cook for Charly. I have to."

"Then," Andrea said, "that is what you will do."

"But how?" Fabiana said.

At the moment, Dante didn't have the slightest idea how he was going to cook for Charly. Nonna had given him the mandate but no direction on how to do it. Then, like a lightning bolt, an idea shot into his mind. "What if we steal Greenjeans' phone and text Charly to meet him at your father's restaurant?"

"What do you mean?" Velia said.

"We tell her that there's been a change in plans. Now he wants to meet at Quattro Uccelli instead of the Trevi Fountain."

"Yes!" Andrea said.

"I think this will work!" Renzo said.

They all went back inside the conference center, Andrea, Velia, and Dante through the front door, Renzo and Fabiana through the loading dock. The plan was for the five of them to split up to look for Greenjeans. Once someone found him, they'd all converge and do their best to get the phone.

Dante duckwalked the hallways, and as he looked for Greenjeans, he found it difficult not to focus on how hard it would be to steal the phone, the risks his friends were taking, and what he would do if the plan didn't work. A half hour passed with no sign of Greenjeans and no text from any of the others that they had found him. He had only four hours until 7:00. He still had to get back to Marcello's—which might take as much as an hour—and get out of his disguise. He'd need to shower all the goop off, which would take at least fifteen minutes. Then he had to get to Quattro Uccelli, and make the gnocchi. Baking the potatoes alone would take forty-five minutes. The finished gnocchi should dry for an hour. That was about three hours in all, which meant they had one hour to get the phone and text Charly. Dante clenched his jaw so tight that he thought his teeth might crack from the pressure.

He stopped outside a session that was just letting out. As people walked by, some not-so-stealthily eying his heft, he visualized seeing Charly at Quattro Uccelli, her eating his food, and saying she loved him. The thought made his heart swell.

That's when his phone buzzed. A text message from Fabiana that she had seen Greenjeans heading into the exhibition hall. Dante hurried to the escalator, which his girth completely blocked. Another text from Fabiana said that she and Andrea had found each other and that they were now in the southwest corner under a black and gold sign for a company called SunPower. A flurry of texts and five minutes later, all were together on the trade show floor.

Greenjeans was engrossed in a conversation at the SunPower booth. His man purse was tucked under his arm.

Dante said in Italian, "I saw him take his phone from the front pocket of his bag earlier. Do you think we should take the entire bag or try to get the phone from it?"

Andrea shook his head. "Neither will be easy."

"We need those street kids who hang around the tourists and rob them blind," Renzo said. "They never get caught and the tourists either never know they've been robbed or they can never catch the little thieves."

"Maybe," Fabiana said, "we can use one of their tricks. One of the kids distracts the mark and holds a newspaper or magazine up to their face while another slips behind and picks the pocket."

"That might work," Dante said.

Velia removed her suit jacket to reveal her white V-neck top and generous bust. "Fab and I will do the distracting. One of you will have to do the picking."

"I don't think I could sneak up on a dead man," Dante said. "And Andrea, he's already met you."

"I will try," Renzo said.

"Velia," Andrea said, "what will you say to him?"

She thought a moment. "Ah! I will tell him I missed his presentation this afternoon and ask if he will be putting a copy on his company's website."

"That sounds perfect," Dante said. "Now we just have to wait for the right chance."

And so they did as Greenjeans talked and talked and talked. At one point, Renzo said, "Does this man ever shut up?"

Finally, after twenty minutes, Greenjeans said, "Thank you so much for the opportunity to meet with you. I look forward to talking more with you."

Renzo leaned in. "I bet he does."

Greenjeans turned and walked in the opposite direction of the group.

"Okay," Renzo said. "Let's move in."

When Velia and Fabiana caught up to him after a few yards, Velia said in English, "Excuse me. Mr. Langston?"

Greenjeans turned and smiled. "Yes?" When he saw Dante standing back, he waved. Dante smiled and waved back.

Velia and Fabiana stepped up as close as they could, Velia nearly putting her breasts on his arm. The rest of the conversation was inaudible from Dante's vantage point, but he watched as closely as he could without seeming obvious. As Velia spoke—and clearly flirted—Renzo moved in behind Greenjeans who, perhaps out of suspicion, tucked his man purse under his arm. Any attempt to touch it now was impossible.

The three returned from their unsuccessful endeavor.

"I'm not sure this is going to work," Dante said. "And the more I hang around, the more suspicious he's going to become. I'm not exactly inconspicuous in this getup. Maybe you should take me back to your parents' house. I can change and go to the restaurant to start cooking. Then maybe I'll come up with an idea that *will* work."

"We cannot give up so quickly," Andrea said.

"That was just one try," Renzo added.

"I don't know," Dante said. "At this point I'm so fried, nothing makes sense anymore."

Renzo's eyes grew wide. "Look, Greenjeans just went into the bathroom. I have an idea."

Dante grabbed his arm. "What are you going to do?"

"It will be best if you go now. And quickly. Meet me back at the car."

"I know this look," Andrea said. "We'd better get out of here."

"Renzo—" Dante said, but Renzo continued without turning around.

Dante, Andrea, Velia, and Fabiana walked as quickly out of the conference center as they could. When they got to the car, Dante squeezed through the window. Just as he righted himself in the back seat, Renzo came running from the back of the building, grinning and holding Greenjeans purse.

"*Andiamo*!" he shouted—Let's go! "Fab, go! I will ride with Andrea!"

Fabiana pulled on her helmet, got on her scooter, and took off.

Velia shot into the back seat next to Dante. Andrea scrambled to the driver side and hopped in. A second later, Renzo dove into the front seat head first, crashing into his twin brother, who fired up the engine and slammed the car into gear.

Renzo roared with laughter. "I caught him with his pants down. Literally! When I got to the bathroom, I saw that he had gone into one of the stalls and put his bag on the floor. I went to the stall next to him, reached under, grabbed the bag, and ran as fast as I could out toward the loading dock. I don't think he even had an idea of what direction I went."

"Renzo, you're crazy," Dante said.

Renzo grinned. "But I got the bag."

He handed it to Dante, who said, "Oh, man this is so wrong." He opened the purse and looked through it. No phone in the main compartment. Or the front zipper pocket. "Shit," he said. "It's not here."

"Are you sure?" Renzo said.

Dante handed the bag back to Renzo who dumped the contents onto his lap. No phone. Then Renzo said. "Oh no."

"What?" the others said in unison.

He held up a passport. "Unless Greenjeans is French . . ." He opened the passport and dropped his head. "I stole the wrong bag."

Chapter 38

As Andrea drove back to his parents' house, Dante ripped off his fake chins, taking a certain satisfaction in the pain it caused his face. "Well, if this isn't the universe telling me I've made a mistake, I don't know what is."

"I made the mistake," Renzo said.

"No, it was my stupid idea to steal the phone. I can't believe I could even stoop so low. And now some poor French guy has lost his passport. Maybe coming to Rome was the mistake. Maybe I'm just not meant to be with Charly."

Velia put her hand on Dante's arm. "You did not make a mistake coming to Rome. You are in love and you only prove it more by being here. We still have"—she looked at her watch—"five hours until Greenjeans is to meet Charly at Fontana di Trevi. We will come up with something."

Dante took a deep breath. "I don't know. Right now, I just want to calm my mind. I don't want to think about anything." He leaned back and closed his eyes and for the rest of the ride back to Marcello's he floated in a black hole where his thoughts drained off into nothingness.

Thirty minutes later, Dante was in Marcello's bathroom, tearing his scalp off, pulling his belly over his head, dropping his ass to the floor. Then he got in the hot shower and as he washed himself clean of his alter ego, Luca Brasi, and all that went with him, his mind cleared. He knew what he must do. Greenjeans—Dante caught himself. From now on he would only refer to Hugh by his real name. *Hugh* would be at Casa della Panna at 7:00. Dante would simply go there (it was less than half a mile from Quattro Uccelli, so he'd just walk it), and ask Gr—Hugh, man-to-man for a chance to see Charly at Quattro Uccelli. For a half hour, even just fifteen minutes. It would settle for everyone involved the question of whether Charly and Dante were meant to be together. If only, Dante would argue, to give himself closure. It would be a hard sell to convince Hugh that Charly must be given this choice. But he had no other alternative at this point. He was done with trickery and deceit and this was the best, most adult course of action. If Hugh said no, he would press the issue, and if he had to, he would wait right there at the Trevi Fountain. Yes, as Nonna said, he might lose Charly forever if she saw him before he served his food, but that was the chance he'd have to take. As the situation stood at the moment, Charly was already lost to him and would remain so if she didn't know he had come to Rome for her.

Out of the bathroom, Dante picked a few things from his suitcase to wear when he saw Charly: a cream short sleeve silk crew neck, black pants, and his Italian black loafers. He'd change into them after he was done cooking. Then he went to the kitchen where Andrea and Renzo talked with Nonna Cara.

Andrea said, "*Sappiamo quanto siate dispiaciuti per il passaporto del francese*"—we know how sorry you are about the Frenchman's passport. "So Velia and Fabiana have gone back to the conference to return the bag to the Lost and Found."

"Thank you," Dante said.

Renzo grinned. "And we have come up with a plan."

"So have I," Dante said. Renzo, Andrea and Nonna nodded expectantly. "I'm going to talk to Hugh at Casa della Panna—"

"*Chi è Hugh*?" Nonna Cara said—who is Hugh?

Andrea leaned over. "It's the boyfriend."

Nonna's eyes bulged.

Dante continued. "And ask him to let me see Charly—"

Nonna Cara shook her head vigorously. "No, no, no, no."

Dante held up his hand. "Hear me out." He then explained what he would say and his reasons for believing this was the best plan. "It's what I need to do," he said.

Nonna Cara again shook her head. "No, no, no."

"Dante," Andrea said, "You cannot believe this will work."

Renzo made a praying gesture, then said, "I would kill you before I would give you fifteen *seconds* with the woman I love."

"Let us tell you our plan," Andrea said.

"I appreciate your wanting to help," Dante said. "And all the help you've already given me. But I've thought this through, and I'm going to talk to Hugh, face-to-face, man-to-man. I will probably need someone to bring Charly to Quattro Uccelli after I've talked to Hugh. If one of you could do that, I'd appreciate it."

"And," Andrea said, "you expect Greenjeans to let you take her to the restaurant?"

"That's what I'm going to ask for."

"Why would he say yes to this?" Renzo said.

"Because he needs to know the answer as much as I do. He needs to know that Charly chooses him, not me. That Charly loves him, not me. The only way either of us will know is for him to let me see her."

Andrea blew out a long breath. "I can see you have made up your mind."

Renzo threw his hands up in disbelief. "But—"

Andrea put his hand on his brother's arm. "It is for Dante to decide."

"Thank you. I think I'm going to head over to Quattro Uccelli now."

"You remember how to get there?" Renzo said.

Dante smiled. "I walked it every day for a year."

He arrived at the restaurant twenty minutes later. It hadn't changed much in the fourteen years since he'd seen it. Out front, simple marble-topped tables (they would be covered with white tablecloths for the dinner service) sat empty in the afternoon sun. The patronless dining room—small, quiet, and in the evening hours, softly lit—looked almost identical to when Dante worked there. The two side walls were painted yellow, the back wall sponge-painted orange. The memories of himself as a young man with the whole world before him flooded his mind. Though he'd accomplished so much, seen great success, since the day he arrived in Rome the first time, he couldn't help longing for those younger days.

Anna came over to Dante and said in Italian, "Marcello is waiting for you in the kitchen, and I am saying prayers for you."

"Thank you, Anna."

The small kitchen was quiet except for a couple of cooks prepping for the night.

Marcello held out his hands and said he had cleared a space for Dante to cook. "*Dovresti essere in grado di lavorare in pace qu*"—You should be able to work here in peace.

The space had a large prep table. Pots and pans hung above. It was only ten feet from the cooktops and ovens of the main kitchen

"You sure I won't be in the way?" Dante said.

"Yes, quite sure. And please help yourself to whatever you need."

Dante closed his eyes and focused on his task. He thought of Charly's face. He gathered his potatoes and placed them in the oven. While he waited for the potatoes, he looked around the kitchen, and noticed a bag of chickpea flour. Maybe he should make panelle, a Sicilian chickpea fritter, as an appetizer. Should he top them with something? He went to the walk-in cooler and found some arugula that looked good. Arugula-walnut pesto would be a nice addition to the panelle.

He gathered up all his ingredients and started with the panelle. He poured water, olive oil, and salt into a large sauté pan, then slowly whisked in the chickpea flour until it thickened. As he continued to whisk, he imagined holding Charly in his arms. When the batter started to pull away from the sides of the pan, he turned it out onto an oiled quarter baking sheet and spread it evenly, filling the pan. He'd let that cool and set. He'd fry a few pieces when Charly arrived.

Next came the pesto. As he toasted the walnuts on the stovetop, he thought of Charly's eyes, her smile. When the walnuts just started to brown, he dumped them in a food processor. He added two cloves of garlic and pulsed them together until they were roughly chopped. Finally he added arugula, extra virgin olive oil, lemon juice and parmesan and mixed them all together until they were smooth.

By the time he finished the panelle and the pesto, it was time to pull the potatoes from the oven. He scooped out the insides of the potatoes and ran them through a china cap to make sure they were fine enough for the gnocchi dough. He added the flour and as he kneaded the dough, he thought of kissing Charly after she told him she loved him. He thought of caressing her beautiful face. He thought of gazing into her gorgeous eyes.

Dante finished the gnocchi and set them aside to dry. It was 6:20. The bulk of the cooking complete, Dante changed his clothes. Anna and Marcello said that Renzo and Andrea would meet him at Casa della Panna. They wished him luck as he left.

During the walk, Dante's mind was filled with what he'd say to Hugh. The words, the arguments. He imagined what Hugh might say and how he'd respond. It seemed like barely five minutes passed when he found himself standing in front of Casa della Panna.

"Dante?"

He looked over to see Hugh sitting at a table out front.

Dante walked over and pointed to the chair opposite Hugh. "May I?"

Hugh furrowed his brow. "Actually, I have a meeting in about a minute."

Dante sat and said, "That meeting was a fake."

"What?"

"My nephew set the meeting with you. I was his associate, the fat man, Luca Brasi"

Hugh's eyes registered *Does Not Compute*. "Why would you—"

"I came here to talk to you about something that's very important to both of us."

"Let me guess. Charly." He stared coldly into Dante's eyes, then finished the last of his cappuccino.

"Yes. I know you're a decent and reasonable person. I'd like to ask you a favor."

"Which is?"

"I would like to see Charly for just fifteen minutes. To talk to her." He expected Hugh to protest, but he remained silent. "So I know. So you know. So she knows, for that matter, where we all stand."

Again, Hugh did not reply.

The silence burned Dante's ears. "I need to know," he said, "that she doesn't love me."

Hugh sighed. Finally, he said, "Dante, Charly's a very smart woman. You think she doesn't know what my plans are here? You think she doesn't know that I'm going to propose tonight? You don't think she would have come all the way to Rome with me to say no, do you? You already expressed your feelings. You already had your chance. The question of which one of us she wants to be with has already been answered by the simple fact that she's here with me now."

He paused to yawn. "I know this is hard for you, but it's time for you to step aside."

"I can't just step aside. Charly has never said she *doesn't* love me and I'd think you'd want to know for sure, too."

Hugh yawned very loudly, then slowly shook his head, accenting each long sweep with a *no*. "No, no, no, no, no." When he stopped his head, he had to steady himself in his chair. "Tonight . . . I . . . am . . . going . . . to . . . pro . . . pose." He closed his eyes.

Renzo and Andrea appeared from behind Dante. Renzo said, "*Questo sarebbe il momento giusto per ritornare al ristorante*"—Now would be a good time for you to go back to the restaurant.

Hugh's eyes remained closed and now he had a goofy smile on his face.

"What did you two do?"

Andrea smiled. "We slipped a little sleepy-sleepy into his coffee."

Renzo shook his head. "Serves him right, ordering a cappuccino in the evening."

"How did—"

"I distracted the waiter," Andrea said.

"And I slipped the powder from Nonna's anxiety medicine into the coffee," Renzo said. "Now get out of here." He took Greenjeans' arm.

Andrea pulled Dante's arm to ease him up. "We will take care of Greenjeans and let him sleep. We hired a horse-drawn carriage to take Charly to Quattro Uccelli. Fabiana is waiting at the Trevi Fountain and will tell Charly that Greenjeans has sent the carriage for her. Mama and papa will have a table all ready for her and tell her that the person she is to meet will appear shortly. The rest is up to you."

"Now, how do you Americans say it?" Renzo said. "Git!"

Dante started to head back toward Quattro Uccelli as the brothers helped up Greenjeans, who said, "I would like to have a nap now."

"Yes, yes," Renzo said. "Which hotel are you at?" He then made a shooing motion to Dante, and mouthed, *Go*!

When Dante got to the restaurant, Velia, Marcello, Anna, and Nonna Cara all stood in the dining room, grinning.

"So you were all in on this?" Dante said.

"Of course," Marcello said.

"Is everything ready in the back?" Anna said.

Dante nodded. "Just some last-minute preparations."

He went back to the kitchen where he cut a few pieces of the panelle from the pan. He fried them lightly in olive oil, then placed them in the warming oven. He put the water on for the gnocchi.

It seemed like only a matter of seconds before Velia came back and said, "She's here."

Dante peeked outside to see Anna seat Charly. Anna, he knew, was telling Charly the chef had prepared a very special meal for tonight and that her party would meet her shortly. Charly smiled and nodded as Anna left.

He went back to the kitchen and plated the panelle with the arugula walnut pesto. He gave it to Anna. "Tell her to get started."

He dropped the gnocchi in the boiling water and poured heavy cream into a saucepan. As the cream thickened he added gorgonzola until it was smoothly incorporated with the cream. Then he added salt and freshly ground black pepper just as the gnocchi began to float to the top of the pot. He removed the tiny dumplings with a slotted spoon and put them directly into the sauce. He gave the pan a few quick flips to toss the gnocchi and coat it in cream sauce, then poured them into a pasta bowl and garnished it with a sprig of parsley.

As Dante walked through the crowded restaurant toward Charly's table on the patio, he noticed an old woman sitting across from her, holding her hand. At first he thought it was Nonna Cara. But then he saw Nonna Cara standing inside the dining room with Velia and Fabiana. When he looked again, he saw it was *his* Nonna with Charly. He heard Nonna's voice across the distance, like a whisper in his ear. Everything around them, all the movement, all the sound, blurred into the background.

"My dear," Nonna said, "close your eyes."

To Dante's utter surprise, Charly closed her eyes.

"Now," Nonna continued, "you must look with your heart, not your eyes. It will show you all you need to know."

Nonna stood and walked away and the rest of the world came back into focus.

When Dante arrived at the table, Charly's eyes remained closed. He put the gnocchi on the table and said, "Charly."

She opened her eyes, which almost crossed as they registered recognition, shock, and elation all at once.

"Dante!"

She stood and hugged him so hard he could barely breathe.

"What are you doing here?"

"I came for you."

She held him so close and Dante's heart swelled with love.

Then Charly caught herself and backed up. She sighed.

"What I said the other day hasn't changed. It's not like you can just show up here and that's going to turn everything around."

He noticed she hadn't touched the panelle, yet. "Please have something to eat."

Charly rolled her eyes. "Don't think your food has some magic power that's going to make me change my mind."

Dante took a deep breath. "All I know is that I made it with every ounce of love I have for you." He tried hard to hold the tears back, but one snuck down his cheek. He quickly turned away and wiped it off with the back of his hand.

Whether out of pity or respect for his effort, Dante wasn't sure, but Charly picked up one of the pesto-topped panelle pieces. She slowly lifted the food to her mouth and tasted it. She didn't look him in the eye when she said, "It's good." Some of the hardness on her face had melted.

"Thank you. I knew you'd like it."

Still refusing to look at Dante, she ate the rest of the panelle. Finally she made eye contact.

"Dante, I know you think you're in love with me now—"

"Charly, I wouldn't be here, I wouldn't have come all the way to Italy, if I weren't absolutely sure I was in love with you. And have been for some time." Her eyes softened, but again Dante wasn't sure if it was out of love or pity.

"Dante," she said, "you're feeling old and I know you're ready to start a family. And somehow I've become the convenient one . . . or some kind of Promised Land."

"That's not it at all."

"What is it, then?"

"It's that you are my love, my life. If I lose you, I lose everything." This time, he made no effort to conceal his tears.

He pointed to the bowl of gnocchi. "Do you remember that this is the very first dish of mine you ever ate?"

Charly leaned forward and smelled the food. She looked up and smiled. "That was a long time ago. I'm surprised you remember." She sat for a moment without moving. Dante wasn't sure if she was going to take a bite.

Finally she picked up the fork and took one of the gnocchi from the bowl. When she put it in her mouth, she closed her eyes. She left them closed for a few seconds, then tears rolled down her cheeks. Without opening her eyes, she said, "I've never tasted anything like it."

"I'm not sure if that's good or bad."

She laughed and opened her eyes. "It's good. It's very good."

"I love you, Charly."

He took her hands. "I know I've been a fool. We should have been together a long time ago and I know it's all my fault that we're not."

"But why have you realized it now?"

He squeezed her hands. "Charly, maybe I've grown up or maybe I needed things to happen in my life without you. But I can tell you I've never been more sure about my heart than I am right now, and if you'll have me, I will love you forever."

Charly released one hand and wiped the tears from her cheek. "I don't—"

"Please, just look into my eyes. If you don't see all the love and truth in my heart, you can go and I won't bother you anymore."

Charly hesitated for several seconds before she finally looked into his eyes. And when she did, Dante knew she saw his heart with hers. They sat staring at each other and as he gazed into her eyes he saw something he'd never seen with anyone else: he saw his future. He saw the two of them with their children, in their home. He saw himself and Charly growing old together and their children and grandchildren visiting on Sundays while Dante made dinner. He saw Thanksgiving and Christmas and birthdays and a life so full of happiness. And he felt not only a tremendous love for Charly, but a calm of knowing that she was, in fact, his one true love and that they would be together forever.

"I love you," he said.

Charly put her hand on Dante's face. "I love you, too."

Then Dante leaned in and kissed her. Marcello, Anna, Velia, and Fabiana all shouted and applauded. Charly and Dante remained lip-locked as the rest of the restaurant patrons joined in the cheering and clapping. Andrea and Renzo pulled up in the car. They cheered and Andrea honked the horn.

Finally, Charly and Dante both started laughing and had to break off the kiss. They sat with their foreheads touching and Dante brushed her cheek with his hand.

As they embraced, the entire city celebrated them. In the golden honey light of the setting sun, love showered them. Dante looked to the sky and silently said, "Thank you, Nonna."

Acknowledgements

There are so many people who have helped me in making this book a reality. Whatever words I put on this page can't express the extent of my gratitude. So I will keep it simple, and thank each one of you for the help and guidance in matters great and small. Holly Payne, Masie Cochran, Alan Rinzler, Greg Molesky, George M. Formaro, Deanna Mackey, Rom Webber, Ani Boursalian, Jennifer Cronin, DeAnna Roberts, Doug Heikkinen, Christie O'Toole, James Eagan, Annick Sjobakken, Joaquin Lowe, Bruna Naitana, Sarah Evans, Cynthia Bates, and Anne Marino. Also thank you to family and friends whose support and encouragement kept me going.

Thanks also to my mother, Gina Formaro, for all she has done for me my entire life, and my father, George P. Formaro, whose spirit continues to guide me.

And special thanks to my beautiful wife, Rachel Formaro. Without her love, support, dedication, and faith, *The Broken Heart Diet* simply would not exist.